W0232635

PENGUIN BOOKS

# MURDER AT THE HAPPY HOME FOR THE AGED

Bulbul Sharma is the author of five collections of short stories, a novel, three books for children and a work of non-fiction. Her books have been translated into several languages. She lives in New Delhi and Goa.

PENGUIN BOOKS

MURDER AT THE HAPPY HOME FOR THE AGED

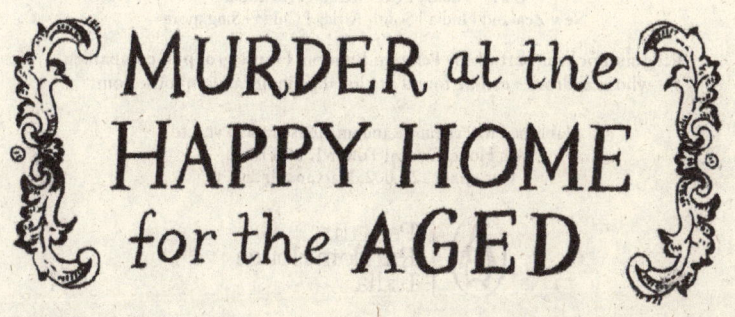

# MURDER at the HAPPY HOME for the AGED

# Bulbul Sharma

PENGUIN BOOKS

An imprint of Penguin Random House

PENGUIN BOOKS

USA | Canada | UK | Ireland | Australia
New Zealand | India | South Africa | China | Singapore

Penguin Books is part of the Penguin Random House group of companies
whose addresses can be found at global.penguinrandomhouse.com

Published by Penguin Random House India Pvt. Ltd
4th Floor, Capital Tower 1, MG Road,
Gurugram 122 002, Haryana, India

First published in Penguin Books by Penguin Random House India 2018

10 9 8 7 6 5 4 3 2

ISBN 9780143442264

Typeset in Minion Pro by Manipal Digital Systems, Manipal

Printed at Repro India Limited

www.penguin.co.in

This is a legitimate digitally printed version of the book and therefore might not
have certain extra finishing on the cover.

*To 'D'*
*And to all my friends in Goa,*
*with love and a big thank you*

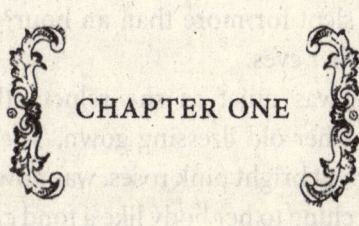

# CHAPTER ONE

THOUGH THE SEA was far away, the breeze tasted salty and warm as it mingled with the scent of jasmine and then floated through the garden. Before it streamed into the house, it briefly touched the body that was hanging limp and broken from the branches of the old mango tree. The breeze did not linger to pick up traces of the nauseating stench of death. The garden stood still and not a single bird called as the breeze circled the house, searching for open windows so that it could flow into every room.

Maria heard the crows declare dawn and opened her eyes, but quickly shut them again as the warm breeze touched her face gently. *It must be 6.00 a.m.*, she thought, keeping her eyes tightly shut, because the crows always begin to call around that time. But she knew she could sleep for another fifteen minutes—the neighbours' dogs were not barking to be let out yet. Maria went back to her dream. She and Francis were sailing on a boat on the Mandovi river. Someone was playing a guitar, but she wanted whoever it was to stop because a very strong smell of rotting fish was making her feel dizzy and sick. Francis was looking deep into her eyes and she was certain he was about to propose when the ship toppled over and a deafening clanging began. That must be the milkman. That meant it was 7.30 a.m. now. Had she slept for more than an hour? Maria forced herself to open her eyes.

The house was quiet as she reluctantly got out of bed and put on her old dressing gown. The print, once a cheerful pattern of bright pink roses, was now faded but the soft old cotton clung to her body like a fond caress. *Another long day at the Happy Home for the Aged*, thought Maria as she brushed her teeth. Her eyes looked puffy and bleary in the bathroom mirror. She had forgotten to take off her eye make-up last night and now two large raccoon-like eyes glared back at her. 'I will try that new eye cream,' she said to her reflection as if to soothe its ruffled feelings, but at the back of her mind she knew she should not have had that third glass of wine.

*All the residents of the Happy Home for the Aged must be at their usual posts, doing exactly what they do every day, and will continue to do till they die*, thought Maria viciously, tugging a brush through her unruly hair. Deven would have left long ago for his morning walk on the beach, Yuri must still be asleep, Cyrilo must be digging in the garden, Prema must be bathing and Rosie must be putting on her make-up. Leela must be in the kitchen coaxing the old stove to life. Everything would be chugging along in the same boring way. Maria thought about her dream, desperately trying to bring the silver-tinged images back, but the boat had vanished into the depths of the river, taking Francis with it. The cruel sunlight that was now blinding her eyes had killed her beautiful dream and plunged her into real life.

* * *

The breeze made the torn muslin curtains flutter as Rosie moved her wheelchair closer to the window. She held up the mirror close to her face to check if she had any new hairs on her chin. There were none, and she heaved a sigh of relief as she put the old ivory-framed mirror, a gift from her late second husband, back into its velvet-lined box. Then, slowly and meticulously, like a surgeon conducting a tricky operation, she began putting her face on. It was difficult because her hands shook badly now and her eyeliner often got smudged, but she was not going to stop doing her make-up just because she was seventy-nine years old.

Even though she never left the boundaries of the Happy Home for the Aged, Rosie made up her face every day as if she was going to a party. First a fine layer of foundation, applied carefully with trembling fingertips, then a careful dusting of powder from her old compact, and finally, a black line over her eyelids that often disappeared into the wrinkled folds of her skin.

After doing her make-up, she put on her large hat and wheeled herself out. The old house had a vast, rambling garden and Maria had kindly paved a path so that her wheelchair could go smoothly from one end of the garden to the other. There was even a ramp for her to go upstairs. Rosie never went out beyond the gates.

Maria Anne Souza, who looked after them all, was pretty in an untidy, careless way and Rosie hoped she would find a nice man soon—she was already thirty-nine and a half. Maria worked so hard to keep the Tip Top Cafe going and looking after the Happy Home that she had no time for herself. *There is time still*, thought Rosie as she wheeled her way along the path. *After all, I married my second husband when I was sixty-four. Poor fellow died on my seventieth birthday.*

The house was silent, though a few windows and doors creaked sadly as they always had, as if still complaining about some long-forgotten hurt. Cyrilo was already up and doing his push-ups in the veranda. Rosie heard him counting breathlessly. *He's still so handsome, even though he must be well past sixty-five*, she mused as she took out a small bottle from her bag and sprayed rose water on her wrists. Cyrilo, always so happy and cheerful, spent all day pottering about in the garden, his strong, muscular arms gleaming in the sunshine as he dug up weeds. He made Rosie's day pass wonderfully when he worked right under her window. She kept talking to him, and though he could not hear her, he looked up and smiled at her from time to time. It was enough for Rosie. At her age, a small gesture like that was enough to keep her happy all day. When she was younger, men would faint with joy when she threw a careless little smile at them. 'Time changes everything, and we have to bow our heads to its harsh commands,' Rosie whispered lines from a half-forgotten poem, picking up the mascara brush with a trembling hand.

Yuri was still asleep and would not wake till noon. He was an insomniac, and Rosie often heard him prowling about on the terrace, muttering to himself in Russian. Sometimes he got drunk and sang loudly for hours, and stopped only when the neighbourhood dogs began to howl. Yuri, who said he was only sixty-eight, was a painter, though he hardly ever sold any of his brightly coloured, strange paintings of Goan villages.

He often told Rosie he was in love with her but she didn't really care for him, though it was fun to flirt sometimes. 'One must flirt to keep alive,' Rosie often said to Maria, whom she thought was too boyish and lacking in femininity. Her eye make-up was always smudged with sweat and her dresses were either too long or too tight. Her beautiful thick hair was never brushed properly and instead hung about her face like a wild shrub. Poor Maria was in love with Francis but she would have to polish herself a bit to catch a playboy like him. Rosie had told her many times to wear false eyelashes and flutter them at him, show a bit of cleavage instead of her plump, unwaxed legs, but Maria just laughed her advice away. 'Where is the time to make myself pretty? I have to rise at dawn, bake for Tip Top, and rush back here to take care of you all.'

Rosie wheeled her chair towards the courtyard to look for Leela. An empty teacup was lying on the table. Deven, the youngest resident of the Happy Home for the Aged, had already left for his yoga class on the beach at dawn and would only return late in the afternoon. He spent his mornings at the temple, cleaning the idols of the gods and goddesses and feeding the cows. Then he went to the church in Trionim, the closest village, and helped the priest teach orphaned children. But Rosie found him too cold and unfriendly; even though they had both been at the Happy Home for ten years he hardly ever spoke to anyone except to bark orders, as if he expected everyone to obey him.

No one knew anything about Deven except that he was sixty-four years old and had lived in Mumbai for many years before coming to the Happy Home. Prema, the bad-tempered old woman who lived in the room next to Rosie, had tried very hard to find out more but Deven had been very rude to her. 'I will never talk to that fellow ever again,' Prema had said to Rosie, but she had continued to chat with the scowling, taciturn Deven, who just ignored her. Prema, who claimed to be two years younger than Rosie, was so bitchy and rude to everyone that they secretly felt it served her right. The only information Rosie had, given by Maria, was that Deven had once been a successful accountant in the Indian civil services and often helped her with the accounts at the Tip Top Cafe. She did not tell this to Prema. It was good to keep little secrets to oneself.

* * *

The crows flew in a wide arc, and then rose in the sky. They hovered briefly over the tree, uncertain because of the foul, strange smell that was drifting on the wind. They twisted their necks and ruffled their glossy black feathers as they watched the body hanging from the branch, each of them knowing by instinct that the smell was not natural. They flew away to another tree and sat brooding, waiting silently for the sun to rise. The breeze avoided the mango tree. The army of red ants walking down the garden wall in a long line stopped and waited, waving their tiny antennas suspiciously, as if afraid of entering the garden gate. The shadow of death hovered over the old house, tapping at the shuttered windows, whispering to be let in.

\* \* \*

The Happy Home for the Aged had been set up by Denzel Souza, Maria's grandfather, almost sixty years ago as a cosy shelter for his friends. He had inherited a vast cashew plantation from his father and never really had to work for a living. A mild-mannered, timid man, he was quite content to sit in his garden and play cards with his friends. Then life struck him a cruel blow when he lost his wife. He could not believe that the strong, cheerful woman who was constantly by his side, taking care of his every need, had gone. After her death, Denzel sat quietly for days in the garden, not speaking to anyone, as if waiting for his wife to reappear. He said he could hear her voice calling out to him. The people of Trionim thought he was going mad. His friends tried very hard to pull him out of his melancholy. Finally, he began to play cards again.

A few years passed and tragedy struck again just as Denzel was becoming reconciled to his beloved wife's death. His son and daughter-in-law were both found dead in the forest, with their five-year-old daughter roaming alone nearby. The old man, once again broken with sorrow, could not cope alone and two of his close friends moved into the huge empty house to take care of him and his granddaughter. They didn't do much except play cards all day but he was consoled by their company. Soon after, a few more friends of his friends who, for various reasons, found they had nowhere else to go moved in.

The old man gradually recovered and the large house sheltered them all. There was plenty of money still coming in from the sales of the cashews and coconuts that grew in the plantations surrounding the spacious house. An old couple from the village moved in and took charge of the kitchen. Meals were cooked, clothes were washed and the rooms were cleaned by seemingly invisible hands. Everyone was happy.

Then, one day, an old woman turned up at the house, claiming to be Denzel's cousin: 'Your mother's youngest sister's eldest daughter.' This stern, steely-eyed woman prayed all day and expected him to do the same. Denzel was not sure where she had come from and often tried to ask her exactly how they were related. But as soon as he tried, she shut her eyes and began to click her prayer beads together. Denzel did not have the courage to persist in his questioning in case the wrath of the heavens befell him. Soon, most of his friends left the house. Only two brave souls remained, who were both very deaf and could not hear her reprimands.

The old man died at the age of 102, lonely and sad, with a glass of feni and three ace cards in his hands. One by one, all the other old residents passed away too, as if Denzel had ordered them to accompany him to the other world so they could continue to amuse and entertain him.

Maria had been only seventeen years old when her grandfather died. She had promised him she would take care of any old people who wished to come and stay at the Happy Home. She was the one who gave the old house this name, and somehow the house responded and lost its gloomy air.

Now, two decades later, the house had only five residents, not counting the cheerful, chattering ghosts who kept Maria awake at night. The living ones—Yuri, Deven, Cyrilo, Prema and Rosie—paid Maria a small amount every month for food and laundry. Leela, an orphan whose parents had once lived in the servant quarters of the house, had taken over the cleaning duties. Despite being only fifteen years old she managed the kitchen and the house with very little help from the two servants who sat in the courtyard all day drinking tea and talking about the good old days when the Happy Home was the grandest residence in the Trionim area.

Maria often said they should do something for Leela, who was very bright and an extremely quick learner. She did not want her to spend her life cleaning and cooking for them. 'I will train her as a nurse so she can look after me when I am old,' Rosie often said. At seventy-nine, Rosie did not consider herself old and knew she had quite a few good years left. She also had plenty of money, though she never told anyone at the Happy Home about the treasure under her bed. Rosie had twenty gold coins hidden under sheets and pillowcases in a steel trunk that she kept locked. She wore the key around her neck on a chain along with a tiny golden cross her mother had given her.

* * *

Maria searched for her slippers and then, shaking them to check if any spiders had crawled in at night, she put them on. 'I am so bored with life,' she said aloud to the damp walls of her room. 'I wish something would happen to break the monotony of these humid, hot days after the monsoon. I want to run away somewhere cold and lonely. Maybe a mountain village where nobody will bother me.' She looked out of the window at the hibiscus shrub. There were three new flowers today. The garden had been created a long time ago by her mother, her grandfather had said, and each time a new flower bloomed Maria felt her mother was talking to her.

She would go to Panjim tomorrow and get some new books for Leela and maybe a new rose plant from the nursery near Porvorim. She needed new napkins for the Tip Top Cafe and some new tablecloths too. Last week's earnings had been good—all the tourists from Delhi seemed to love her cinnamon cupcakes, mushroom patties and chilli jam.

It was strange how many people came to Goa during the monsoon now. They seemed to love the rain-drenched roads, muddy puddles and traffic jams caused by caved-in roads. Trionim was not on the tourist map but somehow more and more new people were coming to explore the old village. Maria was happy that the cafe was doing well but she did not want Trionim to become a sea of tourist shops, like Candolim and Calangute.

'Life changes. The sea brings in new sand and changes colour every hour of the day. Be happy about it, Maria,' her grandfather used to tell her. Maria shrugged her shoulders and forced herself to smile as she went out to greet the day.

* * *

Rosie moved into the veranda because the sunlight was getting stronger and she did not want to spoil her fragile ivory skin. Never going outdoors in the sunlight had its advantages and her skin was as unblemished as a young woman's. She always wore a hat, even indoors, because the rays of the sun could creep in anywhere and put a stain on her skin. She put her hands on the handle of the wheelchair and began to move, singing softly to herself.

Then she heard the scream.

* * *

Maria went downstairs to the kitchen to sort out the lunch menu with Leela. Another day of juggling with food. Though all the residents of the Happy Home were quite old, they still had healthy appetites and ate like teenagers released from boarding school. Maria did not mind that but she hated the task of thinking what to make for lunch and dinner every day. Then she had to plan the menu for the Tip Top Cafe too, and go out and shop, but she loved that part and so did Leela. Every second day they would jump on her old scooter, sling jute bags over their shoulders and go down the winding road to the weekly Mapusa market. There, they would haggle, argue, chat and gossip for one hour and come back loaded with fresh vegetables, fish wrapped in soggy paper, freshly ground spices, bread warm from the oven, tiny sweet bananas and fragrant mangoes. If she was feeling rich, Maria would buy a few live crabs and Leela would hold them high above her head like an offering to the gods as they rode back to the house.

'Do you think we can make soup with the leftover chicken? Is there enough?' Maria asked Leela. The young girl smiled at her and winked. 'Of course. None of them ate the bigger pieces since they cannot chew well,' said Leela. 'I can get some cucumbers from the garden and make a salad for us.'

'That will be fine. We can get some tomatoes and spring onions from the village shop. I won't go to the market today. Francis said he would drop by and maybe stay for lunch. If he comes you can make a cutlet for him,' said Maria, her eyes suddenly bright and shining.

She must run upstairs and change into the new skirt she had bought in Panjim last week. It was a bit tight but if she stood straight and pulled her stomach in, no one would notice. She would not eat lunch today.

'I will have only a small helping of salad. I wish I had not had that jalebi last night. I must learn to zip my mouth shut,' muttered Maria as the taste of the sweet, hot jalebi drenched in syrup rose in her mouth. She hoped Francis would notice her new hairstyle. Joni, her friend who owned the only beauty parlour in Trionim, had said yesterday that it made her look much younger.

'You don't look a day over forty,' said Joni.

'What do you mean? I'm thirty-nine. I just turned thirty-nine six months ago.' Maria was horrified.

'I meant thirty-five,' Joni had quickly said and sold her some new night cream that had just come in from Mumbai. It was very expensive but she claimed 'all the famous movie stars use it'.

Maria had put the cream on at night before she went to sleep and noticed that her skin did look much better in the morning. Francis would certainly notice. Maria looked out of the window at the flowering magnolia and pictured herself walking down the aisle of the church, with all of Trionim admiring her wedding dress. *I will be quite slim by then*, she thought as she picked up a piece of buttered toast. She immediately put it back down on the plate.

Leela watched Maria eat and continued to clean the dining table. She knew Maria was desperately in love with Francis, who she didn't consider a reliable sort of man. Francis worked in Dubai and only came to Goa for a few days a month to visit his old mother. He was very tall and good-looking, with brown eyes that were forever laughing. He was always flirting, flashing his white teeth like a leopard. Leela had seen him driving around with another girl in the village but she had not told Maria.

Leela much preferred Bobby Menezes from the Menezes Spice Farm, who adored Maria but was ignored by her. Bobby would keep giving her herbs and spices as gifts, and Leela often hinted to him that he should bring Maria flowers but he never did. Bobby was very timid and shy, though they said at the farm that he was a very clever botanist and knew the names of all the plants in the garden. Leela had once heard him explain how the trees in the forest behind their house were very rare. 'Goa is a land with many unusual trees. We should protect them,' he had said, but Leela could see that Maria was not listening to him.

Leela picked up the broom and came out into the veranda. There was no one about. Yuri the drunk painter must be sleeping; Cyrilo the happy gardener must be digging in the vegetable patch; Prema the witch must be praying; Rosie the beauty queen must be brushing her hair a hundred times and Deven the headmaster must be scolding the boys in the church school. Leela had given all five residents of the Happy Home nicknames (though she never said them out loud) but she called Maria 'Miss Maria'. When she grew up she wanted to be as smart as Miss Maria and she also wanted to be a beautician. Ever since she had peered into the brand-new beauty parlour that Maria's friend Joni had opened next to the tailor's shop in Trionim, she knew that was what she wanted to do. She wanted to cut the hair on women's heads, put rollers to curl their locks, polish their nails, and put magical stuff on their faces to make them more beautiful. She had not told anyone about her dream. They would just laugh at her, and in any case, no one would care to listen except perhaps Miss Maria. Leela began to hum softly as she swept the dead leaves away.

Then she heard the scream. It sounded strange, as if the person was trying to scream for the first time ever.

Maria heard it at the same time and came running out of the kitchen.

'Who was that? Prema? Or was it Rosie? I hope she hasn't had a fall. Leela, can you go and check?' said Maria.

'I think it came from outside, Miss. Someone screamed in the garden,' said Leela, and they both rushed out. There was no one, and the green shadows of dawn still lingered in the dark corners of the garden as if reluctant to meet the sunlight. The breeze was making the leaves rustle and sing. Maria and Leela looked around, waiting by the door. A small boy was perched on the topmost branch of the old mango tree, his thin hand pointing towards the well located some distance away. He hid his face in the branches.

Maria quickly walked towards the well. Leela stayed near the door. She knew something terrible was lurking inside it. Ever since she was a child she had always avoided going near the well. Once, long ago, she had peered into the green, moss-covered water and seen a dead parakeet, its green feathers almost the same colour as the moss surrounding the well. Its stiff eyelids were covered in black slime. She held her breath as she watched Maria lean over the stone wall encircling the well.

Maria clenched her fists and forced herself to look in. A strange, putrid smell hit her face as if the water was full of dead, rotting things. At first she could not see anything except a dark hole and then, slowly, her eyes managed to focus. The water, dark and full of algae, seemed like a circle of oil with a few white feathers floating on its shimmering surface. There was nothing else. She looked up at the mango tree again and called out to the boy. But he seemed to have jumped over the wall and vanished. Maria was about to turn away when she saw the shoes under the tree. They were polished brown shoes with black laces. A pair of black socks lay discarded near them, looking like two dead rats.

The shadows moved and something made her look up again. That was when she saw the body. It was hanging from the branch right above her head. For a moment she was too shocked to do anything. She opened her mouth to scream but her head began to spin, and she collapsed on the ground.

Leela had seen the body too and she ran towards Maria screaming with terror. She tried to pick Maria up. 'Miss Maria . . . open your eyes. Oh! God protect us from evil,' she muttered. She forced herself not to look up but she knew the bloated face with its protruding tongue was watching them. The birds in the garden suddenly came alive and began to call as if they wanted to announce the tragic death to the world.

\* \* \*

Inspector Chand yawned as he pushed his chair back and leaned his head back. There was a patch of oil on the wall and his head nestled right in the centre of it as if it had been measured out for him. He yawned again, snapped his fingers and looked out of the window. The green paddy fields shimmered quietly in the sunlight in front of his window and a few egrets hopped about. He had recently learnt that these long-legged white birds were called egrets. A young English boy he had briefly arrested last week had told him this as they sat waiting for his bail. The boy had been found smoking marijuana right outside the police station, blowing puffs of aromatic smoke into Constable Robert's face, and Inspector Chand had had no choice but to arrest him. There were so many foreigners roaming about smoking 'ganja', wearing happy, calm expressions on their faces.

They had informed the British consulate and the boy had been released after a few hours, but while he was around he had taught the inspector a number of new

English words, many of them so rude that Inspector Chand had blushed on learning their meanings. He was not sure he would ever use them but it was good to be aware of their existence. He wished all his arrests could be so informative. Inspector Chand liked nothing better than to improve his English and learn new things about the world. He read all the time, mostly comic books he had borrowed from his nieces and nephews; there was not much for a policeman to do in Trionim.

People obeyed rules, rarely fought, and nobody stole anything since everyone in the village knew everyone else. If you stole something you could never use it since the entire village would know at once. You would have to hide the stolen item forever, like those wealthy collectors who stole antiques from museums and kept them hidden in secret places. He had read about this in the newspaper just last week. Inspector Chand stared at the paddy fields and wished he had become a journalist. He was too smart to be only a policeman. He was thirty-five years old and there was not much hope for a promotion in this place.

He had not even found a wife yet, though his mother had been looking for a long time. In fact, everyone in Trionim was looking for a wife for him, and several fathers had approached his mother. They had all been rejected quite rudely by her except those willing to pay a huge dowry. She liked the ugly rich girls with ugly rich fathers while he liked the pretty ones with no financial scope. They could never agree, and now there were six new grey hairs on his head and two on his chest. Sometimes he woke up at night, panic-stricken, thinking, *What if I never find a wife?* He had liked one pretty girl with a BA degree but her father was only giving one lakh rupees in cash, which his mother rejected right away. He had tried several times to stand up to her and tell her that asking for dowry was illegal; she should remember that he was a police officer and his job was to uphold the law and not break it for his own gain. 'You are a police officer; that is why I am asking for two lakh. If you had been a schoolteacher or a railway guard, I would have been happy with fifty thousand rupees. There is a fixed price for every profession and all fathers of marriageable girls know it.'

'We are educated people, not ignorant villagers. And there is no dowry system in Goa. Only Hindus in the north take and give dowry, Ma,' he had said.

'It is a perfectly good system and many families have benefited from it for hundreds of years. My father was educated entirely by my mother's dowry. We should embrace what is useful to us in our religion,' she had announced firmly.

Inspector Chand shut his eyes and thought about Maria. Her beautiful, dusky cheeks, pouting mouth and soft eyes appeared before his eyes. If only she had been a Hindu girl she would have been perfect for both his mother and him. She was not rich but she did own a big house with a lot of land, and she was hard-working too. Her figure was so generous, unlike girls from the city who were as flat-chested as men. Her nose was a bit odd, upturned like a small boy's, but that was a tiny blemish in a girl with a very pretty face and stunning figure. As if this was not enough, she was a really good cook and managed that Tip Top Cafe so well. But Maria was a Christian. His mother had said that she would hang herself from the ceiling fan if he ever married a girl who was not a Hindu and of the same caste as them. 'My ghost will haunt you forever if you marry a Christian girl and take my grandchildren to church every Sunday,' she warned, pointing to the fan whenever he tried to talk to her about Maria. He had never dared to tell Maria about his feelings but he was quite certain she would marry him. He was a policeman, after all, and she would get a very good pension when he died.

The door of the police station creaked open hesitantly and Constable Robert peered in. If there had been a wrestling competition in Goa, Constable Robert would have won it hands down. He was six feet four inches tall, and his shoulders were so wide that he often had to enter rooms sideways. His hands were like a giant's paws and his feet so large that special shoes had to be ordered for him from Mumbai. No other policeman in India had such huge feet. Constable Robert looked like an ancient, mythical giant who had been reborn in Goa but you could not find a more mild-mannered and soft-spoken man than him. It was fortunate that not many people knew about his timid nature because one look at him and the few unruly elements in Trionim fled at once.

'Sir,' squeaked Constable Robert in his shrill, girlish voice. God had given him a giant's body but a woman's voice.

'Yes? What is it, Robert?' asked Inspector Chand, trying to look busy though he had only been cleaning his fingernails with a paper knife. He always liked to give the impression of being a busy man whenever someone walked into his room. 'Look busy, son, and people will respect you,' his late father had often said to him while pacing up and down in front of the house with a preoccupied air.

'A boy has come from the Happy Home to say a man has been found dead there,' said Constable Robert breathlessly, twisting a lock of hair like a small, frightened boy. Both he and the inspector had a morbid fear of dead bodies, and fortunately not many had come their way in Trionim.

'Which one has gone? They are all so old except for Miss Maria. I knew one of them would pop off soon. Just as well. There are too many of them for her to look after. Was it the drunken artist or old Cyrilo? He was a decent chap. Gave me a huge cabbage once. Tell me, which one?' asked Inspector Chand, quite pleased to have a chance to visit the Happy Home and meet Maria again. He would call Eric the undertaker and ask him to take the body away.

'Not any of them. The old people are all alive, sir. Some new dead person. Hanging from the tree,' whispered Robert, looking out of the window anxiously.

'Which tree?' asked Inspector Chand, too shocked to say anything else.

'Don't know, sir. Maybe mango or banyan. The boy just wrote on a piece of paper "dead man hanging from tree" and ran away,' muttered Constable Robert, keeping his head low so that it would not hit the ceiling fan and also to hide his eyes, twitching with fear, from Inspector Chand.

'We should go and find out at once. Get the jeep out. I will ring up Eric and tell him to take the dead body to the morgue,' said Inspector Chand, bile rising in his mouth as he uttered the words 'dead body'.

'But the Happy Home is so close, sir. Just behind the police station. We can cut across the rice fields,' said Constable Robert, scratching his head.

'Robert, get the jeep. It is always best for the police to arrive as quickly as they can. We are here to serve the people, remember. We don't want to stroll down like tourists, do we?' said Inspector Chand, hoping Maria would be there to see him arrive in a flurry of dust in his new police jeep like policemen in TV shows.

It took them a long time to get to the Happy Home since the road circling the village had been dug up in various places and they had to turn around and take a longer route. When they finally arrived, there was a huge crowd outside and their jeep had to stop quite far away, much to Inspector Chand's disappointment. He forced himself to walk calmly and prayed he would not throw up when he saw the body. He was certain Constable Robert would.

Maria had warned Leela not to say anything to the other residents but they already knew because Rosie had seen the body from her window. Cyrilo, who was working in the back garden, had rushed over at once. He told Prema not to go outside but she was already running towards the gate, screaming her head off: 'Evil . . . evil has struck us!'

Many more people from the village had gathered and begun wailing as if they had known the dead man. 'Who is it? Do you know him?' asked Maria. 'No, no one we know. A stranger, but it's so sad,' sobbed a woman whom Maria had never seen before. The noise woke Yuri and he came out half-dressed, his eyes swollen and red. 'Looks like a close relative of the corpse,' hissed Prema. 'Deven is missing all the fun. Serves him right,' she said, and pushed her way through the crowd.

Rosie watched from the other end of the garden; she did not like crowds. She could see the dead man's legs dangling from the branches but could not see his face. *Just as well. It will not be a pretty sight. If he had to kill himself, why not walk into the sea? Much cleaner and better for himself and those who'll have to clean up after him.* The sea would have just taken him into her arms and not a trace, not a finger or a toe, would ever be found again. The sharks would see to that. Hanging from a tree was such a stupid way to die. Trust a man to make a nuisance of himself even after death. People were so selfish; fortunately, both her husbands had died quietly in their sleep. She had organized beautiful funerals for them with music and flowers.

Rosie tried to peer through the shrubs. She saw Inspector Chand strutting about, pointing his baton at the tree. *Now, if he were a good Christian boy, Maria could have married him. He is not as good-looking as Francis or as clever as Bobby from the spice farm but he is a police officer and a man who wears a uniform is always the best suitor.* Both of Rosie's husbands had been civilians but she had always made sure they wore smart blazers with an emblem stamped on the pockets as well as a tie.

'Look, they are bringing the body down,' whispered Leela as a cry went up. The crowd moved forward and fell back as the body hit the ground. 'Move back, move back!' cried Constable Robert, waving a stick about as his giant figure pushed through the crowd. For a brief moment there was a silence so deep that Leela could hear the cicadas chattering. Suddenly someone yelled. 'Oh my god! Look!'

'He is . . . it is a woman!'

'The dead man is a woman!'

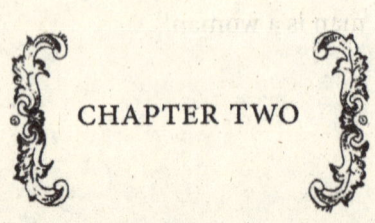

# CHAPTER TWO

GOA, VERDANT GREEN, fragrant and gold, rose from the sea when an arrow was shot from a high mountain peak by Lord Parashurama, the sixth avatar of Vishnu, when he was looking for land on which to build a sacred space for meditation. He stood on the highest peak, his eyes searching for the perfect spot, and then swiftly sent forth an arrow that landed on the sea. Obeying Parashurama's command the sea moved back dutifully and offered a beautiful stretch of land studded with pearls and conches and with sand as pure as gold dust. Thus, Goa came into being.

Geologists have concluded that Goa rose up from the seabed as a result of violent tectonic activity around 10,000 BCE. But it is easier to believe that a heavenly being was responsible for creating Goa, adorning it with endless golden beaches fringed with coconut palms, wide rivers and several natural harbours glowing like half-moons as they kiss the blue-grey waters of the Arabian Sea. The Mauryans included Goa in their empire and so did many other kingdoms down the ages. The rulers of Vizianagaram used Goa as a safe landing place for the priceless horses that Arab traders brought by ship. Many fierce battles were fought over Goa through the centuries and it changed hands constantly. There was an abundance of fish in the rivers, the soil was rich and fertile, and paddy grew effortlessly. There were coconut trees all around. What more could they want?

The Portuguese arrived in 1510 and Afonso de Albuquerque laid siege around Goa, finally defeating the sultan of Bijapur and claiming the land for Christ and his country. By the end of the sixteenth century, Goa became famous as 'Golden Goa' or the 'Lisbon of the East'. Grand churches and beautiful mansions were built along the Mandovi river, and elegant boats carried equally elegantly dressed men and women. The cashew, guava, chickoo, aubergines, tomatoes and chillies they brought with them became a part of Goan life. Each year, ships carried away precious cargo of pepper and other spices, and fabulous stories about the magical land of Golden Goa spread all over Europe.

The inhabitants of Trionim had long forgotten Goa's glorious past and were now focused on the activities in the little village. The twenty-odd houses had been here for more than a hundred years—Maria's Happy Home for the Aged was one of the oldest—but many of them were in a neglected state. Their tall, elegant pillars, red-tiled roofs and shell-studded windows were falling to bits as wild creepers grew like green ropes to strangle the houses. The Happy Home was, fortunately, in good shape thanks to Maria's grandfather's efforts. Denzel Souza had made sure that the house was painted regularly and any missing roof tile was replaced before each monsoon. But after his death, the house went into a sharp decline as if mourning the loss of its beloved owner. The income from the cashew crop also grew less as much of the land was sold to pay for the upkeep.

Now the walls were covered with grey patterns of damp and mould, and a filigree of old cobwebs had embedded their circular patterns into the wooden beams across the high ceilings. The vast garden was neglected except for the vegetable patch tucked away behind the house. The trees, planted almost a hundred years ago, surrounded the old house, leaning over the roof and casting their cool shade over the shuttered windows like trusted old friends. The house still had an air of dignity; when you looked at it, you knew it belonged to an era of grace and elegance and demanded respect.

Several new houses with brightly painted walls and huge, complicated iron gates had recently been built on the outskirts of the village, where once there used to be sprawling paddy fields. They looked like eyesores, like poisonous little mushrooms that had sprung up after the rains, but nothing could be done about them. They all belonged to people from Delhi and Mumbai, who only came here during the winter months. The rest of the year these houses sat lonely and quiet, and stray dogs slept in the empty swimming pools. The village people disliked these new constructions and never tired of criticizing them and their inhabitants. At every gathering they sat around exchanging new gossip about 'those people' but in their hearts they secretly envied them.

They too longed to have bathrooms with tiles that had patterns of pretty English flowers and fruits. They too wanted kitchens that were not blackened with ancient marks of smoke and soot but lined with polished granite. How wonderful to have roofs that did not leak during the rains. But it was not done to praise these new houses standing like cardboard boxes in the paddy fields. Though they discussed them endlessly, when they walked past them, the villagers pretended they did not exist. They shut their eyes and tried to think that the paddy fields were still a sea of green, unscarred by these ugly toadstools.

Maria's grandfather used to own most of the paddy fields and the forest beyond where he had planted hundreds of cashew trees. Every year the family would camp in the forest during the feni-making season, everyone except the old man and his wife, who felt it beneath her dignity to camp with the hired labour from god knows where. Maria's grandmother was a famous beauty in her time and claimed that pure Portuguese blood, untainted by any 'native black', ran in her veins. Her husband, dark-skinned with curly hair, could not claim such noble origins and was proud to say he was of mixed blood like many other people in his village. Maria's mother came from the distant north. Though she was a devout Christian, she was never accepted by her snooty mother-in-law, who called her a barbarian from the wild north—a land she had never visited and had no desire to.

'How my foolish son was caught by this milk-drinking peasant girl, I don't know,' she would mutter as she walked around the garden, holding her parasol like a shield, watching her daughter-in-law through narrow green eyes. Maria's mother, Sonia, did not care and carried on drinking milk and doing whatever she wanted. She created a kitchen garden in the empty space behind the house where the stables used to be long ago. She planted chickoo, guava and mango trees and kept chickens in the barn. She was the one who set up the feni-brewing plant in the cashew plantation much against her husband's wishes. 'You should stay at home and look after our daughter,' he would tell her.

They were found dead by a fisherman who was spreading his net out to dry. No one ever found out how they died. The village people said they had tasted too much freshly brewed feni; others said they had died of snake bite. Maria, fortunately, was safe. She was taken home by the fisherman. 'Protected by the gods,' said everyone in the village.

Maria had a vague memory of her parents but she was not really sure what they had looked like. Their faces kept changing. Their voices she could not remember at all. She had conjured up her mother's face from a single photograph that hung in her grandfather's study; the fake aunt had thrown all the others away. Her mother was smiling under her crooked wedding veil, a naughty, twinkling smile like a young child's, holding her husband's hand.

*In death too they must have been like this*, Maria thought, *lovingly holding hands*. There were many formal photographs of her father taken by the village photographer in various stages of his life—as a plump, fair baby in a frilly dress and cap, as a thin teenager with a strange, jaunty hairstyle and as a handsome young man in a smart suit and hat. The backdrop was always the same: a fountain with three doves perched on its edge. The fountain was still in the garden but the dove figures had crumbled away long ago.

Maria was about five years old when her parents had died and she remembered the 'aunt' telling her that they had gone to heaven and she would never see them again unless she behaved herself and became a very good girl. They were watching her all the time from heaven and would know at once if she told a lie, broke anything or did not finish the food on her plate. If she picked her nose, if she said a rude word, if she showed her panties when she was sitting on a chair, they would know at once. This cruel, thin-lipped woman kept a notebook by her bedside in which she claimed to write down all Maria's misdeeds of the day and listed out the punishments due to her. A broken saucer was a sharp but painful twist on her right ear, a rude word was a rap on her knuckles with a small wooden ruler. Sometimes she would give her a quick slap on her back for no reason at all. 'Just to keep you in order. Children should always be kept in check,' she would hiss, her cruel eyes gleeful.

Till she was twelve Maria was terribly afraid of every little thing because she was sure her parents were watching and writing down all her faults and misdemeanours in their little black books. Her grandfather would try to protect her but he was afraid of the aunt; besides, he could barely hear or see any more. His mind was getting confused and he often thought she was his beloved wife. 'If I say anything to her she will stop talking to me and I cannot bear that,' he would say and give Maria a handful of sweets to stop her tears.

Then, one morning when Maria was thirteen, she woke up with blood on her bed sheet. She cried out in fear, clutching her nightdress. When she ran to her great-aunt's room to beg for her forgiveness and ask to be punished, she saw that the house was filled with people. Strangers hugged her, sobbing loudly, patting her head. The door to her grandfather's room was shut and women dressed in black stood wailing outside. Maria found her great-aunt in the garden, sobbing.

Maria knew something terrible had happened and she was to blame for it. She ran and hid in the coal cellar under the kitchen and did not come out till mice began to nibble at her shoes. The house was strangely quiet and the rocking chair in which her grandfather sat all day was empty. The fake aunt suddenly vanished, taking with her the large black suitcase and grey boots. Her little black book with Maria's misdemeanours lay on the floor of her bedroom. Maria did not dare pick it up but she sat staring at it for a long time, afraid it would fly up any minute and give her a stinging slap on the face.

Her life changed after that day, but Maria could not stop looking up at heaven whenever she broke a saucer or told a white lie, because she knew that now, along with her parents, her grandfather was watching her too—six pairs of eyes. Maria tried her best to be a good girl. She knew that the invisible fake aunt was hovering somewhere nearby, waiting to pounce on her. She said her prayers every night kneeling by her bed, the dust tickling her nose as she whispered under her breath. She never went near the aunt's room, which was locked up, but she sometimes heard the old lady's voice scolding her.

Leela's parents looked after her and let her run around in the garden all day. When she was eighteen, an old lady called Rosie turned up one night with five suitcases and a parakeet in a cage and asked if she could stay. And then the others came, one by one, and the old house filled with people again. People she loved and wanted to look after. Kind, gentle people who never scolded her or looked at her with hatred in their eyes.

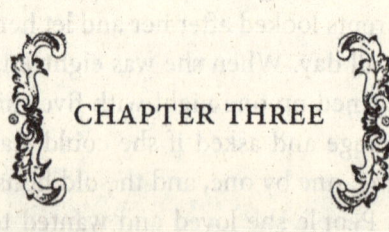

# CHAPTER THREE

IT WAS QUITE late by the time the police took the body away and the crowd left reluctantly. A few young boys lingered at the gate, trying to peer in, while a couple more perched on the garden wall. They seemed to be hoping for more dead bodies to appear or some other sort of drama and went away looking rather disappointed, muttering about the police not being helpful or allowing them to see the body. 'After all, it could have been a friend of mine,' said one young man.

'This was your friend? A woman who dresses like a man?' asked his friend.

'I didn't say she was my friend. I said I might have known her if the policeman had let me see her properly.'

'Yes, I wish we could have had a good look. I've never seen a dead body.'

'Your grandfather died just last week.'

'Yes. But he was family. Dead members of the family do not count since they look the same dead or alive. My father, mother, uncle and aunt all look the same to me.'

The boys then ran off to the tea shop where other people from the village had gathered to discuss this important event in Trionim's history.

Maria closed the garden gate firmly and locked it. She did not want any curious onlookers to come into the house. She then went to the kitchen and washed her face several times with cold water. It made her feel calmer. 'Dinner. Let's plan dinner,' she told Leela, who was singing softly under her breath as she washed dishes in the sink. This morning's gruesome events did not seem to have upset her in any way. *For such a young girl she has really strong nerves*, thought Maria. 'A light dinner should be fine. Chicken soup with boiled vegetables.' She was sure none of the old folks would like any dinner after such a harrowing and sad day.

She was mistaken. None of them had lost their appetite. They had all been a bit subdued at lunch, confused and bewildered by everything that had just happened, but their spirits seemed to have revived. In fact, they were more hungry and lively than usual as they gathered around the dining table, chattering loudly about the other dead bodies they had seen.

It was amazing how many unusual deaths Prema had encountered. Not a single person she had known had passed away peacefully in bed after reaching a ripe old age; each and every one of them had died a violent and sudden death. Prema listed out all her deceased relatives one by one; then Rosie started on her list. Hers was not as shocking but she quickly added, 'One cousin committed suicide just like this,' she said, pointing a painted fingernail at the garden.

'Suicide is the coward's way out,' Deven said to them in a gruff, accusatory tone, as if they were to blame, and Cyrilo muttered something about his late uncle who had drowned in the sea. 'We were never sure if he had really drowned since we never found his body. My aunt would always lay an extra plate for him at the dining table and none of us were allowed to sit in his chair,' he said.

Maria wished they would stop talking. Yuri was the only one who was quiet. It seemed so disrespectful to talk like this, as if they were discussing a horror movie: *The ten best deaths I have seen*. Maria was still quite dazed at what had happened. A dead body in her garden! Why had this woman come here to die? What connection did she have to this house? Maria looked up and saw Yuri watching her. He seemed to have tears in his eyes but he smiled and shrugged his shoulders. She wondered why Francis had not come today. Just as well, because she was still wearing her old dress and her hair was its usual tangled mess since she had had no time to wash it.

Leela bustled around the table, urging them to get up and leave. She had found some leftover dal, tomato curry and rice in the fridge which she had heated up and served after they had each finished a big bowl of chicken soup. But they still wanted more. 'I can smell fish. Are you frying some for us tonight?' asked Prema, sniffing the air. Her eyesight was very bad and she often stumbled over furniture but refused to go to the eye doctor in Panjim to get her eyes checked. 'What can he do? My eyes have seen enough. They need to rest now,' she would say while squinting.

'No. You are not getting any fish till Friday. Just finish what's on your plate and go to bed now,' said Leela, slapping down a plate of rice on the table.

'You are getting too cheeky, girl. I would give you a slap if my wrist was not so stiff with arthritis.' Prema tried to grab Leela's long plait as she went past her.

'How can you talk of fried fish when we have just discovered a dead body?' said Maria, and they all looked at her with surprise.

'Calm down, dear. People die all the time. Nothing to feel so upset about. People are born and then they die. Please pass me the chicken,' said Rosie, patting her hand. Yuri nodded, smiled and said, 'Death is not bad. Worries all gone. All goes well after you are dead.'

'It's just a change of garments according to our holy books. But they mean a proper death, not an ugly one like this,' said Deven in a low voice. Cyrilo helped himself to some more rice while Prema tapped her fingers on the table, still hoping for the elusive fried fish to arrive.

Maria shivered as she watched the old residents chatting and chewing their food noisily. Prema was making a dreadful noise, rattling her false teeth. Maria turned her face away and stared at the garden now bathed in darkness. She just could not get the terrible image of the dead woman's face out of her mind. Why was she dressed in a man's clothes? Inspector Chand and his constable had refused to touch the body.

'Leela, Leela. Is there any ice cream?' shouted Cyrilo. 'It's so hot today.'

'I also feel like eating something sweet. Can we have carrot halva tomorrow, Maria? You make it so well. Please put lots of cashew nuts but make sure you grind them well. My teeth cannot chew whole cashew nuts now,' said Prema.

'The older you get the hungrier you feel. Teeth gone, eyes gone, legs gone but stomach doing very well,' said Cyrilo with a smile.

'The woman was found dead right at our doorstep. Do you people realize that? How can you talk about carrot halva at a time like this?' shouted Maria, suddenly losing her temper.

'Okay, Maria, forget about the carrot halva. Anyway, sugar is bad for you, poison for everyone regardless of their age. In Ayurveda they say you should avoid all white things. Flour, potatoes, sugar.' Deven wagged a finger at them.

'Who cares? I love deep-fried floury, white snacks. What is life without sugar and flour? I have some chocolates in my bag. I saved them from that birthday party we went to. We can have them later. Maria, do calm down. That Inspector Chand will soon find out why that poor woman killed herself. Let us say a prayer for her and then eat our chocolates.' After she said this Rosie turned around in her wheelchair to reach into a large bag that always hung from the handles.

As Deven, Cyrilo, Yuri, Prema and Rosie bowed their heads and began to pray, Maria hesitated and bowed her head too. An old, familiar feeling of guilt flooded her as she thought about the six pairs of eyes watching her from heaven. She quickly began to chant an incoherent prayer.

Leela emerged from the kitchen with a tray on which sat seven glass bowls, filled to the brim with bright pink ice cream, and seven silver teaspoons: the last surviving spoons from Maria's grandmother's cutlery. She carefully placed the tray on the dining table, stuck the teaspoons into the bowls and then folded her hands in prayer. 'Keep us safe, oh lord. Mother Mary protect us. Krishna, please watch over us too,' she sang in a beautiful clear voice. The entire house rang with their prayers and a flock of wood pigeons roosting on the guava tree fluttered their wings in response.

'Ah! Good, good. Strawberry . . . my favourite flavour,' whispered Rosie, her eyes half shut. Everyone stopped praying and quickly opened their eyes. As soon as the sweet, slightly plastic flavour of the ice cream touched her lips, Maria felt sick. She couldn't bear to sit around pretending nothing had happened. She knew she had to do something. She had to find out why this unfortunate woman had died, but before that she had to find out her identity.

Why had she come here? No tourists ever did since the beaches were rocky and there were no good restaurants except the Tip Top Cafe. Though last week a crowd had suddenly arrived to see the old church. Maybe the dead woman was a tourist. Maybe she owned one of the new houses in the paddy fields. But why had she come to the Happy Home? *What a horrible way to die. Poor woman. I hope she won't haunt the Happy Home now. There are so many ghosts here already*, thought Maria.

The residents watched her as they spooned ice cream into their mouths. They sensed that Maria was upset but did not know what to say to make her feel better.

Rosie passed the chocolates around. Everybody took one and the table fell silent as they ate them slowly, noisily, making each one last. 'Mint and dark chocolates . . . so delicious,' Rosie murmured, taking Maria's hand in hers, and Maria felt tears rolling down her cheeks.

\* \* \*

Inspector Chand sighed and looked at his empty cup and Maria knew he wanted more tea. He had spent the entire morning at the Happy Home interrogating Maria. He was a helpful and friendly man; in fact, a bit too friendly, thought Maria. She did not like the way he tried to brush against her hand when she passed him the bowl of sugar. Now if only Francis would do that. But maybe he was just shy and she should encourage him a bit more. Deep in her heart, though, Maria knew very well that Francis was not shy at all, on the contrary, he was quite bold, but she felt better thinking about him as a timid man who needed encouragement. Bobby was shy and timid but she found him boring. All he did was talk about his plants and trees at the spice farm.

As soon as Maria thought about the trees, the dead woman's face rose in front of her again. How long had the poor creature been hanging there? She must have died at night while they were all sleeping peacefully in their beds.

Suddenly, a terrible fear filled Maria's mind. She felt like a child once more, hiding from punishment. Would the police think she had anything to do with this death? She had never seen the woman before in her life, but would they believe her? After all, the body had been found in her garden, hanging from her mango tree. Inspector Chand might be friendly and kind now but if he suspected her he would certainly change his attitude. All his friendly attempts to get close would disappear and he would clamp a pair of handcuffs on her.

Maria rose from her chair and went and stood near the window. The trees in the garden were bathed in a grey light, as if in mourning. Inspector Chand did not seem concerned about the identity of the dead woman and kept asking Maria unrelated questions. What did she think about Hindu gods? Would she ever change her religion? What did she think of mixed marriages? Maria wished he would go away. She had still not planned the menu and Leela was waiting for her in the kitchen. Today was market day at Mapusa and if they did not go early they would not get any fresh fish. 'I don't like that fat policeman. He keeps looking at you as if he is your boyfriend,' Leela had told her earlier, watching him from behind the door.

'Inspector, I need to go out. If you have any more questions I can talk to you in the evening,' said Maria, picking up the empty cups and putting them on a tray.

'Evening? Evening would be best,' said Inspector Chand, a wide smile lighting up his sweaty face. A picture of Maria in a revealing long evening dress rose in his mind and he could feel his heart racing.

'You can talk to the others now if you wish. Shall I call them?' asked Maria.

'No need. Why bother the old people? They can hardly hear or see anything so what will they know, poor things.

Let them rest in peace.' He looked around. *If I marry Maria I will turn this massive house into a five-star hotel. I will take early retirement from the police force and become a hotelier. I know I will do an excellent job,* he thought, staring at the cobwebs on the ceiling.

'Why isn't he talking to us? I have been waiting all morning,' muttered Prema angrily as she watched the inspector get into his jeep.

'Maybe he thinks we're too old to be of any help,' said Cyrilo.

Rosie glanced at Cyrilo. He was looking very smart this morning after combing and brushing his hair. She too had worn her best dress and put a black velvet ribbon in her hair. Yuri had woken before noon for once, and had even taken a bath and worn a clean shirt. Deven had not gone out for his early morning walk. All for nothing. They were not needed. They had waited all morning but the inspector didn't speak to them.

'He said we can hardly see or hear so what is the use of asking us anything. He said this to Maria. I heard him. He sat for hours drinking tea and gobbling up our precious almond biscuits,' said Prema.

'He is not interested in finding out anything. He just wants to spend time ogling Maria. He has a crush on her, I am quite sure.' Rosie was wishing she had not worn her best silk dress. It was all crushed and sweaty now and she would have to get Leela to wash it.

'Are you sure the woman committed suicide? You are a good judge of all these things,' Rosie asked in a serious voice, turning to Deven.

For once, Deven did not turn away. He looked at her thoughtfully and said, 'No one will commit suicide in such a hidden place. They will usually go to a place filled with people, where people they know will find them. They always want to send a message to friends and relatives even in death. Make sure they know they are dead. People who kill themselves want attention even in death.'

'I think that's a cruel thing to say,' said Prema, glaring at him. Rosie could see she was upset because Deven had not spoken to her though she was sitting right next to him on the bench. The five of them had been waiting in the courtyard, hoping to speak to the inspector. But he had left and they were left with nothing to do but wait till lunch was served. Leela had also insisted they sit there since she wanted to clean the drawing room and the dining room.

Rosie looked around her. Cyrilo had started plucking the dead flowers off the marigold plants. He could never sit still and do nothing. Deven was writing something in a notebook. Prema was leaning close to him and trying to read what he had written. How rude of her. Yuri was strangely quiet and had shut his eyes, but she knew he was awake because his fingers were tapping the bench restlessly.

Were they really too old to be useful? How was the inspector so sure of that? They could have seen something, or heard something. One of them could have looked out the window and seen the woman come into the garden at night and climb the tree to hang herself. And how did he know for certain that she had killed herself and not been murdered and put there? Rosie often got up at night to drink water and go to the bathroom around 2 a.m. but last night when this woman was busy hanging herself or being hung right outside her window she had slept through and missed it all. But the inspector did not know that. She could have easily seen the murder/suicide happen. She always sat by the window and knew what was going on in the village because people often stopped and spoke to her, telling her all the gossip.

'I will tell that inspector what I saw whether he asks me or not,' said Cyrilo, getting up suddenly, almost knocking Prema off the bench.

'What did you see?' asked Deven, not looking up from his notebook. Rosie thought he looked just like a detective in a movie. He was very alert this morning, his eyes roaming as if he was a fox out on a hunt. And as she watched him, an idea slowly formed in her head. An idea that would break the tedium of their lives, make them feel alive, and shame the inspector. They would show everyone that they might be old, but they were as clever as anyone younger. They would solve this mystery and prove to that arrogant Inspector Chand that they could still hear and see as well as anyone else in Trionim. Their collective age totalled almost 400 but their eyes were sharp and their ears worked very well and their brains were far superior to his.

# CHAPTER FOUR

MARIA FELT SORRY for the 'sweet oldies' as she secretly called them. They were sitting around dressed in their best clothes looking dejected. Inspector Chand could have asked them a few questions just to make them feel important. Poor things. She would make bread and butter pudding tonight to cheer them up.

Just then, she saw Rosie move her wheelchair towards the bench and all of them huddle together. That was odd. She had never seen them act so friendly towards each other. Most of the time Prema and Rosie were not on talking terms, and Deven would ignore them all. 'They talk nonsense. I have no time for them,' he had said to her the other day. Deven was quite abrupt with her too sometimes and she could see that he had been an arrogant and bad-tempered man in his former life.

Where had he come from? Maria wondered as she looked at him. She did not know much about any of them because she did not like to pry into their affairs. They were like guests in her house. She only knew that Deven had once held a high-powered post in the government, but nothing else. He never got any letters or visitors.

Rosie, who was twice widowed, had no children but many of her nieces and nephews often came to visit her at the Happy Home. 'Hoping I'll leave them something in my will,' she would say and laugh.

Prema had retired as a school headmistress in Pune and come to live at the Happy Home just last year. She never mentioned any relatives and no one ever visited her.

Cyrilo had once lived in a large family house in the village with his wife but after she died and his son emigrated to Australia, Cyrilo decided to move here. A builder from Delhi was very keen to buy his old house, but Cyrilo had not made up his mind yet. Yuri kept urging him to sell it and invest the money in a business Yuri was setting up in Russia. Maria wanted to warn him to do no such thing but Cyrilo had just laughed at her. 'Don't worry your pretty head over such things. I know what Yuri is up to. I know a fool and his money are soon parted. I am old but not a fool, Maria.'

Maria was a bit suspicious of Yuri and hoped he would leave next summer. She did not trust his charming, reckless manner and was wary of his drinking binges with his Russian friends. She wished she had not allowed him to rent the room on the top floor. But she needed the money and he was paying cash.

Meanwhile, in the courtyard, Rosie cleared her throat, turned her wheelchair and said, 'Come closer. I want to talk to you all.' They all looked at her in surprise. Cyrilo smiled and leaned forward, Yuri winked lazily, shifting his long legs, and Deven gave her a serious look as if he knew what she was going to say. Prema sniggered but she moved a bit closer to Deven.

All five of them now formed a closed circle. A pigeon suddenly flew down, so close to their bowed heads that Rosie almost screamed. She controlled herself and said, 'We will find the person who killed that woman. I am certain she did not commit suicide. We will show Inspector Chand that we are not silly old fools, sitting around dribbling into our food as we wait to die. We will catch the murderer and then he will listen to us. He will know that we are very much here, alive and alert, and we are not invisible like everyone thinks old people are.' She stopped to take a deep breath.

For a moment no one spoke and Rosie thought they were going to laugh at her, but then Prema, her arch-enemy, said, 'Rosie. You are quite right. Let's show them. Yuri, Cyrilo, Deven and I can go out and catch that bastard who killed the woman. The four of us will put that fat inspector to shame,' she hissed, showing her missing front tooth.

'Four of us! What do you mean? You can't leave me out. It was my idea,' cried Rosie.

'Good idea, Rosie. I was thinking the same as soon as I saw that woman hanging from the tree,' said Yuri, picking a scab off his finger. His hands were stained with paint and lined with old scars.

'Shall we tell Maria? I don't want to hide anything from her.' Cyrilo looked towards the house. They could see Maria in the veranda with Leela, sifting through a large basket of vegetables.

Rosie didn't say a word. She was still hurt and she couldn't believe that the others were going to leave her out. She didn't care. She would do her own snooping and find out much more than they could. She would show them. Just because she couldn't walk didn't mean she was helpless. She had her own ways and means and was much better than them. She had a network of spies in the village and could find out things much faster. *Four of us. How dare Prema say that.* Rosie felt tears welling up in her eyes and turned her face away.

Cyrilo saw her do this and moved forward to pat her hand gently. 'Of course, Rosie, you will be with us. You can be our chief detective. We will gather information and report to you. You have better brains than . . . most women.' Prema leapt up at once, shouting, 'Better brains. Of course, all women have better brains than you lot. Even a cockroach has better brains than you, Cyrilo.'

'No need to be so rude, Prema,' said Cyrilo, getting to his feet. Yuri jumped up too, as if to show support for his friend, but bumped his toe on the bench and began to howl with pain.

'Sit down. Be quiet, all of you.' Deven spoke in a low, commanding voice they had never heard him use before. All of them fell silent and sat down like obedient schoolchildren. Rosie moved her wheelchair slightly away as if declaring her independence from the group. Cyrilo's kind words had mollified her a bit but she did not want to beg to be included. They should plead with her to join them and then she would give in gracefully.

'I propose that we tell Maria. She may want to help us. After all, that woman practically died on her doorstep. It's her moral duty to find out how and why such a terrible thing happened. She will regret it all her life if she doesn't. The shadow of this unnatural death will always hang over the Happy Home if we don't catch the murderer. The dead woman will haunt us forever,' said Deven.

\* \* \*

Rana Hooda stared at the sea, his eyes unfocused and blurred. He could not remember much from the previous night, but his head was throbbing with pain and his mouth felt as dry as sandpaper. So he must have had a good time, probably drank a whole bottle of wine. Olga and her friends had decided they had had enough of spicy Goan food and needed to give their Russian palates a rest. 'My stomach is grumbling, grumbling all day. Saying to me no more chillies, no more cardamoms or cinnamons,' she had cried, rubbing her stomach. *How beautiful she looks even when she is complaining of a stomach ache,* Rana thought, shutting his eyes to block the sunlight streaming into his room.

So the girls had gone out and bought a huge chunk of meat—it looked like an entire goat—and cooked it on an open fire in the garden. None of them could cook so they had just poured brandy and oil on it and set the meat on fire. Rana couldn't remember what it had tasted like; anyway, he was too drunk to notice anything by the time they took the charred meat off the fire. The entire garden was stinking of burnt flesh, and brandy fumes floated in the air, even making the wasps drunk, but the girls were thrilled. They had screamed with delight and clapped their hands, like cannibals celebrating their first human victim of the day. Olga did behave quite madly sometimes but that was part of her charm. She was a child, a wild, wilful child from Russia, though she claimed her ancestors were from Kazakhstan and ate horse meat for breakfast.

Rana got up from the bed and picked up his phone. He was surprised to see there were no messages or missed calls from his wife. She had left the previous night for Mumbai—that was why Olga had moved in. That was why they were celebrating. 'The old cow has gone,' screamed Olga as soon as she rushed into the house, spraying air freshener. Olga could not stand Rani's rose perfume and always tried to get rid of the strong smell as soon as she came into the house.

It was not easy to keep them away from each other. He had got Olga an apartment near the beach but she said it was too small and did not have a pool. She kept nagging him to get her a villa but Rani would get suspicious if he bought another villa for himself. It was tough to ensure their two worlds never collided, and he was glad Rani had finally gone to Mumbai to visit her friends. He checked his phone again. No calls from Rani. She must have landed by now. She called him at least twenty times a day and sent endless messages, giving him every tiny detail of her day like a commentary in a cricket match. She also gave him instructions on what to do, what to wear and what to eat. 'I'm going to the market. Now I'm at the hairdresser getting my hair dyed. Black streaked with a brown shade this time. I am buying a new fridge for the Goa house. I am having lunch with Rita, she talks too much and now I have a headache. Don't forget your BP medicine. Wear that new shirt I bought you from Armani. Wipe your shoes before you step on my new carpet.' It went on and on like this day after day. Her voice was like a defective tap, dripping non-stop all day. She often even called him late at night and spat abuses at him for no reason. Rana often wished that the mobile phone had not been invented; then his wife would leave him in peace. The good old landline hardly ever worked now but it kept you safe and hidden from prying eyes and ears. Fortunately, she did not know about FaceTime or else he would have had to stare at her angry, scowling face all day. She had once been quite pretty but the cosmetic surgeries she had had done at great expense abroad were losing their effect and her face now looked like a swollen, distorted mask.

Rana glanced at his phone again and wondered why she had not called him yet. *I hope her phone has got lost at the airport. I hope she herself is lost and is never found*, he thought viciously as he threw his phone back on the table and walked out into the balcony.

He knew Olga would be by the pool and that was the sight he longed to see first thing in the morning. Her blonde hair rippling in the sunshine, her young, perfect body stretched out languidly. What a change from Rani's clumsy yoga poses and loud breathing exercises. At the moment there was no one in the pool except for a few doves that were noisily cooing as they drank water from the edge. The waves roared in the sea in the distance, reaching up like walls of foam and mist, and then fell silent. As Rana gazed out at this serene and peaceful landscape, he felt a cold hand touch his spine. He turned around quickly.

There was no one.

Rana came back into the room and sat on the bed again. His heart was racing for no reason and he knew something terrible was going to happen to him that day. A cloud of anxiety now covered his face, its clammy fingers touching his skin. Maybe he had taken too many of those little pink pills Olga had given him. 'Make you feel great. You will be flying in the air. All your tensions, your gloomy thoughts, will vanish,' she had said, waving her hands in the air as if she was a fairy with a magic wand. Rana tried to breathe slowly but another wave of anxiety flooded through him. His hands began to tremble and he reached for his phone again. There were no calls from his wife.

# CHAPTER FIVE

THE RUGGED WALLS of the Chapora fort, black with age, protect nothing except for a few grazing goats and several oddly shaped boulders. One expected to find an ancient sea mariner perched on the ruined walls, looking out at the sea, waiting for his ship to arrive. The vast blue-grey view of the open sea on one side and the mouth of the Chapora river on the other was the perfect place for a fort, and the paranoid Portuguese had built several such forts along the coast. Aguada, Alorna, Tiracol and Chapora stood on the edge of the land like giants made of stone, guarding Portuguese territory from their neighbours, whose favourite pastime was to attack their settlements. They constantly feared an attack from the sea and kept watch from these vantage points to make sure no hostile ships sneaked into their ports, like they had themselves done not so long ago in the past.

They could not forget how in 1510 their great hero Afonso de Albuquerque had had to retreat after nearly taking over Goa to his ships anchored in the harbour.

There he lived in the cramped, wet and filthy space with his men for three months, surviving on rotten rice and meat as the monsoon rain lashed at his ships. Though the sultan of Bijapur's army attacked them relentlessly, they remained safe since the enemy's crude artillery could not harm them.

For three months the furious rains poured down as their flour turned mouldy and fungus grew on their clothes and leather shoes. By the end of the siege, the men were forced to catch river rats to eat. But soon the sun came out again and their fortunes turned. Afonso de Albuquerque managed to take Goa once again. So massive forts facing the sea were built and guns placed on impressive-looking battlements to scare off anyone who thought of mounting another attack. 'That should teach the native savages a lesson,' Albuquerque must have said, feeling very satisfied for once again conquering the gold mine that was Goa. Unfortunately, he did not live long to enjoy his fame and fortune and died in 1515, a sad and lonely man, humiliated by his king and countrymen.

Five hundred years later in one corner of the fort, hidden by the crowds of tourists, sat Alfonso. He was a tiny man, unlike his illustrious almost-namesake, but as agile as a baby monkey. Alfonso was a cat thief. From an early age he had learnt, or rather been taught by his father, to sneak into houses through narrow windows, air conditioner vents and coal holes.

One sultry morning, he sat rubbing his legs with coconut oil to keep them nimble and agile as he looked at his haul from the previous night. Flies buzzed over an open bundle of dirty cloth in which gleamed five gold necklaces, eight bracelets and a few rings. 'Not bad, and the season is yet to begin,' he said and laughed. His assistant, a young boy who looked like an angel in rags, sat by him, looking at a picture book. Alfonso kicked him and said, 'Tony, stop wasting time on that book. I told you not to pick up books from houses; just extra load for us to carry. Now go fetch us some food from the fish shop. Here, take this hundred-rupee note, and remember to bring the change back.' He threw a crumpled note to the boy. Then he began stroking the jewellery with his grubby fingers and tried to slip on the rings but none of them fitted him. 'Thin bastard. Rich beggars too thin these days,' he spat.

Yuri watched the young boy standing quietly in front of the fish shop, turning the pages of a picture book. *He looks like a sepia-toned cherub from a classical painting*, thought Yuri, and wondered who his parents were. He would ask them if he could paint a portrait of this boy. Russian tourists would love to buy a picture of this angelic-looking child in ragged clothes. Pretty images of poor, beautiful Indians always sold well.

'Hey. Come here, boy,' shouted Yuri from his table in the dark corner of the fish shop. This was where he sat every day, eating huge amounts of fried chilli fish, washed down with several glasses of home-brewed feni. The food at the Happy Home was very bland, and he needed these spices to remind himself that his taste buds were still alive.

The boy ignored him and kept reading, his lips moving silently. Yuri lifted his hand and called again, louder this time, and everyone in the fish shop turned to stare at him. The boy picked up his bag of fried fish, the oil already dripping through the thin paper, grabbed a handful of extra onions and chillies from the steel bowl on the counter and ran off without a backward glance.

'Funny boy. I would have given him some money if he had posed for me,' Yuri said, looking at the owner of the fish shop, his old friend Babu.

'He cannot speak or hear. Maybe he's mute or he just does not want to speak to anyone. Not quite right in the head, poor boy,' said Babu. 'Anyway, do not try to speak to him otherwise his master, Alfie, the weasel, will attack you.'

Yuri had often seen Alfie hanging around Morjim beach, trying to sell cheap trinkets to foreigners. He spoke a smattering of German, Russian and French and could tell jokes in each language as well as bargain like an expert but Yuri had never seen the boy before.

He paid Babu for his plate of fish fry and came out of the shop. He stood on the crowded street, not sure where he should go now. The sunlight was so strong that it seemed to set the gulmohur flowers ablaze, though it was still early in the day. A cat ran out on the road, chasing a huge, sleek rat, and then they both ran into a hole in the ground. Yuri heard shrill screeching sounds and wondered which one would come out alive.

A narrow lane led to the beach. Yuri could see the sun gleaming on the sand, turning it into a sheet of gold. The waves rose angrily and then lost their rage and gently fell. Though Yuri was quite far, he heard the soothing rolling sound in his head. A three-legged dog ran across the beach and stood watching the waves like an old sea dog. Every beach in Goa seemed to have its own three-legged resident dog and he was happy to see that this one looked quite well fed.

He turned his eyes away from the sunlit beach, the waves and the dog. He wanted to go and meet Olga but she was not picking up her phone. Something about yesterday was bothering him and he needed to talk to her urgently. He just could not get the dead woman's face out of his mind. He was sure he had seen her before but despite trying very hard he could not remember where. The policeman had covered her face so quickly. In any case her face was swollen and discoloured, as if she had been dead for hours. As Yuri stood by the road, a scooter whizzed past, splashing mud on his feet, and a stray dog came up to sniff his cloth bag filled with charcoal pencils. He desperately hoped Olga would see him today. She had not called him for three days now and there was no way he could find her. Why was she playing hide-and-seek with him?

When he spoke to her last week, she had refused to come to the beach to meet him. 'I will call you only after Rana leaves. He does not let me out of his sight even for a second. He gets up at night to check if I am there. He even waits outside the bathroom door to listen if I'm talking on my phone. He is a creepy swine. First, I have to hide in that gloomy apartment and wait for his stupid wife to leave Goa and now I have to wait for him to go away. It's very boring.'

'Why do you have to be with that toad? Tell him to get lost and come away with me,' he had shouted in Russian.

'Yuri, my little snowflake, Rana the creep lets me stay in this beautiful villa on the beach, he buys me expensive clothes and lovely, lovely diamond necklaces. Why should

I tell him to get lost? He is my golden goose, laying big fat golden eggs for me every morning. I hate hiding when his wife is here but then I have to do it.' Olga had laughed. 'But not for long, my snowflake. Soon I will be a rich woman. You wait and see, my darling Yuri. One day soon.'

Suddenly, Yuri remembered where he had seen the dead woman—in the villa on one of his earlier visits. She had been staring down at them from a framed picture on top of a bookshelf, her dark eyes as bleary and swollen as when she was dead. Yuri had turned his head away, thinking, *Why would someone take a photograph of such an ugly woman? Better to have her blemishes painted over with oil paints.* However, there was a kind of attractive quality in her ugly face; she looked like a wicked witch from a fairy tale, a powerful, evil woman who could destroy you.

Yuri tried Olga's number again but all he heard was a tune from a Bollywood film before the call was disconnected. Yuri knew Olga had seen his number and cut the phone dead. He rubbed his eyes and threw a piece of bread from his pocket to the dog still waiting patiently by his side and started on the way back to the Happy Home, his heart aching with sadness. 'I am an old fool,' he said to himself over and over again as he walked.

* * *

Deven spread out a large sheet of paper on the table as the others watched. They were sitting around the dining table, not eating for once but discussing the murder. Deven had declared he was in charge and when no one protested he appointed Rosie as his assistant. Prema was not pleased at all but after giving Rosie a dark look as if to say, 'You wait and see what I do to you', she kept quiet. Maria had agreed to help them, though she was not sure how. 'You get information from the inspector for us. He is so infatuated by you and will tell you every detail of the case,' Rosie told her. Maria was surprised to see the sparkle in her faded eyes.

Cyrilo had already been to the village and found out from the grocer that the dead woman was a stranger and no one knew where she had come from. A few people said they had seen her driving around in a big car but they hadn't spoken to her. 'Why should we? We have nothing to do with her kind of people,' they said. 'They come and go like summer flies. Why should we care?'

'I asked everyone at the market too but they said they had never seen her in Trionim before this summer. The grocer said a rich woman had come last week to his shop to order a large quantity of bottled water and five family packs of ice cream but sat in the car the whole time so he didn't get a good look at her face. The driver paid and he could hear her scolding him in Hindi for taking so long. She used some really good abuses which the grocer hadn't heard before. He was quite impressed. She was the only stranger around here except for the foreign tourists hanging about near the beach,' said Cyrilo. 'Imagine buying five family packs of ice cream in one go.'

'So at the moment we don't have anything to start with except this.' Deven wrote the following down in bold letters.

1. Woman found dead in Happy Home (hanging from mango tree)
2. Woman's identity not known but could be from Delhi
3. Seems to be very rich

'Why Delhi? How can you be so sure?' asked Yuri. He had not yet told them about the photograph. He wanted to see it once more and then reveal it but he could only do that if Olga called him to the villa. Maybe he would go and hang about there. If that Rana fellow came out, he could always pretend to be a Russian tourist looking for a hotel.

'I know why you wrote that. You think she's from Delhi because she spoke in Hindi and abused the driver. Only people from Delhi are so free with bad words,' said Prema, giving them a gleeful smirk.

'You should know, since you are from Delhi,' muttered Rosie, keeping her voice low. She knew that Prema was hard of hearing and the barb would not reach her.

'I heard what you said, Rosie. I may be from Delhi but I come from a very respectable family. My father was a senior officer in the railways,' said Prema.

'My father was also in the railways,' said Rosie.

'Well, I'm sure he was a railway guard. My father was the station manager in Saharanpur. We always travelled first class. Our cook travelled with us in second class,' Prema retorted.

Rosie kept quiet. Her father was indeed a railway guard and she wondered how Prema had known. He was a brave, honest guard and had been awarded a medal by the local mayor once. She wondered if she should tell Prema that and shut her up.

'If you ladies have finished telling us your family history, may I continue?' asked Deven, looking at them sternly like a schoolteacher. His glasses were perched on his nose and his eyes looked very bright.

'Inspector Chand told me that the woman had been drugged and then killed. She was already dead when they brought her here. It was definitely murder. The body has been sent to Panjim to a forensic team,' said Maria, looking at them. She thought it was very brave of them to help solve the crime but she felt uneasy. Should she allow them to get involved? What if they got hurt? What if the killer was still around? But she had never seen them look so happy and excited. They had huddled together all day talking to each other, planning things. It was sad that an unfortunate woman's death had brought them together but that was what life was like when you got so old. At their age, anything—a broken-down car, a petty theft, a funeral and even a death—was exciting. It broke the monotony of their everyday lives. One day she too would become like them and get a thrill every time she heard of a death in the neighbourhood.

'MURDER.' Deven wrote this in big, bold letters and looked at them. 'I knew that for sure. I knew it was murder the moment I saw the body. I noticed her fingers were badly bruised. She must have put up a fight,' he said quietly.

'Write that down too,' said Yuri.

'What for?' asked Cyrilo.

'Just like that. It'll fill up the sheet a little bit. I hate seeing a blank sheet,' he said.

'Maybe you can draw a dead body hanging from a tree.' Prema threw him a nasty look.

'Good idea. Here, take my pen,' said Cyrilo with a smile, sliding his pen towards Yuri, who quickly picked it up. He began to draw a long, wavering line.

Deven snatched the pen away. 'Don't be idiotic, you two,' he said angrily. 'We must draw up a plan. Enough of this rubbish talk. I will give each of you a task and you must report back to me in the evening. You have to talk to people, find out every little detail. We must follow each clue and link them all together to reach a conclusion. The most important thing is to find a person with a motive. Who gained from this woman's death? We also have to find the boy who saw the body first. He could lead us to other people. Someone must have seen the body being brought into the garden of the Happy Home at night. We have to do this very carefully. I don't want any of you to make mistakes.' He glared at them.

'He thinks he's back in his office and we are his employees,' whispered Rosie to Cyrilo and giggled. Deven was suddenly looking taller and smarter, like a general in the army. Rosie smiled at him, twisting her curls with her fingers and thinking that marrying for the third time might not be a bad idea.

* * *

Inspector Chand wiped his hands on the small towel on his chair and burped. His mother had sent too much food as usual and he had to finish everything otherwise she would get into a bad mood. If he married Maria, he wondered what he would do with his mother. There was no way they could all live together, but that was a worry he would deal with later. At the moment he had to focus on this letter from Panjim. The inspector general was planning a visit to Trionim the following week. What a nightmare. He would have to get into a clean uniform and wear shoes in the hot weather instead of the comfortable rubber slippers he had picked up for fifty rupees at the beach. He looked around the office and called Constable Robert in.

'Tell Eric to send his nephew. He must paint the walls outside, repair the toilet seat and get rid of the garden umbrella.'

'Why, sir? It's so comfortable to sit in the shade in the afternoon. We got it for free, too, from that Russian we arrested last month for drunken driving,' said Robert. He had come to work in thin cotton shorts that day since he had a rash on his legs; he looked like a baby in a crumpled nappy: a big, fat baby with nappy rash.

'And get your uniform out. The IG is coming tomorrow.' Inspector Chand barked and burped once more. The rich, butter-laced tomato curry was sitting in his stomach like a stone. He reached for the bottle of Hajmola pills on his table.

As he chewed thoughtfully on the salty, spicy pill, he wondered if he should visit the market. He had sent Constable Robert to check in the village about the dead woman but nobody seemed to know who she was. Or they knew and weren't willing to tell him. Everyone was so suspicious of the police these days. In the olden days policemen were treated with so much respect. As a child in Punjab he had seen villagers touching the local *daroga*'s feet before giving him a tray of sweets on Diwali. Here, no one ever sent him sweets or even wished him on Diwali. Constable Robert had brought a large chocolate cake filled with cream the other day—sent by the old woman who lived next door after they had found her cat—but it wasn't the same as a tray of sweets being laid at his feet.

He hated going to the crowded market to deal with the sullen shopkeepers and belligerent village women who screamed at him for no reason at all. He hated the fact that he had to walk there because the jeep could not enter the narrow, winding lane. He swallowed the digestive pill, savouring its delicious, sour flavour, and took out one more. Then he rose with a loud clatter as his files and torch fell on the floor, and strode out of the police station like a warrior embarking on an epic journey. Constable Robert, who was reading a comic book, jumped up to salute him and together they went out into the sunshine.

Inspector Chand wished the murder had taken place in the winter when Goa was at its sparkling best and not so hot. That was the perfect time to go looking for a murderer, not this humid weather that gave him prickly heat and made his uniform smell of sweat. He always made sure he sprayed some aftershave lotion on his arms and neck whenever he went to meet Maria.

# CHAPTER SIX

'TURN LEFT. LEFT. When I say left, I mean left,' said Deven in a low voice.

'Your left or mine?' muttered Yuri as the car stalled.

'Your left,' said Deven, raising his eyes to the sky as if praying to the gods to grant him patience.

'You should make that clear. There's a lot of difference between your left and my left. I hope this path leads to the Vaddy village. That's where the boy lives, according to Eric the undertaker,' said Yuri, taking a sharp turn, throwing Cyrilo against Prema. She frowned and pushed him away. 'Sit straight. Why are you trying to climb on my lap, you idiot? Stay on your side or I'll clobber you with my handbag,' she said.

'Watch your tongue, madam,' said Yuri, turning his head around to give her an angry look from the front seat. They heard the sudden screech of brakes and a scooter slam to a halt behind them. The driver raised his arm and shouted at Yuri.

'Hey, watch where you're going,' he said and then added 'sir' reluctantly when Deven put his head out of the window to give him a stern look.

'Don't shout at us. You should not be going so fast on this narrow road,' he said.

'I was going so slowly. You stopped suddenly without giving a signal,' replied the scooterist.

'You want to have a fight with me?' asked Yuri, rolling his window down. His blue eyes flashed in the sunlight as he smiled menacingly.

'No. Just asking you to drive carefully. That is all. Why should we have a fight, uncle?' the scooter rider asked in a mild tone, looking worried. 'Anyway, where are you trying to go? This road only leads to my house. I am Bhola Ram, by the way,' he added, wiping the sweat from his hands with a red handkerchief and reaching forward to shake hands with them.

'I am Yuri, this is Deven, and in the back seat are Cyrilo and Madam Prema. We are from the Happy Home and we are looking for a boy, a small boy with curly hair.'

'Hundreds and thousands of small boys with curly hair in Goa, sir,' said Bhola Ram, grinning. Yuri's little van and Bhola's scooter were both blocking the road and five scooters waited patiently for them to finish their conversation. Bhola now called out to the man who was trying to edge his scooter past them, almost driving into a muddy drain.

'Oh. Hurry, hurry. Lobo. What is your hurry? These gentlemen and the lady are looking for a small boy with curly hair. How many do we have living in Vaddy? One thousand?'

'Maybe one thousand and one. Tony had a son last night. Going for breakfast there.' He laughed as he revved his scooter but didn't move. 'I tell you what. I will take you to Tony de Costa's house. He is celebrating the birth of a baby son. Everyone will be there for breakfast and you can see if the boy you are looking for is there. Okay?'

Deven looked doubtful but everyone else agreed this was an excellent plan. They had not had a proper Goan breakfast for many years. Prema muttered that she was not dressed properly for a feast and had left her teeth at home but when Cyrilo asked her again, she agreed. She took out a comb from her bag and quickly patted her hair in place. 'Does my hair look all right?' she asked.

'You look like the queen of England going to a garden party,' said Cyrilo.

'But without her teeth,' whispered Yuri.

As Bhola Ram had told them, there were at least a hundred small boys running around in the large garden. A few more were climbing trees, and some were racing in the fields nearby. 'Trees. Let us first question the boys on the trees. Remember, Maria said the boy had been perched on a tree that morning. He had pointed out the dead body hanging from it,' said Deven in an excited voice.

'We know. We were there too,' muttered Yuri, picking up a sausage from a plate and dipping it in a rich red tomato sauce. Cyrilo had piled up his plate with chunks of bread, thick slices of roast chicken and three boiled eggs.

Prema was only drinking tea and looking around with a haughty air like a queen at a servant's ball. 'We have not really been invited. You two should not eat like starving beggars,' she hissed when she saw Cyrilo and Yuri going for a second helping.

'Please eat some more,' said an old lady, coming up to them.

'It was very kind of you to let us come,' said Prema in a voice that sounded exactly like Eliza Doolittle's in *My Fair Lady*. Everyone stopped eating and gaped at her. Prema tried to smile, keeping her mouth closed since she did not want to display her toothless gums.

Suddenly, a small boy dressed in a Superman costume came running up to them. 'You are from the dead lady's house,' he shouted, pointing at Yuri. 'I saw you that day. You vomited at the gate.'

'I did not. I did no such thing,' said Yuri, looking around sheepishly. 'I had a bad cough and I just coughed because something was stuck in my throat.' Now some of the other guests gathered around them and someone pushed a little boy forward.

'He found the body,' Tony said proudly, patting the boy on the head. Yuri stared at him and the half-eaten sausage fell from his hand. It was the brown cherub he had seen in the fish shop.

'But the boy cannot speak. It is very sad but otherwise he is a very clever boy. He looks after the garden for us. His name is also Tony.' Tony Senior then moved away to talk to his other guests.

The boy smiled at them and pointed to the gate.

'Is he saying he wants us to leave? How cheeky!' said Prema.

'No, I think he's saying he wants to go out with us to the gate,' said Deven and turned to leave.

'Let us say thanks to our kind host,' said Yuri, but Tony was nowhere to be seen so they walked out quickly, Cyrilo leading the way.

Their white van stood under the shade of a banyan tree and scooters were parked all around it like bees around a honeypot.

'How will we ever get out?' screamed Prema. 'Why did you park in such a stupid way?'

'Relax. Your blood pressure will go up if you shout so much,' said Cyrilo. 'Calm down, take a deep breath.'

The boy moved forward swiftly. As they watched, he took out a bunch of keys and began moving the scooters. Within a few minutes he had cleared a path for the van. Yuri clapped his hands.

'This boy is a genius. We should employ him at the Happy Home. He can help you in the garden, Cyrilo, and maybe we can have some flowers one day instead of a forest of weeds.'

The boy smiled and took out a small notebook from his shirt pocket. 'My name is Tony. The Happy Home has a very good mango tree,' he wrote in clear, neat handwriting.

'Did you see anything that morning when you were sitting on the tree?' asked Prema.

'I will ask him the questions if you don't mind, Prema,' said Deven.

'Yes, good idea. Prema is quite deaf, you know,' whispered Yuri.

'I heard you. I can hear better than you any day. I will not waste my time if you don't need me here. You think you are all so clever. Anyway, my hearing aid batteries are going now.' She started walking away.

'Prema, come back. The boy is going to write his answers down. She can read; it doesn't matter if she can't hear,' said Cyrilo gently. Prema sniffed the air like an offended vixen a few times, adjusted her hearing aid and came back. She didn't want to miss anything.

Tony sat on an upturned drum that had been left on the road and looked up at them. Then he pointed to Yuri.

'What does he mean? Why is he looking at me?' muttered Yuri, moving backwards. His heart was beating very fast. He drummed his fingers on the car nervously. Had the boy seen him talking to Olga? He could have easily seen them together near the villa and now he would tell the others. He must quickly think of an excuse before the others could understand what the boy was trying to say.

But just as Tony was about to write something, he stopped and jumped up. A thin, small man dressed as a clown in bright red and green trousers was walking down the road towards them, followed by a group of children. He waved to Tony, his eyes glaring from his face, painted white, his red mouth angry. The boy started running away from them.

'Alfie. Alfie. Show us tricks,' shouted the children, but the clown ignored them and ran behind the little boy.

* * *

The monsoon rains had turned the fields outside Trionim into vast stretches of green, and some women walked from one paddy field to another carrying tufts of long, green plants. 'See, that is how they plant rice,' said Rana as they sat on his balcony sipping lukewarm coffee. Olga yawned. *Now he is going to lecture me on the monsoon*, she thought, gazing beyond the fields where she could see traffic moving in a long, slow line. Her friends must be heading out to beach parties. She wished she could invite some of them over for dinner, then she would not have to sit alone with Rana. Time hung heavy in the air when she was with him. She would go and call up a few people later after he had finished telling her the boring details of the rainy season that hit Goa every summer. At home in Moscow nobody ever talked about the rain. They just unfolded their raincoats, covered their heads with plastic caps and went out. When they moved into Rana's house in London she would learn to talk about the weather. 'The English love talking about the weather,' her friend Martina had told her. She was well settled in London and spoke really good English now. 'Come here next month. We will both go to classes to learn table decoration,' she had said the previous night.

Olga wished she could run out of the house and escape Rana's voice still going on and on about the monsoon. He was now telling her in great detail about the history of the rains and how they had once flooded the Rajasthan desert many years ago. Olga smiled and nodded at Rana as she stroked his arm. She saw herself plunging a knife into his chest, through his Armani shirt, through his gold chains, through his Mont Blanc pen, right into his heart.

She picked up an apple and sank her teeth into it. *I must call Yuri at the Happy Home as soon as Rana leaves for Delhi. I hope Ziriko comes to the restaurant tonight with my packet. I am running out of pills. Oh god. I really need one now. I will never be able to get through this evening without them,* she thought, her eyes dull as Rana described for the tenth time how he had fallen into a monsoon-created ditch last year and lost the keys to his brand-new BMW.

'Look, Olga, the women have already transplanted half the field,' said Rana, jolting her out of her daydreams. 'They wait for the first monsoon showers and begin their work. The monsoon hits Kerala, then Goa and then slowly travels up to the north. It covers the entire country by the middle of July. It's amazing how that happens. Let me explain it to you. The monsoon is caused by the difference in annual temperature over land and sea. But sometimes a factor called El Nino plays havoc and the monsoon fails.' Rana's nose twitched with excitement. Olga shut her eyes and thought about table decorations. Martina and she would learn to cut vegetables into flowers and which wine glasses were meant for which occasion. She would be Mrs Rana Hooda by then, and she could tell him to take his monsoon saga and go to hell.

Olga got up and went to the bathroom to wash her hands. She had to wash her hands at least twenty times a day. She was afraid of catching an infection in India if her hands became dirty. The skin on her fingers was peeling away but she kept scrubbing them with the strong carbolic soap she had brought with her from Moscow. She was very worried that her supply of soap would finish before her plans to become Mrs Rana Hooda materialized. Once she got this idiot to marry her, she could flee to England and she would not have to wash her hands any more. There were no lethal germs in clean and cool England. The only problem was Rana Hooda's wife. His ugly witch of a wife who stood like a stone pillar in the way of Olga's fabulous life.

* * *

Yuri wondered if he should tell the others about the photograph. But what if he had made a mistake? No, he would wait till he had seen Olga and checked the photograph again. He would definitely go to the villa tonight. Even if Rana was there, she could sneak him in.

'Why did the boy point to you, Yuri?' asked Prema, her eyes narrow with suspicion. 'What was he trying to tell us, I wonder. Do you know that little boy?'

Cyrilo also looked at him but did not say anything. Sometime earlier, Deven had taken an autorickshaw and gone to the market. 'I'm going to talk to some people there. It's better I go alone. You people talk too much and disturb my thoughts. Hercule Poirot did not have to deal with a gaggle of confused minds,' he had said and marched off.

'We should work together and not be so secretive. We are a team,' muttered Yuri, trying not to feel guilty about the photograph. He would tell them when he was really sure it was of the dead woman.

'Look, let us not quarrel. Such a waste of time. So far we have not found out a single thing. I think we should go to the tea shop and ask around there. I have seen that people

always talk a lot at tea shops.' Cyrilo was keen to have a
cup of tea since Deven had not let him finish his breakfast.
*What delicious cupcakes they had at that place. Each one
with a different sugar candy on top*, he thought with regret.
He did not like all this rushing about. It was much better
to settle down somewhere comfortable with a cup of tea
or better still, a glass of chilled beer, rava-fried prawns and
then talk to people. They would certainly find out a few
interesting facts. Who was the dead woman? That was the
main thing.

Prema suddenly gave him a nudge in the ribs and said,
'Get out, slow coach. Always daydreaming. We are trying to
catch a murderer to catch a murderer, not go on a holiday.'

Cyrilo slowly got out of the van, his knees creaking. He
stood for a while to find his balance and Yuri came and
stood by his side, rubbing his back. 'Oh. This van creaking
and whining always gives me a pain in my backside,' he said
loudly and winked at Cyrilo. They both kept a straight face
as Prema glared at them. Her hearing aid was also whining
loudly as if complaining to them.

The tea shop, noisy and filled with smoke, was crowded
with men who had just come off the ferry. Baskets of
vegetables and fish, bundles of newspaper, various odd
bits of luggage and a huge pram filled with books stood
blocking everyone's path. They stepped over it and found
an empty table near a window. Prema immediately picked
up a newspaper and began wiping the table with it. 'So
dirty, I will not eat anything here.'

'Go to a five-star hotel, then,' said a voice next to them.
They turned and found the owner of the tea shop standing

at their table. He began to laugh. 'Just joking, auntie.' Cyrilo, Yuri and Prema stared at him. They could not believe their eyes. It was Tony. But he did not seem to recognize them. They all felt a bit hurt and looked away.

'Hey, what is the matter? Don't feel bad. I will get the table cleaned for you at once. Oi, come here you,' he shouted and a small boy came running. 'Go, clean, clean properly. Can't you see these are high-class people?' He gave the boy a nudge in the ribs and started laughing.

'Not high-class. They are old folks from the Happy Home,' muttered the boy, flicking a wet, stained cloth over the table as Prema wrinkled her nose.

'How do you know, Mr Know-it-all?' asked Tony, surprised.

'They came for breakfast. Didn't you see them, boss? Didn't you see how much they ate?' said the boy, grinning.

'You were at the breakfast party?'

'You have a very short memory, son. Must have it checked. Could be a disease, you know,' said Cyrilo.

'Early stages of dementia,' said Prema, her eyes narrowing with malice.

Tony laughed. He slapped his plump hands on the table and laughed so loudly that everyone at the tea shop stopped talking and began laughing with him. 'It has happened again. You think I'm ignoring you nice uncles and aunties? You think my memory has gone bad like old people who cannot remember if they ate breakfast or not, if they went to the toilet or not? Do you? Do you?' He laughed. 'I remember what you ate, what you were doing just one hour ago. I never forget a face though you three have forgotten mine.'

Cyrilo did not say anything. He was feeling embarrassed. Why was he going on and on? Why could he not just sit down at his counter and take their order?

Prema got up from the table and picked up her handbag. 'I am going. This place is awful. How can we ever find out anything here? Look, they all seem to be asleep in their teacups. Look at him.' She pointed to an old man who was dozing nearby. He was wearing a torn paper hat with ribbons, as if he had been to a birthday party. He, too, looked very familiar. Why was everyone looking so familiar in this dark, gloomy tea shop?

As he stared at the old man Cyrilo suddenly remembered where he had seen him. 'He was at Tony's breakfast party. I saw him throwing a bun at the dog,' he told Yuri.

'Yes, yes, we were all there. I am Tony's twin brother, Roy. We both like confusing people, but this lady does not seem to like our little joke. Learn to laugh, auntie, otherwise life is a burden. Learn to enjoy what each day brings.'

'There is no need to give me advice, young man. I am old enough to be your mother so keep your thoughts to yourself. If you are Tony's twin brother, why did you not tell us before? Why play this silly game? Take my advice and grow up. Now bring us some tea in clean cups, please.'

Roy smiled and scratched his head. 'Okay, mama. Right away.'

'Do you know that little boy who works for Tony? His name is also Tony but he cannot speak. We wanted to talk to him.'

'About the murder at the Happy Home?' said a voice behind them. Cyrilo, Yuri and Prema quickly turned around.

The old man had woken up and was adjusting his paper hat and ribbons as if getting ready to party again. He looked at least ninety years old but his eyes were bright and alert and he was as slim as a young boy. Cyrilo wondered if he would look as fit if he lived to be ninety. He already had a paunch and a double chin. *Maybe your looks improve as you age and by the time you are ninety, you look really good*, he thought.

'The woman was drugged, stabbed and then hung on the tree,' the man said, turning towards Cyrilo. He spoke slowly and clearly, as if talking to a simple-minded person.

Roy pulled up a chair and sat down. 'You really think she was drugged too? That's something new. Who told you? I heard she was stabbed ten times. You saw the body?' His eyes sparkled with curiosity.

'We saw the body but no blood. Her clothes were clean,' said Cyrilo.

The dead body loomed before his eyes. The clean white shirt, the baggy trousers and the expensive shoes. The red handkerchief around her neck. Why had she been dressed like a man? Who was she?

'You want me to tell you, you keep your mouth shut and listen. Don't jabber on. Learn some manners, young man. Lady, move your bag from the table.' The old man wiped his chin with his hand.

Cyrilo noticed his nose was covered with sugar, as if he had dipped his head into the sugar bowl. For once,

Prema did not rise to the challenge of being the rudest person in the room. She just stared at the old man, waiting to hear what he had to say. *She has finally met her match. I should take this old fellow home. Maybe she can marry him and set up her own home and leave us in peace*, thought Cyrilo.

'Eric the undertaker is my younger brother's son. He told me there was a wound on her neck. He told the fat policeman but he said, "Forget about it. She is dead; what difference does one small stab make when your neck is broken and you are dead. If you want me to check her blood pressure, her eyesight and her sugar too, I will do it." A very stupid man. He must have paid a heavy bribe to get into the police. Robert, his constable, is much smarter. Anyway, why do you people want to know? Are you the dead woman's relatives or just nosy people who like to poke their noses in other people's business?'

'Err . . . we just want to know. We are from the Happy Home and since she was found in our garden we thought we should find out more about her,' muttered Cyrilo.

'Aha. You think this is your own little murder and you want to play detective. Well, have fun. No harm, after all at your age, what else can you do? Talk to Eric, he can help you. By the way, the woman had come to Trionim to buy a house. She should have gone to the graveyard and booked a plot instead.' The old man said this and walked out of the tea shop, whistling.

'Who is he?' asked Prema.

'My great-uncle Bob. He claims to be a hundred years old. Drinks like a fish but can still row his fishing boat faster than any other fisherman on the Chapora river. I will get your tea in clean cups right away.' Roy got up from the table.

As they sipped their tea—hot, milky and sweet, just the way Cyrilo liked it—they wondered if they should meet Eric the undertaker or go home.

'My back is hurting a bit and I need to have a nap now,' muttered Yuri.

'Yes, I want to go to the toilet urgently,' said Prema. 'This one must be dirty. I hate dirty toilets.'

As they drove back to the Happy Home, they felt they had done a good day's work. They were tired but also mentally much more energetic, as if life had thrown them a bouquet of fresh flowers and the scent was exhilarating. They felt exhausted by all the hectic physical activities, and their knees hurt, but this was a new kind of ache in their bones. Suddenly the blood in their veins was running briskly and they felt years younger. It was good to have something to do. It was good to wake up in the morning and look ahead to another exciting day. It felt rejuvenating to be alive once more.

When they got back they found Rosie sitting by the door. She was holding her favourite mirror in her hand and looking into it. Her face was flushed with excitement. Her eyes, lined heavily with kohl, sparkled like two glass beads.

'So glad you people are back. I've been waiting for you. I saw the boy again. He was passing by my window and I called out to him. He came in and sat down with me. He told me that the woman had come to the Happy Home last week. He told me the dead woman was here, right outside our door.'

'How did you understand what he was saying?' asked Prema suspiciously. She was sure Rosie was making this up to impress the men. She was always seeking attention.

'He can write, you know. He wrote it all down in a small notepad he carries around his neck. He is so sweet and clever. I might adopt him. He could be my little page.'

'Did he say why the woman had come to the Happy Home?' asked Yuri.

'No. He just wrote that in his notebook and ran away.'

'We found out that the woman had been stabbed in the neck and then hung from the tree. Someone must have killed her and then dragged her body here. But why?' said Cyrilo.

'Poor thing. Imagine being pushed and pulled even when you are dead. May her soul rest in peace,' said Rosie.

'She was obviously being punished for some evil deed from her past life,' said Prema. 'We all have to reap rewards and punishments in our next life for our deeds in this life. That is why I lead such a pure, blameless life.'

'I too have lived a blameless life and will be born as a white swan in my next life,' said Cyrilo.

'This rule applies only to Hindus; you are not included,' said Prema.

'Prema, you will be born as a cat, I'm sure,' said Yuri. 'A sweet, cute cat with sharp teeth.'

'Oh, no, I don't like cats. I must put my teeth in before dinner,' said Prema, and she rushed off to her room.

'Do you think that woman had come to the Happy Home to meet us?' asked Rosie.

'She was looking for a house to buy. A man at the vegetable shop in the market told me that too. Maybe she thought the Happy Home was for sale,' said Deven thoughtfully.

'I hope not. We will be homeless then. Maria will never sell this old house,' said Yuri.

'Listen, I think we should drive to those new villas near the road and see if we can find somebody who knew her. I have a feeling she came from there,' said Deven.

Yuri looked down at his hands. Should he tell them now that he had seen her photograph in one of those very villas? But then he would have to tell them about Olga. Somehow he could not bring himself to talk about her. They would make fun of him. Prema would have something nasty to say. No, he would wait. Let them find out who the woman was. The police must have worked it out and the inspector would be coming soon to tell them.

'Life is so fragile. It's like a pearl necklace that can break any moment and scatter all the precious pearls. One day you are a rich woman driving around in a big car, abusing everyone and the next day you are dead,' said Rosie.

'I hope I have a quick, painless death,' said Yuri.

'I don't want any kind of death just yet. Right now, I just want something to eat. I wish I had eaten a few more cakes at the feast. They had delicious coconut sweets.' Cyrilo headed towards the dining room.

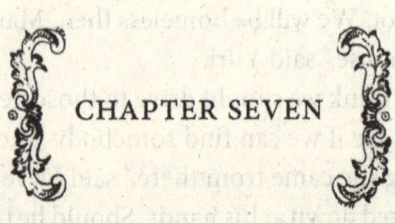

## CHAPTER SEVEN

MARIA AND LEELA were in the kitchen kneading dough for the bread that was baked every afternoon. Leela pushed the dough down on the stone slab and rolled it up again deftly in one quick movement, just the way Maria had taught her. Later, the house would be filled with the delicious aroma of freshly baked bread and the scent would linger till late evening.

Rosie loved the aroma. The next day for breakfast they would have thick slices of hot buttered toast and home-made jam. Sometimes, Maria made them scrambled eggs on freshly baked buns. Rosie watched them working and moved her wheelchair slowly along the shaded path, taking care to avoid the bright sunlight. She tried to keep to the edge of the path but the wheelchair kept rolling down on the grass. She had to struggle to turn the handle to move it back.

Rosie knew she had to buy a new wheelchair, a motorized one that could zip across the garden, but she kept postponing it. She had had this old wheelchair for eight years now and it was like a trusted old friend. Its rubber wheels squeaked in soft tones, and the smooth wooden handle felt warm under her hand. She could not let go of her old wheelchair yet. It would probably last till she died, so why waste money? Rosie looked down at her hands. How thin and scrawny they looked now; she often thought they were not her hands but some old woman's. *I'm an old woman now but in my heart I'm still a young girl.*

Her hands had once been soft and plump like Maria's. She loved painting her nails a vivid shade of red to match her lipstick. Everyone said she looked like the Hollywood actress Ava Gardner, with her large eyes and thick, wavy hair. Rosie had once gone to a movie to see this actress and was shocked to see how ordinary-looking she was. *She has pretty eyes but she looks nothing like me. I think I'm much better looking.* But she couldn't really say that to anyone.

Now when she looked at herself in the mirror, a strange reflection looked back. A woman with gaunt cheeks, mottled skin and puffy eyes. Who was this ugly old woman? Even if she put on a lot of make-up now Rosie could never bring her old self, her real self, back. *When you grow old you become a different person outside though your inner self remains the same, longing to escape from the aged body,* Rosie thought, leaning back in her wheelchair, allowing the evening breeze and the happy birdsong to soothe her sad thoughts.

The cicadas called outside in cheerful notes and the garden lay in darkness like the vast, unending sea. A soft, sweet fragrance floated into the house from the rose bushes. Someone was singing loudly in the house next door and Rosie hummed the words to herself. She remembered singing this song as a young girl. Slowly, as she sang, the years rolled away and she was a young girl running around in her mother's garden. She tripped over rose bushes, jumped over puddles and heard various sweet voices calling out to her. She was so happy, so carefree, climbing the branches of a beautiful tree covered with flowers, and life shimmered in front of her like a mountain, so full of promise and joy. Now she had almost reached the end of her journey. The hill still shimmered with promise but it seemed so far away.

* * *

They had finished dinner at the Happy Home and were now sitting around the dining table. An owl hooted outside and another one replied at once.

Maria pushed the coffee cups away and brought her chair closer. 'Well, now we have three bits of new information,' she said, but before she could add anything further, Deven gave her a look as if to say, 'Now I will take over.'

Maria stopped and gave him a little bow. Deven stood up. He pulled a chair out and started speaking in a loud voice, as if to a large audience instead of just five people.

'I will now give you all the facts. Please listen carefully. Fact number one: she was drugged, strangled and brought here and hung on a tree. Fact number two: she was from outside Goa. Fact number three: she had come to Trionim to buy a house. What can we deduce from all this?' asked

Deven, and when they all stared at him silently, he shook his head with a sigh.

He walked to the blackboard he had placed in one corner of the dining room and then turned around to look at them, his spectacles resting on his nose. No one knew what to say. Cyrilo reached for another coconut biscuit and quickly popped it in his mouth. He began to chew carefully so that Deven would not notice the crunching sound. Coconut cookies were so noisy. He wished he had some soft chocolate cookies with him that he could munch silently. He wondered where Yuri was. He had been acting strange for the last few days. He must talk to him later, find out what was bothering him.

Leela, who was clearing the table, suddenly stopped. She looked at them for a few moments and then said, 'You know, I think I saw her at the beauty parlour when I was cleaning the brushes last week. She was getting a pedicure. A very ugly, tall woman she was. Almost looked like a man. She asked if someone could thread the hair on her chin but none of the girls wanted to. She looked a bit crazy and kept laughing for no reason and talking to herself. She kept shouting to someone on her mobile phone too.'

'Why were you cleaning the brushes at Joni's parlour?' asked Maria. 'I hope she pays you. She is a great one for getting free work done.' The expensive face cream had given her a rash and she was going to ask Joni to refund her money but she knew this time Joni would refuse.

'Listen. This is very important, what Leela has told us. If the woman she saw at the parlour is the dead woman, she was obviously living here and not just visiting from

Panjim. She must have rented one of the new villas on the hillside . . . you know, those expensive ones with swimming pools,' said Deven.

He turned to Maria. 'I want you to go to Joni and ask her if she knew anything about the lady. Be casual so she doesn't suspect we are snooping.' He tapped his pencil on the table.

'I would love to have my own swimming pool. Just imagine getting up in the morning and having a swim,' said Cyrilo, smiling, but he changed his expression and coughed sheepishly when he saw Deven glaring at him. 'Good work, Leela, clever girl.' Cyrilo tried to look serious.

'Please pay attention to what we are discussing,' said Deven.

Rosie glanced at him. *He's really turning into one of those detectives you see in foreign television dramas. Just like that fellow . . . what was his name? No. Not Poirot; he was bald and fat. This detective was very good-looking and always narrowed his eyes and frowned just like Deven. His name was . . . Sherlock Holmes. Yes. That's it. Deven has become the Sherlock Holmes we saw on television last week.* She giggled.

'I will go to the beauty parlour tomorrow and ask Joni,' said Maria and got up. She would return the cream too and try to get her money back. Francis had said he would come tomorrow and she hoped her rash would have cleared up by then.

The trouble with Francis was that he was so unpredictable. He never kept his promises and she was always hanging around waiting for him to show up or send her a message. On the other hand, Bobby Menezes was reliable and always kept his word. He was a real gentleman, so polite and considerate. Even as a young boy, he would always speak to her politely. The other boys would jump and rush about the school garden but Bobby would stand under the banyan tree and examine the leaves. Maybe she should call Bobby over just to make Francis a bit jealous, but that was not fair on poor Bobby. He was such a kind, sweet man. His soft brown eyes always reminded her of a spaniel she had once had. Life was very confusing. You could be cruel to a kind, loving person but love a cruel, heartless person to death. 'I'm not going to hang around like this for Francis. He can't take me for granted. I'll show him that I too can play games,' muttered Maria, but she knew in her heart that she would find it impossible to do so.

The next morning she woke up at dawn, and baked a new batch of cinnamon cakes and two dozen mushroom patties for the Tip Top Cafe. Baking always made her feel calm and she did not think about Francis all day. Kneading the dough, mixing the sugar and butter till her arms ached, watching the cakes rise in the oven and finally taking them out in a cloud of the delicious buttery, cinnamon aroma made her feel good. It took her to a cosy, warm place and made her feel content. Baking was as wonderful and calming as meditation. She also got dozens of cakes to sell at the cafe.

After giving everyone breakfast, Maria got into her car and drove with Leela to Joni's beauty parlour near the Chapora bridge. It was a wet, humid day and her hair rose like a frizzy halo around her head. Maria wondered if she had time for a quick blow-dry at the parlour as she knocked on the glass door. *It's not for Francis. I just want my hair to look good*, she said to herself as she hit her head on the metal wind chime that rang loudly and discordantly in protest.

Joni's beauty parlour was in a mess. A pile of clipped hair lay in one corner and discarded robes were scattered all over the floor. Loud music blared from the radio and hairdryers added their own harsh, whining sounds to the cacophony. In one corner, a big pot of wax bubbled and groaned like a witch's brew. There was such a strong smell of hairspray that Maria began to sneeze. She pushed some robes aside and stepped over a tub of soapy water before waving to Joni, who nodded and pointed to an empty chair, her mouth full of hairpins. Maria moved a pile of old magazines and sat down while Leela stood near the door, looking at everything with great interest. Her large eyes sparkled as if she was in a toy shop and not an untidy beauty parlour. *She really seems to like all this. I will ask Joni to train her next year. I will pay her*, thought Maria.

Joni finally finished and came and sat down next to her. She very reluctantly took the cream back and refunded the money. 'It was a very good cream. You should have a facial done. Must be careful at your age. You already have so many fine lines around your eyes.' Joni pointed to Maria's face, as if she had not understood her. Maria knew she was upset about the cream so she ignored the rude remarks and asked about the woman instead.

'Yes. A peculiar-looking woman did come in last week, Leela is right. We had never seen her before. I remember she had tufts of hair on her chin. She kept boasting that she had just come from London and had had her skin peeled there. It looked awful, almost as bad as your skin. Why do you want to meet her?' asked Joni suspiciously.

'I was told this woman was looking to buy a house here. I know someone who's selling a house near us so could you give me her address?' Maria hoped Joni would not ask who. She knew everyone in Trionim.

'I think she came from one of those new villas. Yes, I'm sure of that. She said her husband had built some of them and was planning to buy more land for a hotel in Trionim. She did mention something about buying a house too. I don't have her name or address. I wasn't really paying much attention. Women who come to the parlour talk so much that my ears get tired of their voices. They should just sit quietly and not go yak, yak, yak,' said Joni, counting out the money for Maria. 'Why don't you buy this new hair colour that has just come from Mumbai? You have quite a few grey hairs now.' Maria quickly walked out of the parlour, dragging Leela away from a tray of nail polish bottles.

'So that woman was from here. It was very clever of you to notice her. Though it's odd that we never saw her in the market,' Maria told Leela as they drove to the cafe.

'She looked like a very rich lady. She had a big diamond ring on every finger and a diamond nose ring too. Rich ladies like her don't come to the market. They send their servants.'

* * *

His face half hidden in the shadows, Yuri stood under a peepal tree, staring at the villa where Olga was staying. The windows were closed. The sun had gone down over the horizon and the sea was a sheet of shimmering grey. Gulls called to each other as if sharing the gossip of the day that had just ended. Yuri wondered what to do. 'Maybe I will go around to the back garden and knock on the kitchen door,' he said to himself. There was a car parked in the driveway, a brand-new red BMW. That meant Rana Hooda was here and Olga would not be able to talk to him, but he had to see the photograph again to make sure it was the dead woman.

It was really urgent. He hated hiding something so important from the others when they were running around trying to find out her identity. If it was the same woman why would her photograph be in Rana Hooda's house? Who was she? His mother? She looked quite old; she could certainly not be his wife. He had to talk to Olga again. Yuri tried not to think of how keen he was to see her again and it wasn't just about the photograph. 'You are an old fool, Yuri,' he whispered as he walked into the garden like a thief, his heart racing madly as if he was running.

Inside the house, Rana looked at his phone again. 'My wife has not called me for twenty-four hours. That's quite amazing. I have never known her to be so uncommunicative. She has to tell me every moment of her day. A blow-by-blow account. She has to find out every detail of what I'm doing. Drives me crazy. Even when I'm in London, she wastes thousands of rupees on stupid, useless phone calls. She cannot go to sleep unless she has called me a few rude names every night.' Rana had now switched the topic of conversation from the route of the monsoon winds to his miserable married life.

Olga did not reply. She was not going to think about anything. She shut her eyes and began planning what to wear if she got invited to the queen's garden party in London. Next year. It had to be next year or she would just go back to Moscow. She could not stand Rana's voice any more. Olga looked down at her fingernails, each one painted with an intricate flower. The new diamond ring flashed on her third finger and suddenly she felt better. Perhaps Rana Hooda, however boring he may be, was not such a bad deal. She could do better but she could do worse too and get hitched to an impoverished Russian drunkard. Olga caressed her ring.

Suddenly, she heard a noise downstairs. The servants were off today. Rana always sent them away because he was scared they would talk to his wife about her, though he always said, 'I like being alone with you, darling.' That was a big bore because she had to fetch and carry for him. Rana could not even make a cup of tea. He was such a lazy slob. Olga got up and peered out of the window. She suddenly saw Yuri and looked around nervously before quickly shutting the window.

'Where are you doing?' asked Rana, looking up.

'Just looking to see if your car is there.'

'Where should my car be?' asked Rana, picking up his phone. He was quite distracted today and kept checking his phone all the time.

'I will be right back, sweetie. Missing you already.' She smiled.

*What is this stupid fool Yuri doing here?* Olga thought as she went downstairs. If Rana saw him there would be trouble. He had smashed all the glasses and broken an expensive vase when he had found Ziriko here one day. She had pretended he was a plumber and had quickly given him a wrench she had found on the shelf. Now Ziriko always carried the wrench around with him like a security blanket. Olga frowned as she looked out at the garden. Ziriko was such a fool and a coward. She hoped he had not messed up what she had asked him to do. Time was running out for her and she was surrounded by a bunch of idiotic men. She must chase Yuri out at once and then call Ziriko.

Olga went back upstairs to Rana and sat down. If she had been away any longer he would've come down to see what she was doing. 'Why did you take so long?' asked Rana, looking irritable.

'Just checking if the garden gate was shut. I'm going downstairs to get a cold beer. Do you want one?'

'Okay. Hurry. Get those masala chips too.' He put his feet on the glass coffee table. It was an expensive Swedish table and it groaned under his weight. Olga made a face behind his back and went out of the room. She quickly washed her hands in the bathroom and ran downstairs, her high heels clicking on the floor.

'Yuri, you fool. Why are you here? You'll get me into real trouble. He will smash your face along with all the glasses in the house,' hissed Olga through the half-open window in the downstairs hall.

'Why don't you answer my calls? I had to see you. I miss you so much. Listen, just fetch me that photograph from the drawing room. You know, that big one in a silver frame on the top shelf,' said Yuri.

'Why? Are you trading in stolen silver now?' whispered Olga.

'I just want to see the photograph, please. I called you so many times but you keep cutting me off. You don't care for me any more,' said Yuri, his voice breaking as a wave of self-pity rose to flood him.

'I do. I do. You are my snowflake. Listen, sweetie, you wait here. I will get the silver photo frame. You can have the silver ashtrays too. He will never notice they're missing. Alfie at Morjim beach will give you a good price for them.'

'No. No. I don't want the silver frame. I want to see the photograph. I think she is the dead woman.'

'Dead woman? What are you talking about? What dead woman? Where?' Olga said, forgetting to keep her voice low.

'The dead woman who was found hanging in the Happy Home garden. Don't you know about it?' said Yuri.

'Darling. What are you doing? Come back,' Rana shouted from the upstairs room.

'Go. Go away, you old fool!' said Olga, and she began to laugh hysterically. She sat down on the floor, covered her mouth, and screamed with laughter. Yuri stared at her, and just when he was about to reach out through the window and touch her hand, he heard footsteps coming down the stairs. He turned around and ran, his heart racing. This time he was truly afraid and his whole body began to shake wildly. He found he could not breathe and had to sit down near the garden wall to catch his breath. 'What is happening to me? Why have I got myself into this trap? She does not care two hoots for me. I must get out of her clutches. I must forget her. She is mad,' he said to himself as he listened to Olga's manic laughter. Yuri's hands began to tremble. He was very afraid.

* * *

'Breathe in, pause, count to five, breathe out and bend to your left,' chanted Maria in a low voice. Her soothing words floated out into the garden and made the leaves of the hibiscus plant tremble. 'Now turn to your right slowly and touch your toes,' she murmured as five pairs of stiff knees squeaked in protest. Her sole student under the age of sixty nimbly touched her toes and sprang back, her firm young body poised like an arrow for the next yoga exercise.

Maria had decided the previous week to start these yoga classes in the courtyard of the Tip Top Cafe to earn some extra income during the off season. On weekdays she had only a few students, mostly Russians on their way back from the beach and a lone Japanese girl who was as agile as a young child. Now all the members of the Happy Home had decided to join, including Rosie in her wheelchair. Maria was surprised but very pleased to see them there.

They were all looking very different for some reason. Deven was dressed as usual in his neatly ironed shirt and black cotton trousers, looking like a lawyer, but the others too had made an effort. Rosie was wearing a pink tracksuit with sequins on her back declaring she was 'Ready for love' while Prema was dressed in an all-black salwar kurta and looked like a female dacoit as she glowered at everyone with her narrow, foxlike eyes.

Cyrilo was wearing shorts and a T-shirt but not one of his usual faded, crumpled ones. He was looking very smart in Nike shorts and a Desigual T-shirt with his grey hair slicked back with gel. Only Yuri was missing. He always woke up late and hated doing yoga in any case.

Maria chanted the instructions as she watched them bend and stretch, their aged limbs awkward and stiff but with smiles on all their faces. She wondered if this horrible murder was the best thing that could have happened to them, and then immediately felt guilty. Some poor woman had died and she was feeling happy. Tomorrow she would go to St Antony's Church in Siolim and light a candle.

Maria stretched and exhaled. A Russian girl was now doing very quick, energetic jumps that were not a part of the yoga class and everyone had stopped to look at her. Maria looked too. A huge diamond and emerald ring on the girl's finger flashed in the bright sunlight as she twisted her body into a perfect triangle and then jumped back again to stand still, tall and beautiful like a marble statue. Maria noticed she was wearing a big red bindi on her forehead.

\* \* \*

The sea rippled in the fading light as a few fishing boats slowly made their way into the tiny Chapora bay. Gulls screeched, making aggressive sorties in the air as they searched for any fish that had fallen off the boats. They swooped down as soon as they saw some movement on the water and then rose in the air again, disappointed, their angry screams getting louder and louder.

Tiny wooden huts painted in bright pink and blue shades lined the edge of the road and each one had a forest of green plants shielding it from the busy traffic. Huge fishing nets were stretched out to dry on the ground and stray dogs lay curled up on their rough surface. A few long-legged white birds hopped amongst them but they were ignored by the dogs, which continued sleeping peacefully.

Alfie cursed as he watched the young man twist a rope around a pole on which a torn fishing net was drying. Then he shook his head angrily and shouted, 'Ziriko, idiot. You are not doing it right. Make the knot the other way. The way I showed you.' But the young man continued, singing loudly to himself. Alfie picked up a stick and threw it at him but it had no effect. Ziriko began singing even louder, leaning on the fragile wooden crate, and his tall, angular figure looked like a crooked wooden pole rising out of the sea. His long, matted hair flew around his face like wriggling worms and Alfie was surprised the birds did not fly down to perch on it in search of food.

Alfie did not like the taciturn, shifty-eyed man but he was the best person to repair fishing nets in Chapora. The best and the cheapest since he was quite happy to be paid in feni or weed instead of cash, but sometimes he was so drugged he just did his own thing and made a mess of the fishing net. Alfie was also a bit scared of this strange fellow with red scars on his hands. It looked as if he liked cutting his own flesh. Ziriko hardly ever spoke and only grunted out short replies but he sang all the time. Alfie was not sure where he came from. He looked Russian but spoke another language that sounded like French but very often he sang in Konkani too. Alfie was quite sure he was a bit off his head. *Too much feni or maybe drugs*, he thought and went down the wet stones to the boat. Ziriko had neatly untangled the fishing net and tied it to the pole. Now he was half in the water, laughing and talking to himself as he tried to catch a plastic bag that was floating past.

'Crazy, stupid fellow,' muttered Alfie, shaking his head. The previous night Ziriko had brought a cloth bag filled with silver ornaments and dumped it on the table. 'You want me to sell them?' Alfie had asked, knowing very well that they were stolen from one of the big villas on the beach. Ziriko nodded and clapped his hands like a child. 'Olga, Olga, my little sparrow, Olga,' he had crooned.

\* \* \*

Inspector Chand tried to focus his binoculars but the sweat trickling from his forehead down to his nose had now reached his eyes and all he could see were two blurred figures trembling like reeds in the glittering sea.

'Here, you take a look and tell me what they are doing.' He handed the binoculars reluctantly to Constable Robert, who was gazing out to sea, holding his large paw over his eyes. The binoculars looked like a tiny toy in his giant hands when Robert picked them up. 'It all looks very far to me, sir,' he said, suddenly speaking in Konkani.

'You idiot, hold it the right way around. Have you never used binoculars before?' asked Inspector Chand.

'No, sir. This is the first time,' said Robert, turning the binoculars around and resting them on his nose. Then he held his breath and slowly shut one eye.

'You don't have to shut one eye. Use both eyes,' shouted Inspector Chand. A few people stopped by to see what was going on. Soon a small crowd had gathered on the beach and everyone was pointing to the boats.

'They caught a thief escaping on that boat,' said one man, squatting on the roadside and washing his mouth at a tap.

'No. He was a smuggler. They catch a smuggler every day around this time. The fat cop and the giant cop share the loot with him and then let him go,' said another man.

'Why are they looking there with those binoculars?' asked a boy, climbing up on a water tank to get a better look. 'O! I can see Alfie and that druggie fellow with long hair.' He said this so loudly that Inspector Chand heard him and turned around. The inspector and the constable walked over to him.

'You know that man?' he asked.

The crowd suddenly melted away but the boy perched on the water tank just froze. 'Yes. Yes. Everyone knows him,' he muttered nervously, looking down at them from his perch.

He was almost at eye level with Constable Robert, who now jabbed a finger as thick as a stick into his chest. 'Who is he? Tell us his name, son. Don't be shy now,' he said in a gentle voice.

'Alfie, and that other man is . . . I am not sure. I cannot see that far.' The boy quickly jumped down from the water tank.

'Here, use these,' said Inspector Chand, handing the boy the binoculars. He hoped he did not have an eye infection. Children had so many dangerous infections; he never went near any child if he could help it. He must remember to disinfect the binoculars before using them again.

'I think . . . I don't know. He could be Ziriko. He comes here sometimes to repair the fishing nets but he never talks to anyone. He is from Mumbai,' said the boy, looking around furtively for an escape route.

'Come on. This is a waste of time. That old fellow from the Happy Home was talking rubbish. Someone must have played a trick on him and told him that something fishy was going on in that house by the beach. These old folks have nothing better to do than waste my time,' grumbled Inspector Chand.

'Something fishy,' said Robert and giggled.

'Find out who that villa belongs to and also ask that Russian in the Happy Home for a description of the woman he thinks is the dead woman. We can give him the photograph that the Panjim police department sent us of her,' said Inspector Chand.

'It is a terrible photograph, sir. I feel scared looking at it,' said Robert.

'Well, it is not a beauty contest we are judging, Robert. We are looking for clues which will lead us to the identity of the dead woman. We don't know who she is. If we don't know who she is, how will we find out who killed her?'

He looked around as if hoping to find the murderer lurking behind them.

'I think I will go to the Happy Home now and try to get some more details from the Russian fellow. You go talk to this Alfonso fellow who calls himself Alfie. Find out if he was near the Happy Home last night. Ask the shopkeepers in Trionim,' said Inspector Chand and turned to get into the car, holding his binoculars far away from his face. He must wash them with Dettol as soon as he got home.

\* \* \*

Eric the undertaker was showing Alfie the new coffins that had just come in from Panjim. He opened the lid of one and then got in as swiftly and gracefully as a dancer.

'Look, it is lined with satin even on the inside. Not that it matters to the poor deceased since he or she can hardly admire its softness now. But little details like this matter to me. I always order my coffins from Berimanza and Sons in Margao. Look, the handles have a pure bronze finish. They are plastic, mind you, and will come off if you pull them. But then, who needs to pull them once the funeral is over. You are six feet under and safe in the bosom of mother earth. I can order you one, if you like, Alfie. They are going at a cheap rate since the season has not yet begun,' said Eric, lisping through his broken teeth.

'I don't want a coffin. I want to be cremated . . . much cheaper, Eric, tell me. How well do you know this woman called Olga?' said Alfie, taking out a packet of cigarettes from his shirt pocket and passing it to Eric.

'Gave them up, man. You will certainly need a coffin soon if you keep smoking like this,' said Eric with a smirk.

'I saw you talking to her the other day. Do you know where she is now? She isn't answering her phone,' said Alfie, blowing smoke out of his nostrils.

'Does she owe you money? I always take an advance payment from these girls if I do some work for them. You can never trust women when it comes to money, especially these smart young Russian girls. I always keep my wallet hidden from my wife too. Would you like a cheaper imitation wooden one? I can show you the one that the police use to transport corpses from one place to another. Cheap and sturdy but no frills.'

'No. No, thanks,' said Alfie, taking another long pull on his cigarette, and then he began coughing.

'Bad cough. A cough like that can take you to your grave. I will see you soon in my parlour, my boy.' Eric laughed. He stared at Alfie and then said, 'Go to that Ziriko. That long-haired boy with scars on his arm. He knows where she is but you have to get him to talk.' He paused and then said, 'You can buy this discounted coffin for yourself. I used it to carry that woman's body to the Panjim morgue and she travelled like a queen in it. I had to wash it with soap and water but it's as good as new now. No one can tell,' said Eric as he sat down on the coffin and opened his lunch box. As Alfie walked away he heard him mutter, 'Soggy veg sandwich again. I will kill that woman one day.'

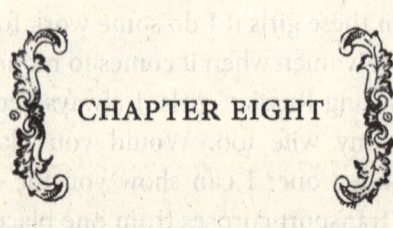

# CHAPTER EIGHT

MARIA WAS GAZING up at Francis, holding her breath in so that her skirt would not feel so tight around her waist.

They were sitting in a quiet corner of the Tip Top Cafe, sipping cappuccinos laced with cherry brandy. Francis had put on weight since the last time she had seen him but Maria did not say anything. Much better if he got fat; then he would not notice her spreading waistline. He was wearing a brand-new cream-coloured Hugo Boss jacket and polished brown leather shoes with pointed toes. His feet looked like baby alligators as he moved them closer to her sneaker-clad feet. Maria would make him throw those shoes out when they were married. She hated them. Francis was obsessed with clothes and was always buying really expensive things. She thought it was odd for a man to be so fashion-conscious.

'Are you sure nobody knows who the dead woman was?' asked Francis once more.

'Not yet. But Yuri found a clue. He saw a photograph in someone's house and he told the police about it. They are now asking the police station in Panjim in case someone has reported a missing person. They don't seem to believe him,' said Maria.

'By police you mean that fat Inspector Chand who keeps drooling all over you?' said Francis, laughing.

*How perfect and white his teeth are*, thought Maria, and quickly resolved to go to the dentist to get her teeth polished. 'What bothers me is how she got there. How did someone drag her dead body and hang it up on the branch of the tree?' said Maria, moving her hand a bit closer to Francis, hoping he would hold it.

'Must have been two or three people doing the job. Are you sure you never heard anything that night?' Francis ignored her hand. He took out a comb and began combing his hair.

'No. Nothing at all.' Maria moved her hand back. She hated it when a man combed his hair in public. Only loafer-type boys did that. Bobby would never do such a thing. Bobby probably never ever combed his curly hair. Maria looked at Francis and suddenly remembered that she had woken up that night to drink water and had stood at the window to look at the moon. But she had been thinking of Francis and did not bother to look into the garden. If only she had. She would have probably seen the murderers dragging the woman's body up the tree.

Maria shivered.

'Are you cold? Shall I switch the fan off?' asked Francis.

'No. I'm fine. Shall we walk back to the Happy Home now? I have to organize dinner,' said Maria, feeling a warm glow of joy. How considerate he was. She loved the way he had looked at her, asking her if she was feeling cold: a gallant Prince Charming with sparkling white teeth. If only he would propose.

'How long are you going to look after those old folks? They should make some other arrangements. You can easily turn your house into a nice little hotel, you know. They are called boutique hotels and foreign tourists love them. Your Happy Home is a heritage building too. Chuck that bunch of oldies out. You are sitting on a pile of money. I can get you a buyer tomorrow if you say yes. So many people from Delhi are looking for heritage houses. They will happily pay any amount you ask.' Francis smiled at her.

Maria stared at him as her happy thoughts vanished into the cool evening air. She could not believe what he had said. Throw her old friends out? This was their home. The Happy Home was their only home and it was her duty to look after them as long as they lived. She had promised her grandfather that. She loved it; she really cared for them and they were her only family. Throw them out! Sell the Happy Home! How could Francis say such a terrible thing? Could he really be serious? Maria turned her face and looked at him as if she had never seen him before. He caught her staring at him and smiled. Then he winked and put his fingers on his lips and blew her a kiss. His eyes seemed to glow with love and Maria forgot about what he had just said as his fingers gently touched her hand and her heart leapt with joy.

* * *

Yuri raised his head to the sky and began singing an aria from Puccini's *Tosca* so loudly that the chickens flew up into the air and then sank down, flapping their wings in agitation. One of them ran straight to the bucket of water and leapt in as if bent on committing suicide. Yuri pulled her out, cooing, 'My sweet little Misha. Calm down. I sing this song only for you, my darling.' He threw a handful of puffed rice to the other chickens but they huddled in one corner, eyeing him suspiciously, wondering what was going to happen to their unfortunate relative who Yuri was holding in his hands.

The chicken stared at him, blinked her yellow eyes a few times rapidly and then shut them as if she could not bear to see him. Yuri was looking really terrible. He had not slept all night and his eyes were bloodshot after the hours of heavy drinking. His breath was so awful that he could smell the stale fumes himself each time he exhaled. The chicken looked as if she was choking on his foul breath and her eyelids trembled with fear and loathing.

Yuri put the chicken down gently and she fled to the safety of the water tank at once. The others followed quickly and the courtyard was soon empty except for a crow that now rushed in and began picking up the puffed rice. Yuri sat on a wooden box and put his head in his hands. He was so confused. He had tried to tell the others about the photograph but Deven had just dismissed it saying he must have made a mistake. 'How could the dead woman come from one of those expensive villas? She was dressed like a man in crumpled, stained clothes. I spoke to Eric and he told me she looked like one of those mad women who roam the beach bothering foreign tourists. If you really believed the photograph is of her, why didn't you get it to show us? Then it would be proper evidence. Who will believe us without proof?' Deven had said, tapping his stick impatiently.

Yuri had gone again and tried to tell the inspector about the photograph but he did not believe him. 'We went to the villa and found no one missing. You gave us wrong information. Don't waste valuable police time.' He had then been thrown out of the room.

Yuri looked at the chickens, shook his head and shouted, 'You old fool. Forget it. No one believes you.'

The chickens gave a frightened squeak. Yuri whispered a few words in Russian and threw them a handful of puffed rice again. They hesitated and then came out one by one to pick up the grains, their feathers still ruffled with suspicion. 'I will talk to Olga. Why did she not give me the photograph? She said she would give it to me later. I will go up to the house again and face that man too. What can he do to me? He cannot kill me. I will say I am her friend and want to talk to her about something urgent. I will speak in Russian to her.' He took care to speak softly to himself this time so the chickens would not get frightened.

\* \* \*

Rosie sat at the window and gazed at the garden lit up by the moonlight. It was a warm night but the breeze was so cool on her face that she felt like someone had splashed water on her. One night, a long time ago when she could walk, Rosie had run all the way to the sea on a moonlit night like this. The sea looked dark, as if it was not the sea but a stretch of bleak land. The moon played hide-and-seek behind the clouds. She had wanted to see the turtles come out of the sea to lay their eggs on the sand. She had waited all night with several other people from her village but no turtles had emerged. She was walking away disappointed but then she heard someone shout, 'Come back. Come back.' She had run so fast over the wet sand that she had to gasp for breath and finally stop. Then she saw a round, dark shape struggling up the sand, leaving a trail of water like a narrow stream. A guard told them to stay away, waving a stick. They had stood silently, holding their breath as the turtle laid its eggs and slowly went back to the foaming sea. The waves rose up to greet it like an old friend and then its shape was lost forever.

How easy it had been to walk. You just put one foot forward and then the other. You didn't even think about it and moved forward. You could go from one place to another so easily. You could climb stairs, walk in the garden or just stroll up and down in the veranda. Sometimes Rosie dreamt that she could still walk. She was on the beach, running, the wind salty on her lips, the sand rough yet soft under her feet. Someone was running with her but she could not see the person's face. She tried to run faster but the face kept vanishing into the mist that rose like waves from the sea. On some nights she climbed a high, snow-capped mountain, something she had never done in her life, and when she woke up she found herself on the floor. She had to wait till Leela came into the room and helped her back on to the bed. They would laugh about it together but she could see the pity in the young girl's eyes as she lifted up her shrivelled, useless legs.

'Poor Rosie, a pathetic cripple. How terrible to live like this. Better to die than be confined to a wheelchair.' She heard people whisper behind her back. But she did not want to die. There were so many things in this world you could do even if you couldn't walk any more. She could admire sunsets from her window, hear the birds chatter in the garden and smell the scent of a new rose when it first opened its petals. She could still eat really hot vindaloo, drink beer and laugh. Why should she die now when there was so much still left to do? Besides, they had to catch the murderer, didn't they?

These days, they sat around the dining table every evening after dinner and Deven discussed what they had found out during the day. Nobody had really found out anything important yet. Deven often scolded them like a headmaster. How smart he looked when he spoke in that firm, loud voice, so masterful and macho. Rosie put on her best perfume every evening and sat very close to him, though she could feel Prema's angry looks jabbing her like darts on her back.

Rosie shut the window and drew the curtains. She wheeled herself around and slowly rolled herself on to the bed, pulling up her lifeless legs. It took her a long time but she succeeded after a struggle. She said her prayers and lay awake wondering when the long night would pass and the birds would begin to call in the garden. The moon travelled slowly past her window, gazing at her like an old friend, and then hid behind a cloud. Her room was plunged into darkness. 'Soon it will be dawn. Soon the sky will turn light and the birds will begin to sing. Soon, it will be another new day and I will be alive to enjoy it,' she whispered and smiled as the moon emerged from behind the clouds to join her.

The next day as they sat around the dining table with steaming cups of coffee, Deven was complaining to the group that Cyrilo was birdwatching when he was supposed to be keeping an eye on the suspect.

'I was keeping an eye on that man but this lovely little green bee-eater just came and perched on the branch right above my head,' said Cyrilo with a grin. Rosie could not help smiling back at him. He was such a child even at this age, with his mop of curly, grey hair and sparkling eyes. How well he played the piano.

'Yes, while you were watching this bee-eater or whatever it is called, the man you were supposed to watch just drove away.' Deven gave him an angry look.

'I forgot why we were supposed to keep an eye on this fellow. Who is he?' Cyrilo scratched his head.

'That man is the owner of the house where Yuri saw the photograph of the dead woman. We want to know who else lives there,' explained Deven and sighed.

'I know who lives there.' Leela picked up an empty cup.

'How do you know, Miss Know-it-all?' asked Prema.

'Doesn't matter how she knows, Prema. Tell us, Leela. Who is he?' asked Rosie.

Leela said nothing and just stood by the table watching them all. She wasn't going to give them this important information so easily. She would make sure they appreciated her efforts by making them wait. She wished Maria would come back but she was still out with Francis. So far Deven had not asked her to do anything to help in this case. Leela was keen to help but they all thought she was too young and stupid. But she was not too young and stupid to cook their meals, clean their rooms, wash their clothes, give them their medicines, listen to their complaints.

She would make them wait. Leela picked up the coffee cups one by one and slowly placed them on the tray. She counted the spoons, pretended one was missing, and took the tray back to the kitchen, humming under her breath. She knew they were all watching her. She wanted to giggle but stopped herself.

'She knows nothing, silly girl. She's just showing off,' hissed Prema.

'She's not silly. She's a very smart girl,' said Rosie.

'Is Leela playing games with us? This is a serious investigation and not a hobby we are indulging in. A woman was found dead right on our doorstep and we must find out who killed her,' said Deven, pointing to the blackboard.

Cyrilo, who was drawing lines on a piece of paper, quickly looked up. 'Where is Yuri tonight?' he asked.

'I don't know. I haven't seen him all day,' said Deven.

'Maybe he's painting on Vagator beach. You know, that place he likes so much above the rocks,' said Prema.

'It's so dangerous. The rocks rise up like a fort and druggies often hide there. I have told him not to go there but he just laughs at me. Mad fellow,' said Deven.

'Yes, he is a bit mad. Wait, I think I saw him near the villa,' said Cyrilo.

'Which villa, Cyrilo?' asked Deven, looking at him sharply.

'That villa you told me to watch. The green bee-eater had flown away and as I looked up at the tree, I saw Yuri standing far away. I waited for him to come to the van but he just vanished. I forgot to tell you about him, sorry,' said Cyrilo, twisting the pencil in his hand.

'Your memory is really bad. Anyway, he will turn up later. When you see him tomorrow ask him if he had seen the owner of the house. I hope he wasn't birdwatching like some people we know,' said Deven, wiping the blackboard with a damp cloth. Though his back was to them, they could all feel his disapproval. Leela watched him from the kitchen door and decided she would wait for Maria to come back and tell them what she knew. It would be good to announce the name of the owner of the villa and watch their mouths fall open in surprise.

Rosie moved her wheelchair closer to the table and patted Cyrilo's hand. He looked up at her and smiled.

'Why is everyone in such a bad mood? Play the piano for us, Cyrilo, please,' she whispered.

Cyrilo got up from the table at once, wiped his hands on a napkin and sat down at the old piano and began to play. The liquid notes drifted into the garden, lingered on the leaves of the plants and then wafted in the moonlight like dewdrops. As the warm, scented air filled the house, a beam of moonlight stole into the room. It touched all those seated around the table and in this magical, silvery light their old, lined faces shed the years and turned young once again. As they sat listening to the lyrical, smooth notes, they remembered how they had danced once, walked on the sand and run wild, chasing their friends on the beach. They remembered the laughter and joy of their younger days and wondered how they had grown so old so quickly. When had time stolen everything while they were not looking? They had never thought they would grow old. Other people grew old but not them. Their youth seemed such a long time ago that it felt like another lifetime. Cyrilo played for a long time before his fingers began to ache. He slowly brought the lid down as everyone clapped.

Leela, feeling much calmer now, decided this was the right time to disclose her little gem. 'The man who lives in that house is the husband of the dead woman,' she said in a voice so low that the others had to ask her to repeat what she had said.

'Really? How do you know that?' asked Deven, walking up to her. The others just stared, their eyes full of surprise. Leela felt a ribbon of thrill run down her spine. There! She had made them all sit up and take notice of her. She wondered if she should milk this a bit more and make them beg but decided it was better not to. Better not play it out too long or else they might just go off to sleep. Anyway, she was dying to tell them everything. She could not wait for Maria.

Leela came and sat with them. Cyrilo, Prema, Deven and Rosie kept staring at her. Each of them wore a different expression. Cyrilo was curious, Prema suspicious, Rosie surprised, while Deven combined all these emotions and glared at her, his face lined with anger, suspicion and disbelief.

Leela lifted up her chin and said, 'I know the young boy who works in that house. His name is Tony. He cannot talk but we communicate in sign language. He told me that this man lives in Delhi but comes to Goa, to this villa, every Sunday. His wife came for the first time last week but then disappeared. Tony saw her photograph in the house. He also saw Yuri there once with a Russian girl. This Russian girl also lives in the house but only when the other lady is not there,' said Leela, feeling a bit breathless.

'That is amazing, girl. You have found out more than any of us,' said Cyrilo, and Rosie reached her hand out to pat Leela on the back. Prema muttered something and almost smiled but Deven did not say anything. He only nodded his head but Leela could see he was impressed. 'This boy, can you call him here tomorrow? I must talk to him. We must find out what else he knows,' he said.

Leela was upset that Deven had not thanked her. The others looked impressed but not this sour-faced headmaster Deven. She was not going to help him any more. She would go straight to the fat police inspector now but first she would tell Maria what she had found out.

'You cannot talk to him. I told you he's mute. He will only talk to me. Only I can understand him,' said Leela and went back to the kitchen. She began banging pots and pans to show them she was upset. Ungrateful old biddies. She would not make any pudding for them tomorrow.

\* \* \*

The rain lashed the windows and Rana wished he had not built the house so close to the sea. The architect had said that it was high up on the cliff and quite safe. 'Look at the view. People will kill for this view,' he had said. Rana wondered if they would be killed *by* the view if a really big storm came up. His head was aching badly, and he could not move his arms. What had he drunk last night at the noisy bar Olga had dragged him to? Something had happened after they got out of the smoky room. He remembered getting into the car but nothing after that. Had she mixed something in his drink? That girl had so many pills in her bag. 'My colourful little friends always help me,' she would say, forever popping some pink or yellow pill. Rana rubbed his forehead. He suddenly noticed that his hands were covered with a white powder. He tried to focus his eyes.

There was a peculiar smell in the room, and marigold garlands all over the sofa along with a huge box of sweets. A lamp had overturned, spilling oil all over the carpet. He glanced at the shelf and saw that Rani's photograph was missing. Olga must have removed it, probably while screaming, 'I hate your ugly wife staring at us all day. When will you divorce her?'

Rana tried to pick up his phone from the table but his hands would not obey. Suddenly a wave of fear flooded over him. What had happened to him? Why could he not move his hands? Where was Olga? He opened his mouth to shout but no sound came out. All he could hear was the oil dripping on the marble floor and the faint sound of a woman laughing somewhere in the house.

* * *

When she was a child Rosie could recite all the poems of William Wordsworth. Her parents were very proud of this talent and at every family function she was trotted out to perform her piece. Most people were not keen to listen to poetry, and the strange words describing fields of daffodils and white clouds meant nothing to them. What on earth were daffodils? They would rather sing familiar songs and clap their hands but they were too polite to say that to Rosie's father. Too polite and too scared since he was a very bad-tempered man. He often broke plates and cups in the house if there was too much salt in his food or his slippers were not dried properly by the servants. Her mother had to rush out and buy new plates every week. The people in the village always joked and said, 'Husband in bad temper again?' Her family members were all in heaven now and they had taken their bad tempers with them. Her first husband and her second husband were in their graves and she was all alone in the world. The Happy Home was her last home. They would carry her out of here one day. The gold coins she had hidden would pay for a grand funeral.

Rosie gazed out of the window, turning her wheelchair so she could see the ocean. All she could make out was a tiny fragment of the water but it made her feel happy to know it was there, a massive waterbody with millions of creatures living in its depth. Suddenly, Rosie saw a small boy climbing up the wall. She was about to shout out to him but then she stopped. *Let me see what he will do.* The boy climbed up the garden wall, agile as a squirrel, and caught hold of one of the branches of the mango tree and swung himself on it. Rosie craned her neck but she could not see him any more. She waited, tapping her finger impatiently on the wheelchair, feeling frustrated with her lifeless legs.

Rosie remembered that she had seen the same boy before. He had come and stood near her window the other day and she had called him in. He had written in the notepad that he always carried that the dead woman had visited the Happy Home the week before she became a corpse. As Rosie watched, wondering if she should call Leela, the boy's face appeared, half hidden by the mango leaves.

'Hey, come here,' she shouted. The boy, startled, looked down at her, his large eyes full of fear.

'I won't scold you. Take the mangoes, they are green and sour, but first come here. You know I'm in a wheelchair. I cannot walk so I will not chase you. Come here, boy. I will give you potato chips. Look.' Rosie waved a packet of chips she had taken out of her bag. 'Come. We met that day, do you remember?'

The boy hesitated and slowly climbed down from the tree. He wiped his hands on his shirt and came forward, not taking his eyes off the packet of chips in Rosie's hands.

'Here, take it,' she said gently.

The boy stood quietly and his face broke into a smile. It was as if the sun had come out from behind the clouds after a shower of rain. Rosie could not help smiling back at him. His face, streaked with mud and black dust, reminded her of a painting of a cherub she had seen in the church long ago. If he were dressed in white robes he could have been a little angel flying down from heaven.

'Listen, you wait here. Eat the chips. I will call Leela. You know Leela, don't you?' asked Rosie.

The boy nodded but did not take the chips. He pointed to a magnifying glass on her dressing table, the one she used to see the hairs on her chin.

'You want to see this? Okay, just be careful.' Rosie handed him the box with the magnifying glass. 'Don't break it. I need it for my make-up,' she said, laughing.

'Hey, what are you doing here?' Prema appeared behind them. 'Why have you let this thief into the garden? This is how things get stolen from the house. Get out, you dirty urchin,' shouted Prema. 'Look, he has pinched your magnifying glass. Give it back,' she screamed, trying to snatch the box away, but the boy quickly moved back.

'He is not a thief,' said Leela, walking into the room. 'I'm so glad he has come here because I was about to go out to look for him.'

As they watched, Leela twisted her fingers into strange dancing gestures and the boy nodded. Rosie realized Leela was speaking to him in sign language and though she tried to follow what they were saying to each other she could not understand anything except that the boy was very excited and pleased.

'What is going on here? This is all rubbish. I'm going to call Deven and get this boy thrown out right now. Rosie, you are a fool to let him into the garden. Next you will have the entire village camping here.' Prema marched out of the room.

Finally, after a few confusing nods and gestures, Leela stopped and turned to Rosie. 'We should call the others.

The boy saw the murderer, I think. I will ask him to write it out for us.' But when they had turned around the boy had vanished. The path where he had stood just a minute ago was empty except for a pair of doves searching for seeds. The branches of the mango tree shook as a breeze swept through the garden, bringing in the scent of the sea, and then the leaves became so still it was as if they had never moved at all. The magnifying glass shone on the table by the window, winking at them like one large eye.

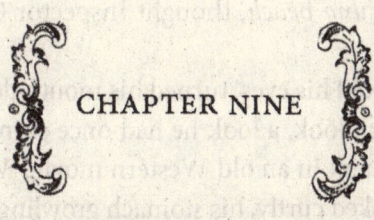

# CHAPTER NINE

INSPECTOR CHAND LOOKED at Deven and frowned. These people from the Happy Home were driving him mad. Four of them had turned up at the police station early in the morning, including the old lady in the wheelchair, when he had not even had his first cup of tea. He had marched out of his house in a rage because his mother had insisted he visit Panjim again to see yet another girl, one more plain and rich girl. For once Inspector Chand had refused and had walked out, regretfully leaving the hot parathas she had just made. But he had to show her he wasn't going to be bullied any more.

Constable Robert had gone to fetch tea and samosas from the tea shop when this group arrived in their old van. The Russian was not with them. Must be sleeping his booze off. Why had they not brought Maria along? That would have been so much better. He could ask her questions all day long and offer her tea and samosas while the old people sat around watching.

They were all above seventy but looked quite fit for their age. Rosie was glowing with her face all made up;

117

Prema, despite her frown, looked sturdy; Deven was dapper as always in his neatly pressed white shirt and black pants while Cyrilo looked like a movie star in dark glasses and a smart denim jacket. *Must have got it cheap at the flea market at Anjuna beach*, thought Inspector Chand with a stab of envy.

He narrowed his eyes, turned his mouth down and gave them all a stern look, a look he had once seen John Wayne give his opponent in an old Western movie. 'What can I do for you?' he asked curtly, his stomach growling with hunger.

'Yuri is missing. He has not come home for two days,' said Deven.

'He must be drinking somewhere. You know how these Russians are. They find a quiet beach shack and then spend a few days boozing happily. Drink, drink and drink; that is all they do. How they sent a man to the moon I don't know,' said Inspector Chand.

'The Americans sent a man to the moon. The Russians sent only a dog,' muttered Cyrilo.

'Who was Yuri Gagarin then? A vet?' asked Inspector Chand, giving Cyrilo an angry look.

'Inspector, you are right. Yuri must be lying on the beach drunk. I said the same thing but this lot would not listen to me,' muttered Prema, leaning on his table heavily. The paperweight slid off and landed on the floor near Rosie's wheelchair.

'Don't worry. He will turn up soon.' He bent down to pick up the paperweight. A sharp pain stabbed his back and he groaned as he tried to straighten up. All four watched him with sympathy in their old eyes.

'You will become like us one day. Your bones will creak and your lungs will sound like an old engine,' they seemed to be saying. Inspector Chand straightened his shoulders and pulled his stomach in.

'Yoga. Do yoga, young man. At your age, you are really in very bad shape.' Deven sounded so uncannily like his late father that Inspector Chand almost burst into tears. Suddenly he was a small, fat boy looking up at his father as he held a stolen laddu in his hand.

'We would like you to file a missing person's report. Please ask the police station in Panjim if they have seen a person who looks like Yuri,' said Cyrilo, taking off his dark glasses.

'I think we should wait a few more days. Then if he does not show up we will send out a notice. Though I already have at least twenty missing Russians on my list,' said Inspector Chand with a loud sigh. He could smell the samosas and he knew the constable was already attacking his breakfast outside in the veranda. He would kill him if he forgot to leave at least two samosas for him along with chutney.

'Okay. Come back tomorrow and we will file a report,' said Inspector Chand quickly.

'No. Please do it now. We must hurry because anything can happen to him. We think he was involved in some way with the woman's murder at the Happy Home,' said Rosie.

'What? How do you know that? Where did you find that information? Why have you not told me this before?' shouted Inspector Chand.

'First you file that report and then we will tell you,' said Deven.

'Okay. You want to bargain with me. But it's a waste of our valuable police time. We have many other important tasks to perform. Our IG is visiting Trionim next week, you know.' Inspector Chand pulled out a crumpled form from the drawer. A photograph of Maria fell out along with the paper and everyone stared at it. Rosie began to giggle as Inspector Chand quickly put it back in the drawer.

'Love is in the air,' hummed Cyrilo under his breath.

'Why don't you tell her you love her?' asked Rosie. 'You're not getting any younger, you know. Tell her quickly otherwise that handsome Francis will marry her and take her off to Dubai any day now.'

'Francis? Francis? Who is this Francis?' asked Inspector Chand, coughing, his mouth agape as if he had swallowed a fish bone.

'Yes, dear boy. Francis has been bringing her flowers and taking her out to dinner. You'd better get your act together, man, or you will miss the boat. You have to watch out for our Bobby too. He is second in line. You'd better hurry,' said Cyrilo.

'Listen. We are here to make a missing person's report and not to discuss the inspector's love life,' said Deven coldly, frowning at everyone. Prema looked at him in awe. She liked men who asserted themselves. Deven was just the kind of man she would have married if she had met him when they were young. *But now it is too late*, she thought, and sighed.

'Love is in the air,' hummed Cyrilo once more, under his breath.

Inspector Chand picked up a pen, shook it a few times and began to fill out the form slowly and laboriously, watched by four pairs of eyes. Suddenly Cyrilo raised his hand, stuck out his little finger and whispered, 'Is there a toilet in the police station? I need to go urgently.' He twisted his legs and pulled the seat of his tight denim jeans. Inspector Chand looked up. He pointed to the tin shed outside. He was sure this old man would take hours there. Old men always did. He knew his samosas would get stone cold.

\* \* \*

The sea was calm except for a few waves that rose and fell together as if doing a coordinated dance. A faint line of white foam circled the bay like a moving fence and the fishing boats bobbed up and down next to it like toys. Children ran around on the rocks, trying to jump on the waves as the tide came in, and then ran back laughing as they missed the rush of water. The gulls hovered above them, unusually quiet this morning as if they could sense something was wrong.

Something was very wrong, Yuri thought as he tried to open his eyes. He could see a faint light shimmering above his nose and nothing more. He put his hand on his arm and felt something warm and wet. It was blood. He must have cut himself when he fell but he couldn't feel any pain. Yuri shut his eyes again and tried to remember what had happened. The last thing he could remember was going to the villa where Olga was staying. He remembered standing at the gate and looking up to see if the light was on in her bedroom. It was dark, but a huge moon, large as a silver plate, hung in the sky. Someone called out his name and he turned his head. After that everything went blank.

Yuri moved his feet and tried to get up slowly, holding the rocks for support. His hand slipped on the wet moss and he sank back on the sand once again. A tiny crab climbed on his foot and rolled down again, waving its pin-like claws in rage. Yuri wanted to laugh but his face hurt. He felt his jaw. It was swollen and wet with blood. He forced himself to get up, ignoring the pain that suddenly sliced through him like a knife, but he could not tell which part of his body was injured. He stood unsteadily for a few seconds and then began to walk slowly over the rocks, carefully, one step in front of the other, like he had seen very old people do. At least he could see a little better now, though things kept going out of focus.

He was an old man, even though he did not feel it. He felt like a lovesick teen yearning for his sweetheart but Olga had told him he was an old fool. She had screamed at him, hit him with a glass ashtray and pushed him out of the villa. He had stood outside the gate, gazing up at her window like a besotted fool, and then someone had pounced on him.

He really was a big fool. He should have realized that Olga was just using him. She wanted him to transfer money from his bank into some account in Dubai. She handed him large amounts of cash and then made him sign a cheque in her name. Yuri was not sure what was going on but he had agreed just to keep her happy. He desperately wanted Olga to be happy.

He looked up and saw that he had reached the end of the rocky path and now the sand was smooth under his bare feet. He sat down and wiped his face with a piece of paper he found on the sand. The paper was stained red now and he quickly threw it away.

'You fell down, sir?' someone asked. Yuri tried to focus his eyes to follow the voice. A man was standing near him, holding a large crab tied with string. When the man moved, the crab moved too, trying to free itself.

'Want to buy crab? I just caught it in the Zuari river. I will give it to you for Rs 600 only since you are an injured man.' The man swung the imprisoned crab up and down like a baby.

Yuri shook his head. 'I have no money. Sorry,' he muttered.

'Sir, you can pay me later. I know where you live.'

Yuri turned to look at him in surprise and suddenly remembered where he had seen him. 'You were at the tea shop. You were with that boy who cannot speak,' he said. His face was hurting.

'Yes, sir. I am Alfie, or Alfonso. I will take you home. You have had a bad fall. Those rocks are very slippery. Come. I have my scooter here and it will not take long. The traffic is bad but I can take a shortcut through the paddy fields. My scooter is used to it,' said the man. 'Then you buy this crab and cook it for all those old people in the Happy Home. How happy they will be.' The man roared with laughter.

Yuri nodded and saw that the crab was no longer moving its claws as they made their way to the scooter. Alfie told him to sit straight and hold on to the crab tightly. 'He is your dinner, sir. Do not let your dinner escape.' Yuri did not want to ride on the scooter but he knew he had to get home somehow. He held the now-comatose crab in one hand and clutched Alfie's shirt with the other as the scooter took off, its horn blaring loudly like a ship coming into the harbour.

When he was a child in Russia, Yuri's mother would often send him out to the river to catch fish. They had nothing to eat at home and survived on whatever Yuri could catch. He sometimes got tiny fish or, if he was lucky, a rare big one and they would all eat well that day. The war had ended long ago, taking his father and uncles in its cruel, bloodthirsty jaws, but the people of Russia were still starving.

Yuri's mother had brought him and his younger brother to the old hut that had once belonged to her parents, who were both dead—killed by bandits who had stormed the country, looting and murdering people. They thought they would starve to death, but suddenly everything became all right; they had food to eat and warm clothes to wear. Yuri had new shoes for the first time in his life. Every time he bought a new pair of shoes now, his younger brother's face rose before his eyes. 'Can I have your old ones?' he seemed to be saying from the other world. He had died many years ago. Their mother, too, had gone.

Yuri gazed at the green rice fields as Alfie drove past them. He hoped he would meet his dead mother and brother in his next life. His father was someone he could not remember at all. Yuri was not afraid of death any more. Living in India had taught him to face death with joy. 'Mamushka, I will meet you soon but not too soon, I hope,' he said, ignoring the pain creeping over his face and arms. Alfie shouted back, 'Soon. We will be in Trionim soon and then you pay me for the crab. Okay? Scooter fare is extra.'

Alfie parked the scooter and immediately went to the wall by the gate to relieve himself. Yuri, holding the crab in one hand, knocked on the door with the other. His head was reeling now. Leela came out and stared at him. Then she quickly ran back to call the others.

'Where have you been? We went to the police station to report you, I mean about you,' shouted Prema. Her voice pierced through his head like a sharp knife.

'Please, someone pay this kind man who brought me home, and take this crab from my hands.' Yuri sank down on the chair by the door.

'Poor fellow. He is injured. Can't you people see?' said Leela, reaching her hand out to take the crab. 'Wait here. I will get some water and Dettol to wash your face and hands.'

'How did this happen? Where were you, Yuri? We were getting worried,' said Maria, wiping his hands with a clean napkin. 'Shall I get a doctor? I think I will call him. Your face looks badly cut.' She reached for the telephone.

Deven came out of his room and stared at Yuri. 'The inspector was right. We should not have bothered to go to him. You have been on a drinking spree, I can see. I hope you enjoyed yourself while we were running around all over Goa looking for you,' he said.

'We didn't go looking for him. We only told the policeman to. Leave him alone. He has hurt himself badly.' Rosie came up to him, patted his arm and pulled her hand away when she saw the blood. 'He's bleeding. Did someone attack you?'

Maria took the wet towel Leela had brought and gently wiped his face and hands. Then she poured a few drops of Dettol on a piece of cotton wool and dabbed his face. The sharp stinging felt better than the pain that was now flooding his head. Yuri closed his eyes. He was home and he was safe, he thought, but then a sudden dizzy spell made him gasp and he knocked away the bottle of Dettol from Maria's hands.

Deven and Cyrilo helped Yuri up to his room, changed his clothes and made him lie down. They came back and sat down in the veranda. They were all quite shaken to see Yuri in such a state.

'Do you think someone has beaten him up? I wish he would tell us where he has been. Why would someone do this?' asked Cyrilo.

Prema looked at him and said, 'You should know Yuri by now. He is always getting into fights after drinking on the beach with his Russian buddies. I wonder if we will get samosas today. Maria did promise me some,' she said, looking at the kitchen door expectantly.

'Why are you always thinking of food? At your age you must eat only one meal a day,' said Rosie, fanning herself with her favourite red Chinese fan. It was already humid though it was quite early in the day. She felt beads of perspiration on her forehead and hoped her eyeliner would not get smudged.

'If I'm alive next year I will apply for a US visa. They are giving it for ten years now,' said Cyrilo.

'At our age we should not plan so far ahead. You should apply for only a five-year visa,' said Prema.

'Life and death is all in god's hands. Our life span is decided already,' said Deven, pointing to the sky, and they all looked up as if they could see the extent of their lives written in bold letters.

'It is important to keep fit at our age and not sit around moping. I'm doing those yoga exercises Maria showed us that day. I've also started doing some running on the spot,' said Cyrilo.

'Better be careful or you'll drop dead running on the spot one day,' said Prema.

'Not a bad way to go. I would actually like to die playing the piano. You know, I wanted to be a pianist but my father insisted I mind the hardware shop we owned,' said Cyrilo.

'I wanted to be a dancer but my father said only women from disreputable families choose such a profession; so I became a teacher. My father was right because I was a hopeless dancer but I was a very good teacher. Some of my students still write such sweet letters to me,' said Prema.

Rosie had never seen Prema receive any letters but she kept quiet. Why shatter Prema's false belief if it made her feel happy. What else was there for her?

*We all become invisible as we age. Everyone forgets that we are still alive*, she thought. Aloud, she said, 'If only we could choose our own deaths. I would like to die in my own bed, surrounded by my family. Unfortunately, my family members are all dead. People wish for a long life but it is not so wonderful to be the last pillar of your family standing all alone.'

\* \* \*

Morjim beach stretched far and deep into the curve of the land, forming a graceful crescent, like a new moon emerging from the sea. It was a quiet beach, not as crowded as the more popular beaches in Candolim and Calangute filled with rubber-slippered and sun-hatted tourists. For some reason, people from outside Goa began to behave in a raucous manner as soon as they landed here. Mild-mannered accountants from Mumbai, sullen shopkeepers and their jolly wives from Delhi, and slick young techies from Bengaluru wired to their laptops—all turned into bawdy, loud holidaymakers in the blink of an eye. The locals would watch in dismay and some would even grumble. 'These people bring money. We have to put up with them,' they would say, shrugging their shoulders.

The new houses on the hills near the Chapora river had made the people of Trionim unhappy but they had no choice. The builder from Delhi, Rana Hooda, was rich and powerful and he knew all the important people in the city.

As Maria drove past the building site she suddenly remembered Francis talking about Rana. 'He is really loaded; you should invite him to the Tip Top Cafe one day.

He will bring all the other rich tourists with him,' he had said. She was surprised that Francis knew him so well. She reached the cafe and parked in a small space under a tree. The cafe was crowded today with a lot of young college students and someone was playing a guitar. It was an old tune and Maria began to hum. The others looked at her in surprise and began to sing. Soon the cafe was alive with their voices and even the lone waiter stopped his service and joined in, drumming out a jaunty beat on a tin tray.

*This is how I want my cafe to be*, thought Maria as she cleared tables. She did not want rich people to hang out here, complaining about the rickety tables and faded posters on the wall. The Tip Top Cafe was shabby, friendly, cheap and cosy and that was the way she was going to keep it. She did not want Rana Hooda and his type to come here.

Baboo, the waiter who had been working with her for ten years, waved his hands when he saw her. 'Good afternoon. We need some more peanut butter. All the cinnamon cakes you made are finished.' He said this with a broad grin as he pointed to the empty shelf proudly.

'Good. I will bake some more tonight,' said Maria.

'Bake at least four dozen. One lady came this morning and wanted two dozen cakes for a party. She kept nagging me to go and get some from the Happy Home right away. I refused,' said Baboo, picking up a tray of empty glasses. Baboo hated any customer ordering him about and liked to take his own time to serve them. Most people who came to the cafe knew that and made sure they spoke to him very politely. Otherwise they would not get any food.

'Who was she? How did she know the cinnamon cakes were made in the Happy Home? Did you tell her?' asked Maria, picking up the rest of the empty beer glasses. How much these college students drank.

'Why should I tell her? Was she my auntie? She seemed to know you too and asked when you were coming here. I said I don't know. I didn't like her. She looked very smart and rich and spoke to me only in English; as if I could not tell she was from here,' muttered Baboo.

Maria went into the kitchen and began setting out the food she had brought from the Happy Home. She only served very simple food at the cafe and most people seemed happy with it. Next month she was going to get a wood-fired oven and start making pizzas. Yuri had offered to set it up. He had once worked at a five-star hotel in Panjim as a kitchen helper but after his illness he had had to leave. Maria had never asked him about it but she assumed it was his alcohol problem. She recognized a fellow sufferer in him. Francis never drank at all. If she married him she would have to give up drinking totally. Suddenly the rosy picture of their future wedded life together began to be tinged with anxiety and worry.

Maria went into the kitchen to arrange the sandwiches Baboo had made on a plate and suddenly thought about the strange woman who had been asking about her.

'She said she was a very good friend of your friend Francis,' said Baboo behind her, giving her a start.

Maria turned to look at him. 'She said she was Francis's friend? What was her name?' she asked, her voice shrill with anger.

'How do I know? She didn't introduce herself to me. I'm only a lowly waiter. Why don't you ask your dear friend Francis?' he muttered, giving her a sly glance.

Maria finished the accounts, put the register away in the drawer and picked up her car keys. She was about to switch off the lights in the cafe when she saw the car. A red BMW with a Delhi number plate but no one inside was parked right behind her car and there was no way she could get out now. Baboo had already left. Maria grumbled angrily under her breath as she locked the cafe. *What should I do now?* she thought. There were a few young boys strolling on the road and she raised her hand to call them. Maybe they could help her push her car out.

Then she saw the girl.

The boys had seen her too and had stopped in their tracks. She was a tall blonde girl. Her golden hair seemed to make ripples in the breeze. She stood in the middle of the road looking like a mermaid who had just emerged from the sea in shiny blue Lycra pants and a loose transparent shirt. She was the most beautiful girl Maria had ever seen, like the golden-haired doll she had once seen in a toy shop, a very expensive doll with blue eyes and golden curls.

'Excuse me. Are you Maria from the Happy Home?' asked the girl, coming forward.

'Yes, I am. Is this your car? It's blocking my way.' Maria suddenly felt irritated with the girl's stunning looks. It was not fair to be so beautiful. *I'm sure she's very dumb and has bad breath.* Maria gave the girl a cold, unfriendly look.

'I am Olga. I am so happy to meet you at last. I am a very good friend of Yuri who is staying in your Happy Home.'

She smiled. Her blue eyes crinkled slightly and sparkled as she extended her hand to Maria. She had a squeaky, high-pitched voice and yellow, stained teeth. The ethereal mermaid vibe vanished as soon as she spoke and she looked like a pretty, young girl, but nothing more.

Maria felt ashamed for feeling so jealous. Despite the large baby-blue eyes and rosy cheeks, the girl's smile was sly and cunning like a fox's. She noticed that her hands were covered with red patches, as if someone had tried to scrub the skin off.

'Yes. Yuri stays with us at the Happy Home. Sorry, but could you please move your car? I am in a bit of a hurry,' said Maria.

'I will just move the car. Please wait and I will come to the Happy Home. Or maybe you can give this packet to Yuri, please. If it's not too much trouble for you?' she asked, taking a small packet out of her handbag. Maria noticed it was a Louis Vuitton. She wondered if it was a genuine one or a copy from the Anjuna flea market.

'Sure. I'll give it to him.' Maria put the packet in her own bag. It was a bit heavy and she wondered what it was.

'Just some Russian stones he had asked me to bring him. Medicinal stones, you know, which you put in a sauna bath to heal pain in the back. Thank you and goodbye, Miss Maria. Take care,' she said and quickly opened the car with a remote key and jumped in. She reversed so fast that two dogs sleeping in the shade of a tree yelped and leapt up in the air. The girl laughed, showing her bad teeth, and drove away at top speed. The boys stood in a line, frozen like statues, staring after her.

Maria shrugged her shoulders and got into her own car. She hoped it would start without her having to push it. One day she would buy a new one. Maybe Francis would buy her a BMW as a wedding present.

Maria drove home slowly, daydreaming about the wedding. She was quite sure that Francis would propose very soon. She must start saving money for her trousseau. The Happy Home roof needed repairs and the kitchen sink had to be replaced, but she would manage. The Tip Top Cafe was doing so well and she would work extra hard baking new things to sell. Maybe croissants and small quiches filled with mushrooms and cottage cheese.

Rosie had given her a recipe for meat loaf. She would try and make that this weekend. Maria stopped at the traffic lights at the Trionim market crossing. It was quite busy today since it was market day. She was wondering if she should pick up some fruit for the Happy Home when she saw them.

They were both standing near the road, holding hands, looking at a vegetable stall. The girl's face was turned away, but Maria, her heart pounding with rage, knew it was Tina. Tina, the red-haired witch whom she hated so much that sometimes she felt she could kill her. Tina, who had been chasing Francis for years.

Francis and Tina were shopping for vegetables. They looked like a married couple out doing household chores. Maria wanted to rush out and rain blows on both of them with her fists. Her car stalled and drivers behind her began to honk loudly. A man trying to cross the road shouted, and Maria rolled her window down and yelled back. 'Learn to drive, lady, or stay at home,' shouted a young boy on a scooter.

Francis and Tina turned to look at the commotion on the road. Then they saw her.

Maria stared at Tina and Tina stared back, a smug smile on her heavily made-up face. She was sweating but she still managed to look fresh and pretty. She was wearing the new kind of skinny jeans, ripped at the knees, and she was as slim as a teenage girl.

Maria knew Francis was looking at her too but she couldn't bear to meet his glance. She knew he would be looking sheepish and guilty and she hated that expression on his face; she had seen it so often.

Maria drove blindly to the Happy Home, sobbing all the way. She parked her car and got out, hitting her foot on the stone near the gate. She cursed loudly and began to cry again as she hobbled into the house. She hoped no one was in the veranda because she couldn't face any questions right now. She wanted to bring down that old sword and slice off Tina's glossy, sleek-haired head. She paused for a brief moment to think about beheading Francis too but decided against it. 'I hope she falls down and breaks her leg in the market. I hope she slips on a banana skin and breaks her head and goes into a coma,' shouted Maria, throwing her bag on to the floor.

The packet fell out of it and she remembered she had to give it to Yuri. Maria went into the bathroom and washed her face with cold water. She saw her reflection in the mirror and began to laugh. The rash from the new skin cream was worse than ever and she looked like an adolescent with spots and puffy eyes. Tina's unblemished, beautiful face rose before her and she wanted to cry once more. Maria blew her nose and went out to look for Yuri. She needed a drink desperately and knew Yuri would join her happily though it wasn't yet evening. Together they would sit under the coconut grove and curse everyone as they drank cheap wine to drown their sorrows.

'What is the matter? You look very upset,' said Yuri once they were both sitting with their drinks. His hands were shaking a bit. Maria had given him the packet but he hadn't opened it yet. 'Olga. You met Olga? Why did she not come here to give me this packet? What is it? I don't care. I don't care about anything in this world any more. I'm ready to die,' he said gloomily and stared into his glass.

Maria was regretting her decision to drink with Yuri. She had forgotten how depressing and morbid he got after a few drinks. He always sang melancholy Russian songs and moaned about long-lost loves. He had still not recovered fully from his injuries and had to walk unsteadily with the help of a stick. Drinking with him was a bad idea anyway, but today he seemed to be sad even before he took his first sip. He seemed genuinely upset about something; however, Maria was too distraught to care about anything except her own pain.

'I saw Francis with that red-haired bitch, Tina. They were buying vegetables together,' said Maria, tears welling up in her eyes.

'Oh. Only buying vegetables? That's not so bad. You didn't find them kissing or something worse, did you?' asked Yuri, suddenly looking happier, as if she had said something to cheer him up. Other's troubles always made people happy.

'I don't care if they were kissing or buying potatoes. I'm fed up with this life. Francis is always playing cat-and-mouse games with me,' said Maria, taking a big gulp. The wine was certainly off and tasted like sour vinegar, but that was the only alcohol in the house. Bloody Francis was supposed to bring her some from Panjim but he was busy buying pumpkins and carrots with that tart. How happy they looked, like an old, happily married couple. Maria shut her eyes and saw Francis and Tina strolling hand in hand followed by three small, neatly dressed children. She saw herself sitting all alone on a rocking chair in the Happy Home, knitting socks.

'You know what my mother used to do when she was angry with someone?' asked Yuri.

'How do I know? I've never met your mother, Yuri,' said Maria, feeling very irritated now.

'She learnt this trick from a gypsy woman. She would write the name of the person she hated on a small piece of paper, roll it up, spit on it and burn it. She said it made her feel much better,' said Yuri, his eyes sparkling.

'Nothing like hatred to cheer a person up,' muttered Maria. She mentally wrote out 'Tina' in bold letters and spat. It did make her feel slightly better, or maybe it was the bad wine, dulling the ache in her heart.

They both sat silently staring at the crows picking up scraps of food from the floor outside the kitchen. They were not fighting over the pieces and took turns to pick them up like polite guests at a wedding feast. Then Yuri began to sing under his breath. His voice was so velvety smooth that even though he could not sing in tune the unfamiliar Russian words sounded beautiful and haunting. Maria let the tears fall from her eyes but she was not feeling that sad any more. Life was not so bad. She would bake hundreds of cinnamon cakes and sell them at the Tip Top Cafe and make a lot of money. She would buy a red BMW and drive all over Trionim dressed in tight Lycra shorts. Young boys would stare and whistle at her in admiration. She would go on a diet from tomorrow and become slim and sexy. Francis and Tina could go to hell in a vegetable cart.

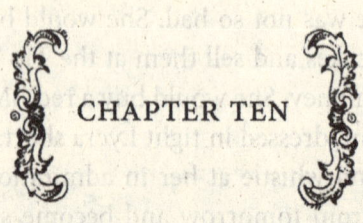

# CHAPTER TEN

JUST THEN, THEY heard a car outside. It sounded like a jeep. Leela came out of the kitchen and after giving them both a stern, disapproving look went into the hall to open the door.

Maria picked up the bottle and gave it to Yuri, who quickly hid it under the rose bush. 'I think it's the big policeman. Your admirer,' he said as they heard Inspector Chand's booming voice at the door.

'Good afternoon,' he said, walking up to them. He was looking very smart in a khaki jacket and blue scarf and Maria nodded her head and smiled. He would not be bad-looking if he lost some weight. He could make a good replacement for that philandering Francis. Maybe she could marry him. It wouldn't be so bad to be a policeman's wife but Inspector Chand was so dull and boring. Maybe she was better off single instead of chained to this tedious man. Why did she have to get married to anyone? She was quite happy alone. She just needed a few weeks to get over Francis. She was an independent woman and quite capable of looking after herself.

Inspector Chand stared at her, his eyes shining with joy. He looked like a golden retriever about to get a bone to munch. Maria did not dare speak because she knew he would smell the wine on her breath. She waved her hand weakly towards a chair and moved back, knocking over a table.

'I hope you are not too busy,' said Inspector Chand, staring at her suspiciously now. *Why is her face so puffy? Has she been drinking this early in the day?* Inspector Chand heard his mother's shrill voice ring in his ears. 'She drinks alcohol? You want to marry a girl who drinks alcohol? Over my dead body,' his mother screamed in his mental image, her finger pointing as usual to the ceiling fan.

'How nice to see you. Will you have some coffee, Inspector? We can sit outside. It's so cool in the shade,' said Rosie, coming out of her room. She moved her wheelchair slowly towards the veranda. Maria knew she was taking the inspector away to give her a chance to escape. She nodded a silent thanks to Rosie and quickly ran upstairs before the inspector could turn around.

'Thanks so much, Mrs Rosie. I would love some coffee,' replied Inspector Chand, wondering why Maria had vanished so suddenly.

Yuri was still sitting in the veranda, humming under his breath as he carved a piece of wood with a penknife. The inspector noted that his face was bruised with angry blue and black marks, as if he had fallen down and injured himself badly. A red bundle lay next to him on the table.

It was exactly like the one the Russian girl had described.

* * *

A few hours ago, as the inspector and his constable were having their third cup of tea, a red BMW drove up to the station, waking every stray dog in the street. A crowd of curious children had gathered as a tall, slim girl got out of it. Constable Robert almost fell down from his bench and Inspector Chand too had to restrain his mouth from falling open. He put a hand up to smooth his hair and pulled his stomach in as he got up from his chair. The girl was stunningly beautiful, a James Bond beauty who had appeared out of the blue in Trionim. And she had come to see him! The old police station suddenly became a magical place full of promise.

'You are the policeman in charge here?' she asked with a lisp.

'Yes. Yes. I am Inspector Chand of the Goa Police.' He was tempted to say 'Inspector General' but he couldn't bring himself to lie so blatantly.

'Oh! Inspector Commissioner,' said the girl breathlessly, her blue eyes sparkling like gems. Inspector Chand almost fainted with joy. 'I want to report that my jewels are missing from my house. Last night I look and I cannot find my diamond and ruby necklace. I cannot find my gold earrings and bracelets. They were all wrapped in a red handkerchief. In a bundle . . . is that what you say in English?' she asked, smiling at him through half-closed eyes. She had such a pretty smile but her teeth were stained and yellow. Inspector Chand wondered if she smoked marijuana.

'I am very sorry to hear such a terrible thing has happened to you. I apologize for this. We want all our tourists to be safe and secure in Goa. I will look into this matter at once. Losing jewels is a very bad thing,' he said, reaching for his stick and tapping it on the table to show he meant to act at once.

'You want my address and phone number?' asked the girl, looking bored.

'Yes. Yes.' Inspector Chand opened his notebook.

'I am Olga Hooda. My address is 45 Greenside Villa, Vaddy. Trionim.'

'You live here?' asked Inspector Chand, surprised that the girl had an Indian last name. Who was this Hooda? She was obviously married to him. He stopped writing and stared at the girl. Where had he heard that name before?

Olga smiled, showing her crooked yellow teeth. She looked like a weasel about to sink its sharp teeth into its prey and Inspector Chand did not smile back at her.

'You could search the Happy Home. I saw a man going in there with a red bundle. I was too scared to follow him. But you can. You are a big, strong policeman,' said the girl and got up to leave. As her car drove away with a roar that thrilled all the little boys watching, Inspector Chand knew he had to go to the Happy Home at once.

* * *

Inspector Chand rose from his chair and walked out into the veranda. Yuri was still humming away. He looked quite drunk as he waved his hands about as if conducting an invisible orchestra. Inspector Chand picked up the cloth bundle lying next to him near two empty wine glasses. Yuri did not notice him and continued to sing.

'Where did you get this?' asked Inspector Chand, tapping the red bundle with his fingers. Yuri turned his head and looked up at him, surprised.

'Oh. Hello, Inspector. I did not see you. When did you come?' he asked, trying to focus his eyes.

'Whose is this? Is it yours?' asked Inspector Chand.

Maria had come down after quickly washing her face and spraying some perfume to disguise the smell of alcohol. She went and stood next to Yuri. Rosie watched them from her wheelchair and behind her Leela hid in the shadows. Everyone was silent.

'Where did you get this bundle? Please open it,' said Inspector Chand, picking it up and putting it on the table.

Yuri stood up, looking confused, and then when Maria asked him to open the red bundle, he sat down again. With trembling fingers, he tore open the string. As they watched, holding their collective breath, a small shiny object fell out. Inspector Chand picked it up. It was a diamond ring. Yuri quickly pulled up the cloth and a pile of more jewellery tumbled out. A string of pearls, a few gold bracelets and a diamond and ruby necklace winked at them.

Yuri gave a cry of surprise and jumped up.

'Where did you get this?' asked Inspector Chand.

'I have never seen these things before. I don't know where they came from. What is all this?' he muttered, rubbing his eyes.

'This jewellery was reported missing by one Olga this morning. It is fortunate I came by to ask Miss Maria something. You should not be so greedy, Mr Yuri. Stealing at your age is not good.'

'Listen. I gave that bundle to Yuri. That girl Olga came to the cafe today and gave it to me. She said it contained some stones for the sauna Yuri is building in the outhouse,' said Maria, looking worried. She hoped she had not got Yuri into trouble.

'You did not check the bundle?' asked Inspector Chand.

Maria shook her head.

'This is not a good thing to do. You should always check when some unknown person hands you a parcel. You know we have a drug problem here. You must be careful, Maria. Why did you not call me?' asked Inspector Chand, gazing at her like a lovesick puppy. *Maria, you are so innocent. You need my protection*, his eyes seemed to be saying.

Maria did not reply and stood looking at Yuri. He was leaning against the wall, his face pale and anxious. His hands were trembling.

Inspector Chand turned reluctantly to him. 'So you have no idea who this girl is? Then why did she send you this jewellery and pretend it was stolen?' he asked.

'I know her but I don't know why she sent me this stuff. I really don't know.'

'Maybe she's trying to frame him. Where does she live? You said her name was Olga Hooda . . . strange . . . the same last name as the dead woman,' said Rosie.

'How do you know that?' said Inspector Chand.

'Leela told me. The dead woman's name was Rani Hooda. She also lived in one of those new villas,' said Rosie.

'Yes. I knew she did. I saw her photograph in the house. I told you all this before but you did not believe me,' said Yuri, holding his head in his hands.

'Are you blaming the police now? That does not sound good. You knew the victim and you also knew this girl and you did not tell us. Obstructing the course of justice is a serious offence, Mr Yuri. It is the duty of all citizens to help the police. You must never lie or conceal the truth from us,' said Inspector Chand and turned to Maria to see if she was impressed with his speech.

Maria had put her hand on Yuri's shoulder and was whispering something to him. Inspector Chand gave a quick cough of disapproval.

Yuri turned to look at him, his face white as a sheet. 'I told you I had seen the dead woman but I could not get the photograph to prove it. I am sorry. I have been a fool.' Yuri raised his head to look at Maria.

'Who is this Olga woman? Why is she trying to frame you? Do you know her well?' asked Inspector Chand loudly. This Russian fellow was irritating him now. Why was Maria protecting him? He could have easily killed that woman and hung her up in the garden. These Russians were all crazy. All he had to do was establish a motive for this murder and arrest Yuri, who was now resting his head on Maria's shoulders. Inspector Chand glared at him and said, 'You have to come to the police station with me. Please bring your papers and passport along.'

'No. No,' mumbled Yuri, rolling his eyes till they could see the whites trembling. Then he fainted, hitting his head as he fell to the ground.

'Oh no! Leela, bring water, quick. Poor fellow. He has fainted,' shouted Maria, quickly sitting down next to Yuri and putting his head in her lap. Rosie moved her wheelchair closer to the veranda steps and tried to lift Yuri's arm. Leela ran to the table and picked up a bottle of water. She began sprinkling it on Yuri's face as he lay on the ground. Inspector Chand stood by the steps, looking sheepishly at them. He felt a wave of guilt sweep over him as they all turned to stare at him accusingly, including Yuri, who had now fluttered open one blue eye like a fish about to die. The diamond and ruby necklace and the gold bracelets, piled up on the bench, reflected the fading sunlight like bits of broken glass.

* * *

The Chapora river flowed quietly, red-hot and blazing in the fierce afternoon sun, and the gulls, squabbling amicably, sought shelter underneath the anchored boats. A lone Brahminy kite hunted in the sky, its rust-coloured wings glowing like embers as it glided in the air. As the river meandered lazily towards the sea, it changed colour and began to swirl around. Then it calmed down, found its path and merged into the sea, creating high circles of waves, happy at last to meet the water. The village was asleep and the shutters of the blue and pink houses firmly closed so that not a single ray of light could steal in. Even the stray dogs lay comatose in the shade of the cashew trees.

The little van hiccupped, breaking the afternoon silence, and came to a noisy halt in front of the fish market.

No one was about except for Alfie and Tony, who were sitting under a tin sheet shelling prawns. A strong smell of drying fish hit Deven's nose and he grimaced and quickly brought out his handkerchief to cover it.

'We'll never find anyone here. We are wasting our time. I must have my afternoon nap otherwise my blood pressure will go up. Must be high already in this heat,' muttered Prema from the car, her face half hidden by a large straw hat with daisies on the brim.

'Then you should have stayed at home with Rosie and had your nap. Why did you come with us?' said Deven curtly.

'Why could we not have come in the evening after tea?' asked Prema with a scowl. She did not like this new Deven any more. He was behaving like a dictator, ordering them about. There was a difference between being masterful and strong and being a mean, rude bully.

'Listen to the madam. We are trying to catch a ruthless murderer. But you think we should have our nap and then our tea, go for our evening walk on the beach and then go and look for him. Is he waiting for us like a docile lamb under the coconut tree?' Deven hissed, his nostrils flaring.

'Stop it, you two. Look, I can see Alfie,' pointed out Cyrilo.

They all looked towards the shed as Alfie raised his head and waved. 'Here come the Happy Home oldies. Let us try and sell them some prawns,' he said softly to Tony who grinned and shook his head.

'Why not? I won't charge them extra, son, like I do the shopkeeper,' said Alfie, wiping his hands on his shirt and getting up to greet Deven.

'Good afternoon. We wanted to ask you something.' Deven tried to speak through his handkerchief-covered mouth.

'You look like a dacoit, sir, if you don't mind my saying so. A very smart dacoit.' Alfie laughed. 'I have some very fresh prawns here. Just came on that boat.' He pointed to a boat bobbing far away on the river.

'That is the ferry boat so don't try to fool me. Anyway, I don't want prawns. Tell me. Do you know any tall Russian girl who lives in one of the new villas?' he asked.

'So many Russian girls going all over the place on their scooters. How do I know which one you want? Anyway, at your age you should be careful.' He winked.

Cyrilo could see that Deven's temper was rising and he quickly stepped in. 'Hey, man. Your name is Alfie, is it not? I think I know your brother. He was in the same school as me in Siolim.' He smiled.

'No one in my family ever went to school, sir, but we are doing fine,' said Alfie. Tony smiled as he continued to shell the prawns, his small hands quickly discarding the pink shells in one quick move.

'I wish I could shell prawns so fast, son,' said Cyrilo in Konkani and Tony looked up at him with a shy grin.

'I will teach you,' said Alfie in Konkani. 'But not this puffed-up rooster with you. Looks like he has a boil on his backside, man.'

Cyrilo burst out laughing and then quickly stopped.

'What is he saying? I think this man knows nothing. He's just wasting our time.' Deven turned to go.

Prema rolled down the window of the van and waved her hand. Alfie looked at her and said, 'Who is she? The queen of Mapusa? You hang out with some weird people, man. Where did you find these oldies? I can get you a nice, plump lady friend if you like,' he said with a wink.

'No, thanks. At my age I am very happy to be alone with my friends since we are all oldies now,' said Cyrilo.

'Listen, fellow, we will pay you. Not asking for free information. You tell us the girl's address and we will give you a hundred rupees,' Prema shouted from the car.

Alfie turned to her and saluted. 'Smart lady. The girl's name is Olga and her address is 45 Greenside Villa, Vaddy. She lives very close to the Happy Home so you can invite her for tea if you like. She is damn good-looking, like a Russian doll.'

'We don't want to invite her for tea, so stop being cheeky. We just want to find out why she's trying to get our friend into trouble with the police.' Cyrilo took out a hundred-rupee note and handed it to Alfie who quickly tucked it into his vest.

'Which friend? The Russian chap with long hair?' asked Alfie, narrowing his eyes. 'The painter?'

'No need for you to know,' said Deven, walking away.

'Why didn't you ask him for her address? You could have saved yourself a hundred. He thinks the golden-haired witch is his sweetheart, the poor old fellow, as do many other men in Goa. You should see the queue of men panting for her when she jogs on the beach every morning,' said Alfie, slapping his thigh and roaring with laughter. Tony put his head down and sat very still, the prawns slipping from his hands as if they were still alive and trying to escape. He looked up at Cyrilo and put his finger on his lips as if he wanted to share a secret, but when Alfie turned his head, he looked down again to hide his face.

They came back to the Happy Home after stopping for ice cream at the new gelato place since Prema was feeling very hot. They packed a large tub to take for Leela, Maria and Rosie. As soon as they walked into the house, Deven quickly called an emergency meeting. Prema shook her head at him and went into her room for a nap. Yuri was still fast asleep in his room. Rosie and Maria were nowhere to be seen. They could hear Leela washing dishes in the kitchen.

'I don't know what Yuri is up to. He is not telling us the truth. Why did the Russian girl send the jewellery to him and then report it stolen to the police? The inspector will lock him up now since he is very keen to show he's doing some work to the IG, who is coming next week to Trionim,' said Deven to Cyrilo, the only member of his team present. Their investigations were going so slowly. Deven wished he had not started all this. Maybe the inspector was right: they were too old to handle this. He was the only one who seemed keen on solving the case. The others were treating it as entertainment, something to break the monotony of their dull lives.

'We will get to the truth. You don't worry. I can see us catching the murderer very soon. You have the brains to outwit him or her and we are all standing right behind you. We are a team,' said Cyrilo.

Deven gave him a quick glance. Cyrilo was right. They would somehow manage. They might be old and not very quick on their feet but they would catch the culprit. The optimistic look in Cyrilo's eyes made him feel much better. It made such a difference when a friendly voice supported you.

'Yes. You are a great help, Cyrilo, but I am not sure about the others. Still, I think we might just get there. I think I will go for a short nap too. I never sleep in the afternoon but today I am feeling a bit tired. Too much sugar is not good for me.' Deven got up and left for his room.

Soon the Happy Home fell into a quiet slumber. The afternoon sun travelled languidly over the house, painting the dusty glass windows with its light, creating shadows in hidden corners. The trees in the garden watched the rays of the sun touch their branches and then glide away. The breeze was very still, as if waiting for the sun to set before deciding which way to blow. Far away in the village, children played in shaded gardens, keeping their voices very quiet so that they would not wake up parents sleeping in darkened rooms. Sometimes a child would forget and shout with laughter but then the others would quickly pounce to silence him or her. A few urchin boys, including Tony, ran around the deserted beach gathering shells. They did not mind the hot sand burning their bare feet; when it got too much they would run with their treasure trove of shells to dip their feet in the water.

Many centuries ago, a prisoner with chains on his bleeding feet had walked on the same beach scavenging for food. He had tried to escape to one of the ships anchored far way on the high seas but no boatman would take him to it since they were afraid of the prison guards. The Goa

Inquisition, which aimed to punish heresy and persecute everyone who was not a Catholic, had eyes everywhere, and even helping anyone accused of the above 'crime' was punishable by death. More than 800 people were burnt at the stake between 1600 and 1775, according to historical records of that time, and many others jailed for years on the slightest suspicion. The sea had washed away those terrible times with its warm, soothing waters and very few people now were even aware of the cruelty that had once swept through the golden land of Goa.

* * *

Rosie put a fine layer of rose-scented powder on her cheeks, dabbed perfume on her wrists and then wrapped a silk scarf carefully around herself so that the wrinkles on her neck would not show. It was much cooler now when she went out into the garden, moving her wheelchair slowly with her hands. The sun had disappeared but the sky was still glowing with a pink and gold light which made all the plants in the garden appear different shades of green. Leela would soon bring her a cup of tea and maybe a snack. Prema had been asking for samosas and Maria had promised she would get some from the sweet shop in the market. It was the only shop that sold north Indian snacks. Prema thought about food all the time and was putting on quite a bit of weight, though she got angry if anyone mentioned it. She sometimes forgot that she had had breakfast and kept demanding tea and toast. 'Short-term memory loss. It happens at her age. You forget recent things but clearly remember everything that happened a long time ago,' Deven told the others. Rosie was afraid she too might lose her memory one day. *Though it might not be a bad thing. I could forget all the bad times and live only in the past when I was young, beautiful and as agile as a deer.*

Rosie rubbed cream on her hands as she sat waiting for her tea. She heard the door open with a loud creak and saw Bobby walk in with a big basket of guavas. He gave her a shy smile and then tripped over the rug, spilling all the fruits.

'How lovely to see you, Bobby, after so long. Maria is still at the Tip Top Cafe,' said Rosie, pleased to have company. Bobby said he was happy to sit and wait for Maria and he pulled up a chair. Bobby always smelt so clean and fresh, as if he had just bathed in lemongrass and cinnamon, unlike Francis, who reeked of expensive aftershave lotion that always made Rosie sneeze. Bobby had brought little packets of fresh herbs for them from his spice garden and he now took them out one by one and placed them on the table. He cleared his throat a few times and said, 'The weather has turned a bit cooler now that the rains have finished.'

Rosie patted his hand and said, 'You have heard about the terrible death that happened here?'

'Yes, auntie. That's why I have come. I thought Maria might need some help. I wanted to come earlier but we were planting new herb cuttings and I couldn't leave. I hope Maria and all of you are all right,' said Bobby, his gentle brown eyes full of concern. Hearing this, Rosie was even more convinced that Maria should marry him and make him live here at the Happy Home. He could then treat all their aches and pains with herbs since he knew so much about herbal medicine. His grandfather had been a famous herbalist, and even the wealthy Portuguese were said to have frequented his spice farm in Ponda. They believed he had a herbal pill to cure both impotence and frigidity. 'Two in one joy', it was called. Not that either of her husbands had ever needed it. Both men had died before they reached the incontinence and impotence stage. Just as well. A long life came with so many humiliating things, and not just endless aches and pains. Her joints hurt, her eyes watered and her mouth always felt dry. Her legs, though lifeless, still had phantom darts of pain. 'Yet, I don't want to die,' said Rosie, and Bobby, startled by her voice, stared at her.

'Why should you die? You are looking very well, if I may say so, Rosie Auntie. Not constipated, are you? I will bring some aloe vera juice for you next time,' he said with a smile.

'Why don't you ask Maria to marry you? Do it soon. There are so many men waiting in the queue and you might lose out. Don't be shy, Bobby, my son. Just pop the question.' Just then they heard the front door open with its usual complaining whine and Maria walked in.

Bobby quickly got up, his face flushed with embarrassment for no reason.

'Hello. How are you, Maria?' he mumbled, handing her a guava and knocking over a vase at the same time.

Maria looked at him and smiled. Bobby, her old faithful Bobby, who had been sweet on her since they were kids in school. He used to give her some fruit almost every day and the other girls would laugh at him as he stood at the school gate waiting for her. Bobby was tall and good-looking in an old-fashioned kind of way. His eyes were bright green, twinkling shyly behind his glasses, and his skin was very fair; he blushed easily. He always wore crumpled grey shirts that looked faded even when they were brand new. Bobby knew the names of more than a thousand plants in Goa and had often told her he would help her replant the garden at Happy Home. 'Grow your own organic vegetables and you can sell them at the Tip Top Cafe.'

Maria had still not done anything about that. She had been so busy planning her future life with Francis, and then her mind became occupied with this terrible murder. She looked at Bobby and smiled absent-mindedly as she bit into the guava. It was pink, fragrant and sweet but Maria could hardly taste its delicious flavour. In her mind, the image of Francis buying vegetables with Tina rose like a jagged knife and she shivered with anger.

'So sweet. This is the sweetest guava I have ever tasted. Here, Bobby, you take a bite and see,' she said, trying to calm herself down.

Bobby's heart began to thump so loudly that he was afraid he would faint. He quickly sat down next to Rosie and held on to the handle of her wheelchair for support. He gazed at Maria with adoring eyes and she smiled at him, wishing he didn't love her so much. It made her feel guilty that she could not reciprocate.

Bobby sighed and took the guava from Maria. How lovely she looked, her hair cascading down her shoulders in unruly waves, her beautiful mouth glistening with guava juice. Her eyes looked sad, though, and Bobby wondered what had happened. He knew it must be something to do with that rascal Francis, but he did not want to talk to her about it; it was safer to pretend that dark, slimy villain did not exist.

'The Portuguese brought guavas to Goa along with chickoos. They brought chillies and eggplants for us too,' he said.

*Why am I telling her about the history of vegetables and fruits when I should be telling her how much I love her and want to marry her? Why can't I say those words? Why should a girl like her be interested in guavas? I'm sure Francis would never talk to her like this. He must be taking her to dinners in expensive restaurants in Panjim and whispering sweet nothings into those pearl-like ears while I stand here like a moron lecturing her on the history of the guava fruit.* As these anxious thoughts raced through Bobby's head, he continued to blabber nervously about the guava, how it had come to Goa, how other fruits and plants were brought to Goa by the Portuguese hundreds of years ago, and so on.

Maria nodded and smiled at him, her fingers twisting her hair restlessly. *Now he'll start telling me about the rare lily discovered in the last century in his spice garden, how many coconut trees are in Goa, how many cashew nuts were produced this year. Bobby is such a kind and sweet man but why can't he talk about anything except plants? Francis . . . Francis talks to me about all the amazing things he sees on his travels, the celebrities he meets, the fancy restaurants he dines in. But Francis is a liar and is just making a fool of me. I never want to see him again.*

Bobby's voice was making her fall asleep. Maria quickly took another bite of the guava to keep herself awake. She wondered if she should offer Bobby a beer and have one herself too. Then she remembered that Bobby did not drink anything except fruit juice and sighed.

*Why is he going on and on about guavas? Why can't he talk to her about his love for her? Look deep into her eyes and say 'Maria, you are the woman of my dreams. How I long to hold you in my arms and kiss your sweet lips. Marry me, Maria, and make me a happy man.' Stupid man.* Rosie glared at Bobby, willing him to read her mind.

Bobby suddenly stopped talking and stared at Maria. 'Oh, I forgot. What a terrible thing to happen to you. Have they found out who the dead woman was?' he asked, glancing about him nervously as if he expected her body to suddenly appear in the veranda.

'Yes. Her name was Rani Hooda. She lived in one of those new villas on the other side of Trionim. You know, those huge fancy ones with swimming pools and fountains,' said Maria.

'I went to one of those villas last week, to do some landscaping,' said Bobby.

'This unfortunate lady apparently came to the Happy Home a few days before she was murdered, looking for a house to buy. None of us met her though,' said Maria.

'She was a very rich woman and wore a diamond ring on each of her fingers. Leela told us,' said Rosie.

'Oh. I remember her. She had come to the spice garden also. She wanted some medicinal plants for her garden. In fact, she wanted me to set up her garden for her, and when I told her I had no time she became quite aggressive and rude. "You are all so lazy. Don't want to do any honest work. I'm offering to pay anything you want and yet you refuse. In Delhi people would jump at such a chance. You don't know who I am", and so on. I was horrified.' Bobby looked so worried and anxious that Maria couldn't help feeling sorry for him. Bobby was so timid. The woman must have really scared him.

'Did she tell you why she was there? Why was she roaming around alone in Trionim? Where was her husband?' asked Rosie, turning to Maria. 'Maria, this is a good chance to find out more. Bobby seems to be the only one who talked to her. Bobby can tell us something about the dead woman that could lead us to her murderer. Bobby, you stay here now.'

Rosie called out to Leela. 'Tell Mr Deven to come here, please. We must hold a meeting at once with Mr Bobby.' Bobby looked at her in surprise, tapping his fingers nervously on the chair.

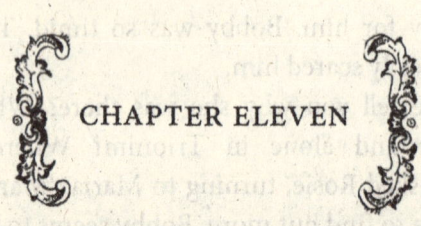

# CHAPTER ELEVEN

AFTER A QUICK cup of tea without any snacks, they gathered around the dining table. Deven, looking very serious as usual, sat at the head of the table, holding a pen in his hand like a magic wand. Prema was slouching at the table with an ice pack on her head, and had already announced several times that she had a splitting headache. Cyrilo was dapper in his blue denim jacket, placid as always, and Rosie, her usual immaculate self, sat very still in her wheelchair. Yuri was missing.

After he recovered from his fainting fit the previous day, Cyrilo had helped him to his room and Maria had told the inspector to leave. Inspector Chand had reluctantly got into his jeep, muttering something about coming back to make an arrest later, but one sharp look from Maria and he drove quietly away, forgetting his constable, who was in the kitchen drinking tea with Leela.

Yuri was still in a state of shock and rambling on as if delirious. Cyrilo had given him some pills which he said were a hangover cure and Prema offered to make some

158

of her foul-tasting herbal brew. Yuri had refused at once, sitting up in bed and saying he felt much better. But he had not come down for lunch today.

Cyrilo pulled up an extra chair for Bobby, who sat down, head bowed low as if he was a new boy at school. Deven cleared his throat and everyone looked at him. 'We welcome a new member to our committee, Mr Robert Menezes,' he said, giving Bobby a quick glance, and everyone clapped.

'Who is this Robert now?' asked Prema in an irritated voice.

'It is Bobby's real name, you silly,' whispered Rosie.

'Okay, Miss Know-it-all,' hissed Prema. Her hearing aid gave a sharp whine as she turned her head.

'Ladies, if you have finished your chit-chat, allow me to proceed,' said Deven coldly and rose from the dining table.

Leela giggled and hid behind the kitchen door. Deven pulled out the blackboard and began writing on it. Everyone watched quietly as the chalk, damp with moisture, made squeaking sounds. They couldn't really make out what Deven had written but no one dared to ask.

'So you see, Bobby. This is all that we have been able to find out. Three days have passed but we have not gathered much information, sadly.' He gave Cyrilo a quick look. Cyrilo smiled back and shrugged.

'Err. I cannot really make out what you have written,' muttered Bobby and quickly added, 'I have not brought my spectacles with me, uncle.'

Deven stared at him and everyone waited quietly for him to explode with rage but he only said, 'Not to worry.

Let me tell you all the facts. We know the woman was murdered. How do we know? We know because . . .' he said, turning to the blackboard.

'Because we all saw her strung up on the mango tree,' said Prema.

'I did not ask you a question. I was merely stating a fact, Prema,' said Deven coldly.

'Sorry,' said Prema and stuck her tongue out when Deven turned to the blackboard again.

'We know her name was Rani Hooda. How do we know?' This time no one spoke though Leela was dying to say 'I found out her name' but she did not dare speak. She knew Deven hated being interrupted.

'We know because two people confirmed it. The police inspector and Leela,' said Deven, underlining a word on the blackboard.

'Now we also know that she was in Trionim because she was looking for a house to buy. What we don't know for sure is where she lived. She was seen in Trionim often but where did she actually live?' he continued as Prema yawned loudly, snapping her fingers in front of her gaping mouth.

'If you are not interested, Prema, please go to your room and take another nap. We can continue without your presence,' said Deven.

'No. No. Just feeling sleepy. My blood pressure is low today. Do you have any herbs for controlling high blood pressure, Bobby? Mine keeps going up and then down again,' she said.

'I . . . am not sure. You can take fenugreek in hot water,' mumbled Bobby and then stopped, looking up at Deven.

'If you stop eating so much, it may help,' said Deven.

'I eat too much? What about you? Stuffing your face with ghee-smeared chapattis every morning? Drinking all those glasses of milk like a baby. Telling me I eat too much. What nonsense you talk.' Her voice rose hysterically.

'You eat like a bird, Prema. Deven just meant you should eat less salt,' said Cyrilo.

'Yes, less salt, less sugar, less oil. Might as well be dead. At least I have a brain unlike all of you. I might forget things but I can remember all the rude things you said to me five years ago and I don't forgive easily.' Prema slapped the wet ice pack back on her forehead.

'I think I can find out which villa this lady lived in,' said Bobby, and everyone fell silent and stared at him. He tugged at his shirtsleeves and gazed into the garden as if waiting for someone to prompt him.

'How will you do that, Bobby?' asked Maria gently. She always forgot what a kind and helpful person Bobby was. Even in school he was always the one who would wait for her at the school gate and carry her school bag.

'She gave me her address when she came to the spice farm. I am sure I still have it in my office. I will check today and call you, Maria.' Bobby suddenly looked very pleased with himself. He smiled at everyone, a smile so infectious and full of affection that they all smiled back at him, even Prema giving a rare, crooked grin.

Maria suddenly got up and said, 'Listen, let's all go to the spice farm right now. I have to get some cinnamon and we could all do with an outing. Leela, you come too.' Leela jumped up and gave a broad grin, clapping her hands. She loved going to Bobby's spice farm. It had a pool with goldfish and huge water lilies. Frogs perched on the massive leaves and stuck their tongues out to catch insects. There were magical trees with perfumed flowers, and shrubs with leaves that left a strong scent of spices on your fingers when you crushed them. Bobby always gave her fresh coconut water to drink and she would scoop out the sweet, creamy tender coconut with a spoon made from the coconut shell.

'What about poor Yuri?' asked Rosie.

'Let him sleep; he'll wake up feeling much better. I'll leave some chicken broth for him. He loves it. He says his mother used to make it for him in Russia,' said Maria. 'Come on, Leela, hurry, let's put some water bottles in the car.' She picked up her bag.

Rosie turned her wheelchair around and moved quickly towards her room. She must take a big hat, her rose water bottle and an extra pair of socks in case her feet got wet like last time. The wheelchair had got stuck on the wooden bridge and she had to be carried over the stream, water dripping all over her legs. Everyone had stared but Rosie did not mind. She had got used to people looking agápe at her, calling her names. She hoped the toilets were cleaner this time—on their previous visit they had had to wade through a pile of manure and dog poo. The problem was when she had to go she really had to go. Waiting for a clean toilet was no longer an option at her age.

'Prema, are you coming with us or do you want to rest? You'd better rest since you have such a bad headache,' said Deven, his eyes glinting with malice.

'Oh. Leave her alone. Of course, she'll come with us. The fresh air will do you good, Prema. Go to the bathroom, please, otherwise you'll make me stop the car on the highway like last time,' said Cyrilo. 'I'd better go too, you know, my bladder does not listen to me. Deven, I'll drive the van so that Rosie's wheelchair can fit. Prema and you come with me. Maria, you go with Bobby in his car. Leela, you want to go with them or us?' he shouted through the kitchen door.

'I will go with Miss Maria. We should take the big baskets to bring some vegetables back. Miss Maria, please wait for me.' Leela ran to the kitchen.

'Please take a flask of soup up to Yuri's room and leave it by his bedside table. I'm waiting,' said Maria, picking up the baskets.

Bobby's face fell. He had been looking forward to a long drive alone with Maria. He was hoping they would get stuck in traffic and he could tell her how he felt about her. But with little Leela sitting in the back seat it would not be possible.

Maria noticed the look on Bobby's crestfallen face and wanted to laugh. He really did have a big crush on her. She must treat him with more kindness. Who knew, she might just end up marrying him. Francis was so unreliable and unfaithful; Inspector Chand so boring and vain. Bobby was not rich but was kind and gentle. 'Rich man, poor man, beggar man, thief,' she suddenly said to herself, remembering a silly song they used to chant in school while playing with pebbles. Would a thief come into her life now or would it be a murderer? But she should forget about marrying anyone and concentrate on building her little cafe into a big restaurant, big but cosy and friendly where all old people would get a heavy discount.

'Come, Bobby, let's go wait in your car while Leela gets the other baskets from the kitchen. Should we take some leftover cake with us and have a picnic near the water lily pond?' she asked, putting her hand on Bobby's arm.

Bobby stared at her, his green eyes brimming with joy. He could not believe his luck. *A few precious minutes alone with my beloved Maria. What more can I ask for? I must not ruin it by talking about fruits and vegetables. I will tell her how much I love her, how much I long to make her my wife and live with her in a cottage by the water lily pond on the spice farm. I will plant a flower garden for her with roses, lilies, gardenia . . . no no, no talking about plants now.* Bobby looked at Maria shyly as they went out into the garden.

The parakeets swooped down, greeting them with shrill cries as if celebrating some event in the garden. 'Look. That's where we found her. I cannot go out of the house without getting a shiver down my spine. Each time I look at the tree, I see her body hanging, her hair flying in the wind.' Maria shuddered and Bobby quickly pulled her away.

'Wait. I just thought of something. It was odd that her hair was not tied up. Leela said she was a very fashionable lady with a big bun on top of her head. Who had untied her hair? Why do all this before killing someone?' She turned her head away from the tree.

'You said she was dressed like a man. Did her clothes fit properly?' asked Bobby.

'What do you mean?' Maria looked puzzled.

'I mean, did it look as if she was wearing trousers and a shirt like some women do? I have a lawyer friend who always wears a white shirt and black pants. In fact, she dresses very much like Deven,' said Bobby.

Maria wondered briefly who this lady lawyer friend was. She could not imagine Bobby knowing any other woman except her.

'No. Her trousers were very baggy and loose and the shirtsleeves were so long that her hands were hidden.' Maria shut her eyes to visualize the image of the dead woman. She hated doing it but it seemed important all of a sudden.

'That means she was dressed in someone else's clothes. I think the murderer was trying to hide her identity, delaying the police from starting their investigation.'

Maria stopped and stared at him. 'That's very clever of you, Bobby. We never thought of that. I must tell Deven. No, wait. Let's go to the spice farm first, otherwise he'll get that blackboard out again and it'll get late.'

Bobby laughed and opened the car door for her. 'There is a very healthy crop of tender fruit on the mango tree. You will get lots of mangoes this season if the rains do not damage the fruits.' *There I go again, wasting the precious time I had alone with her,* he thought as Leela emerged from the house carrying two huge baskets and a large fruit cake.

* * *

Rana Hooda slowly made his way to the other room. The floor was wet and slippery with oil and he was afraid he would slip and break his neck. He had recently heard of a man in Delhi cracking his head on a glass table and dying instantly, with a glass of whisky still in his hands. Where was Olga and why had she brought so many marigold necklaces? It was as if they had been at a wedding. Suddenly, Rana stopped. His heart froze and he found he could not breathe. He looked at his fingertips and saw they were stained red . . . no . . . vermilion. What had he done? Had he married that girl? But he couldn't remember anything at all.

Rani would kill him if she found out. She would take everything away from him: his cars, his factory, his farm, and even his dog. Everything belonged to her. *You came as a lowly clerk to work in my father's office and you earned nothing. All this is mine and will remain mine till I die*, he heard his wife's shrill voice scream in his head. No. He could have never married Olga. It would be bigamy. She knew that. She was not a fool. She kept nagging him to divorce Rani but he didn't have the courage to tell her that he would be ruined, he would be on the street, if he ever did that. This fantastic villa, the BMW and the yacht anchored on the Mandovi river would all vanish with one snap of Rani's fingers. They could do nothing while she was alive. He was a prisoner and the jailer was his wife.

Rana carefully stepped over a marigold garland and picked up his phone. There was still no call from his wife. Three days had passed. Rana hoped nothing was wrong, at the same time wishing she was at the bottom of the sea along with her stupid mobile phone. He was surprised that no one had called to find out where she was. If she hadn't reached Mumbai her relatives would have called him. Maybe she had gone somewhere else from Mumbai. But she would have told him about her plans. Where was that woman?

\* \* \*

Yuri opened his eyes and saw the light dance on his hands, making strange patterns. He wondered if he had died. The room was bathed in soft grey shadows that glided across the wall, floated over his bed and gently covered his face. His entire body seemed to sway and dance in the grey light and he felt at peace. He never wanted this feeling to go. He shut his eyes and let the shadows caress him. Then he heard the sound. It was a faint whisper but he knew someone was in the room. Yuri could hear whoever it was breathing. He dared not open his eyes. He did not want to see death standing by his bedside.

The breathing was louder now and someone touched his arm. A shiver ran through his entire body and the shadows suddenly vanished. The room was lit up. He could sense the glow seeping through his closed eyelids. He waited, his breath tight as a fist in his chest.

Why should he be afraid if he was dead already? There was nothing to fear now. He had always wondered how he would die and how calmly he would face the end, but now that he was being held in its embrace, he could not feel anything but this intense fear. Yuri wanted to scream, to escape, but he felt his breath being snuffed out. The last thing he saw was a pale white hand with long, twisted fingernails hovering over his face.

* * *

As they huddled in Bobby's office, Maria could hear the frogs calling in the pond. She was reminded of her childhood days when the rains would bring hundreds of frogs out in the garden and she would sit in the veranda and count them with her grandfather. The scent of lemongrass swirled around her, making her feel so relaxed and calm that Maria thought she would fall asleep. She wanted to stay at the spice farm forever. If she married Bobby, she would build a small cottage by this pond and spend weekends here. She would have to bring all the old folks with her but they could roam around happily and enjoy the ancient trees, spice plants and coconut palms.

'Here it is. Mrs Rani Hooda. 45 Greenside Villa, Vaddy, Trionim. It has her phone number too,' said Bobby, pulling out a crumpled piece of paper from a drawer in his desk.

'Shall we call her?' asked Prema.

'Have you no brains left? Are you going senile? What do you mean call her? Is she going to answer the phone and say "Hello. Remember me? I am the woman you saw hanging from the tree in your garden. I am dead but will try to return your call as soon as I can,"' said Deven.

Leela giggled and then kept quiet as Prema glared at her.

'Listen, Deven, you smarty-pants. What I meant was let us try the dead woman's number and see who answers.

There is no need to be so sarcastic and rude. I think *you* are getting senile. You are certainly a very grumpy old man,' Prema muttered.

'A bad temper is the first sign of dementia, my father used to say,' said Cyrilo.

'Well, we all know *your* father was not senile. He was just plain insane,' said Prema.

'As far as I know, Prema, you never met my late father. So kindly keep your opinions to yourself. My father was a noble and kind man. The entire village still remembers him with respect.'

'I hope they'll remember you as a silly old man,' said Prema and Cyrilo make a face at her.

'They will certainly remember you as the rudest woman to have ever lived in Trionim. Maybe they'll erect a statue in your honour and the pigeons will lovingly decorate your head with droppings,' muttered Cyrilo.

Leela smiled. She knew the oldies were going to argue for at least the next fifteen minutes. They really enjoyed attacking each other like crows fighting over food. Maybe it made them feel alive and young. She picked up the piece of paper and looked at it again.

'This is the same address as the Russian girl's, Miss Maria. Isn't it? The inspector told us that day,' said Leela.

Everyone stared at her. Maria read the address again and said, 'Yes, it is. You are right, Leela. Do you think there are several apartments at this address?'

'Could be. These new villas are built cheek by jowl like on an anthill. The builders want to pack in as much as they can to maximize their profits,' said Cyrilo.

'Yet people are happy to buy them, happy to pay huge prices for a tiny flat,' said Bobby. 'This lady said her husband was a top builder in Delhi and they wanted to take over the entire stretch along the Chapora river to build hotels and luxury apartments. Very expensive, exclusive villas and not those cheap types you see everywhere now in Goa. Then she offered me the job of doing the landscaping.'

'She would have paid you lots of money. Why didn't you accept it?' asked Rosie as he wheeled her out of the office.

'I'm very happy working here on the spice farm. I do not want to go anywhere else. This is my whole life. The trees, plants and seedlings I have grown in the greenhouse and the spice shed are like my children and I can never leave them. I am planning to build a bigger greenhouse next month to grow rare medicinal plants. Anyway, I did not like that woman. She began ordering me about as if I was her bonded slave, even though I had not accepted her offer.'

Rosie noticed that Bobby was less shy and timid now. It was as if his beloved trees and the fragrant groves of cinnamon and cardamom had given him the power to be a confident man. Bobby in his spice kingdom was a noble prince.

Maria too looked at Bobby, surprised at the change in him. *This is his life and it gives him so much joy. He is lucky to have found a passion that also gives him an income. He does not want to be rich desperately, like Francis. Francis is so eager to get ahead that he would do anything, go anywhere as long as he makes money. He wants me to sell the*

*Happy Home too*. Maria suddenly remembered Tina and her perfect hourglass figure. Tina was the daughter of one of Goa's wealthiest builders. Now she knew why Francis was courting her. He had tried to get her to sell the Happy Home and when she had refused he had lost interest in her. He had found another girl with a bigger house and more money. Francis never wasted time.

Standing in the shade of a mulberry tree, the birds singing all around her, Maria knew she did not love Francis any more. She suddenly felt free and, as a wave of happiness swept over her, she wanted to laugh. She wanted to shake the mulberry tree for some reason and eat all the fruit that would fall on her but then she remembered the dead woman's face and felt all her happiness wash away.

'We will go and check this address. Will you come with me, Bobby?' Maria turned to look at him. He stood uncertainly, his hands on Rosie's wheelchair, and then he smiled and said in a low voice, 'I will always be happy to help you. Have I not been there for you all my life, Maria? You mean everything to me.'

Rosie in her wheelchair, Deven under the pepper vine, Prema by the coconut tree, Cyrilo on the bench and Leela at the lily pond behind them all gave a happy sigh of relief. Bobby had spoken at last. The trees smiled down at them and the frogs croaked suddenly, as if they were offering congratulations. Bobby had finally declared his love for Maria. The mulberry tree shed a few leaves as Maria looked up at Bobby with surprise and love in her eyes. Rosie began planning the dress she would wear at Maria's wedding. She slowly started moving her wheelchair away so that the

couple could be alone. The others followed her and the
heady scent of jasmine, roses and cloves mingled with love
floated over all of them.

* * *

'I just can't understand what has happened to Yuri. He is
so confused. I think he is trying to tell us something but his
speech is so slurred I cannot understand what he says. That
doctor has given him a very strong painkiller since he keeps
groaning in pain,' said Deven.

'I really don't know how he injured himself. Do you
think he fell down in his room? He seems so fit. He's in
much better shape than you, Cyrilo,' said Prema.

'I know that, Prema. But how did he get back to the
bed? He should have been lying on the floor. He has very
bad bruises on his wrists and neck too,' said Cyrilo.

'Poor fellow. We should not have left him alone. Maria
could have gone to the spice farm to get the address from
Bobby,' said Deven.

'The one good thing is that the doctor will not allow
the inspector to take him to the police station to question
him about the stolen jewellery till he recovers fully,' said
Prema.

'At his age that could take months. He may not recover
from this fall. My uncle fell down the other day and now
he cannot recognize his own wife,' said Cyrilo. 'Though he
could just be pretending to escape from her tongue-lashing.
Poor man, one day dashing around on his scooter, the next
like a vegetable dribbling all over his bib.'

'I hope I die before my brain goes all soft and dim. I pray to god every day and ask him to take me while I am still fit and able,' said Prema.

'Glad to know you are fit and able. Now we will not have to hear the list of your ailments every day, I hope?' said Deven.

'Don't be so proud. Death is waiting for us around the corner; waiting and watching. Your turn will come soon,' hissed Prema, pointing a finger at Deven and then at the kitchen where Leela was loudly clanging pots and pans as she washed them.

'I did not know death was waiting for us in our kitchen. You'd better not eat so much, Prema, or else Mr Death will pounce on your stomach tomorrow at breakfast,' said Cyrilo.

'Death is not very far from us. We are all waiting in the departure lounge. We should be happy and content with whatever extra time the Almighty is giving us and not quarrel and say cruel things to each other. Each day is a precious gift from heaven, each breath is a bonus,' said Rosie in a quiet voice.

The others looked at her sheepishly and Deven patted her hand.

'You are so right, Rosie. We must be grateful for everything we have. We must make sure Yuri recovers soon. The doctor has given him some strong antibiotics so that he does not get an infection from the wound on his arm. He suspects Yuri had a mild stroke and that is probably what made him fall down suddenly,' said Deven.

'I will keep my bedroom door open in case he needs anything at night. Poor fellow, he looks terrible,' said Cyrilo.

'I think he's trying to tell us something because every time I go into his room, he points to the window. He cannot talk. But he still manages to raise one arm and point to the window,' said Rosie.

'Let's go and see him. I want to give him some amla juice. We can all have some,' said Prema.

'Amla juice gives me wind but you three have some. I will have coconut water later,' said Rosie, moving her wheelchair towards the door. Prema went into the kitchen to fetch the bottle of amla juice and behind her back Cyrilo made a grimace and pointed to his throat.

'Yuck,' he whispered.

'Why is it that everything that is good for you tastes so bad?' Rosie asked Cyrilo. He shook his head and laughed.

When they reached the veranda, Cyrilo and Deven lifted Rosie's wheelchair and placed it on the ramp that led to Yuri's studio. The sky was grey today and the leaves on the trees seemed much darker, as if they had been drenched in sepia ink. The sparrows were missing from the rose shrub and only a pair of doves cooed quietly to each other. Leela was now chopping vegetables in the kitchen, her knife making loud tapping noises on the wooden board. She was singing softly and looked up and smiled when they passed the kitchen window.

'What are you giving us for lunch today?' asked Cyrilo.

'Boiled cabbage and stale bread,' said Leela.

'Excellent. My favourite,' said Cyrilo, laughing.

'You know very well that today is Wednesday and we are having rava-fried bananas, tomato rice and dal,' said Prema.

'And custard and cake,' added Rosie.

'When I was a child my mother used to give me fried bananas if she was in a good mood. It was not very often since she was always so angry with me. I tried so hard to please her but failed,' said Deven.

Rosie was surprised to hear him talk about his childhood. He very rarely shared his memories with them. Cyrilo, Yuri and Prema had all told Maria about their lives before they came to live at the Happy Home but Deven was a closed door. Anyway, she would never ask him. Why show vulgar curiosity like Prema. But it was all very mysterious. At their age the past was a close companion; they spent so much time travelling back to the good old days.

'How far back can you remember?' asked Rosie.

'Well, I can remember I was about five. We used to live in a huge old house in a village in Punjab. My mother said we had moved there after Partition. It was her uncle's house and since he had no children he invited her to stay there with his family. He was a kind man and knew so many stories from mythology. It's strange I cannot remember my father at all. He died when I was seven. I wish I had got to know him a little bit,' said Deven. Rosie was surprised at how easily he was talking today. Usually he was quiet and polite but never this chatty. This horrible murder business had certainly made them closer. *I hope we stay like this all the time. I don't want only bad and evil things to bring us together*, thought Rosie.

'I can remember swinging on a tree swing my father made for me. He put a strong rope through a plank of wood and hung it on the mango tree. The swing is still there, you know. My nieces and nephews must be playing on it. It makes me so happy that my father's handiwork is still giving so much joy to children,' said Cyrilo.

'Why did you come to live in the Happy Home when you have your own home in Goa?' asked Prema.

No one spoke. It was an unwritten rule that none of them asked each other why they chose to live here instead of with their families. It was assumed that the subject was too painful to discuss, a dark, hurtful thing they had pushed to a remote corner of their minds. The Happy Home had given them shelter. They were fortunate to be here. They had each other, and Maria and Leela looked after them better than their own families. Their twilight years were going to pass here.

'I like staying here. We all like staying here, don't we? This is our only home. Family is something only lucky people have. Anyway, who needs them? Family only demands things from you and gives you very little. As long as I have you all as my friends I am very happy.' Cyrilo opened the door to Yuri's studio.

The room was in darkness and a strong smell of turpentine floated out as soon as they opened the door and stepped in. There were crushed tubes of oil paint scattered on the table, and dirty rags stained with colour hung from the window, blocking the light. Yuri was lying crookedly on the bed, his blue eyes fixed on the ceiling. He was very still.

'Is he dead?' Rosie whispered to Prema.

'Looks pretty dead to me but you can't tell with Yuri. He is so pale. When we brown people die you can tell at once but one can never be sure with these foreigners,' said Prema, putting her hand out to pull Yuri's toes.

He did not move. A mynah came and perched on the window and began tapping its beak on the glass.

'Look, the vulture has arrived, so he must be dead,' said Prema. 'Now this amla juice will be wasted.'

'That is not a vulture. It is Yuri's pet mynah. He feeds the bird every day. Must have come for its food, poor thing. Look, there are the seeds he gives it,' said Cyrilo, picking up a jar from the table. He took out a handful, opened the window and scattered them on the ground. The mynah flew down at once to peck at them and soon two other birds joined in and began squabbling, calling out in harsh notes.

Yuri turned his head towards the window.

'Oh! Good. He is alive.' Prema pulled his toe again. 'Have some amla juice, Yuri. Good for your liver which you have damaged with your excessive drinking,' she said, putting the bottle down on the table by his bed.

'Leave him alone, Prema,' said Cyrilo.

Then, as they watched, Yuri moved his hand and began twisting the bed sheet with his fingers, groaning loudly.

'Are you in pain?' asked Cyrilo, putting his hand on Yuri's forehead.

'Look, he's pointing to the window again,' said Rosie, moving her wheelchair closer to the bed. Yuri had lifted his hand and was moving it up and down agitatedly.

'He's saying hello to those wretched mynahs. Well, now we know he's definitely not dead,' said Prema.

Deven put his head very close to Yuri's face and said, 'Can you hear me, Yuri? Blink your eyes if you can understand what I am saying.'

As they all waited, holding their breath, Yuri's eyes stayed still and suddenly blinked.

'Oh, my friend. Good. You can hear me. Do not worry. You will recover soon. Blink once if you are not in pain,' said Deven.

Yuri blinked once, his hands twitching as he pointed to the window again.

'What is it? You want the window shut? Lift your hand for no and blink for yes,' said Deven.

Yuri lifted his hand.

'Is the light from the window hurting your eyes?' asked Rosie.

Yuri raised his hand once more and his blue eyes filled with tears.

'Did you see anyone at the window?' asked Rosie. She knew that one could sit at the window all day waiting for someone to pass by. That was what she did all day. It was good to see another human face even if it was a stranger's. Sometimes if she was lucky people even stopped and talked to her.

Yuri blinked rapidly.

'Yes. He is saying yes. I think he saw someone at the window. Yuri, did someone come in here? Did someone come into your room?' asked Cyrilo.

Yuri blinked again and slowly tried to move his hand towards his neck. The sheet fell away and they saw that Yuri's neck was lined with red marks.

'My god. Yuri, did someone hurt you? Look, his neck is bruised. We only thought his arm was injured by the fall. Why did the doctor not check this? It looks quite bad,' said Cyrilo.

Yuri blinked once and shut his eyes as tears rolled down his cheeks. He slowly raised one arm and then closed his eyes. They heard him breathing heavily and after a while they all quietly went out of the room. 'What was he trying to tell us? Could someone have attacked him when he was alone in the house?' asked Deven. No one had an answer.

* * *

Rana Hooda walked towards the window and opened it. He took a deep breath and looked out. The dark and threatening monsoon clouds marched across the sky but the sea seemed calm. The waves were gentle. Rana thought about checking the monsoon's travel path on the laptop but he couldn't muster up the enthusiasm to do it. He couldn't focus on anything except Olga's whereabouts. How could she have disappeared like this, leaving the apartment in such a mess? He suddenly wondered if his car was still there. It was actually Rani's car, a sixtieth birthday present to herself. Rana picked up his phone, checked once more for any missed calls and opened the door. The car was missing. Olga must have taken it. As Rana stared at the empty spot in the driveway he suddenly felt a stab of fear tear into him. He imagined Olga dancing on the beach, dressed in that skimpy red dress she loved wearing. Her hair was flying in the wind and her mouth was painted red.

This was the woman he wanted to spend his life with. The woman he was going to leave his wife and home for.

He was going to lose everything, and he knew he was going to lose Olga too. Maybe she had gone already. Taken his car and god knows what else. For the first time since he had set eyes on Olga, Rana allowed himself to look at the truth. She only wanted his money. She desperately wanted his house in London. She wanted to use him in every way possible but she did not realize that he had nothing to give her. Without Rani he had nothing at all. Rani held the purse strings very firmly in her bejewelled, scrawny hands.

Rana thought of those hands, the nails painted a horrible shade of crimson red, the five diamonds rings flashing like demon's eyes every time she moved her hands. She had hit him once in a rage and a diamond had cut his cheek open. She wore a huge glittering stone on each finger because her guru had told her it would bring peace and harmony to her life. Rana wished the man had given her some kind of magic stone to cure her foul temper. It was getting worse every day and the slightest thing would make her insane with anger. She would scream and howl like a mad woman, tearing her hair and throwing things at him. Rana shut his eyes and pictured her. She thought it made her look beautiful, all this make-up and cosmetic surgery which had cost a fortune, but she looked like a clown—an evil, malicious clown with swollen lips and puffy eyes. He wished she were dead.

Rana suddenly began to shiver. His hands were sweaty and damp, yet he was feeling so cold. He tried to remember what he had drunk the previous night. He needed air. The smell of incense and dead flowers was suffocating him. A sharp pain flashed behind his eyes as he stumbled into the blazing sunshine.

\* \* \*

'Keep your head down,' Alfie whispered to Maria as they crouched behind the shrubs outside the gate. Maria, Bobby and Alfie had been waiting for hours for someone to come out of the villa. Maria's neck was hurting and she wanted to leave, when Alfie suddenly jabbed her arm and said, 'There is your man.'

Maria was not sure what to do and stood uncertainly behind the wall, twisting her handkerchief. The previous day Leela had found a piece of paper under the almirah near Yuri's bed. It was a dry-cleaning bill and this was the address written on it. Someone from this house had come to the Happy Home that day. This person could have attacked Yuri, but when they told the inspector he refused to believe it.

'Old age causes a lot of confusion. The brain cells are slowly dying one by one. It is like the lights going off in your house. My mother is so active yet she forgot to wash my vest the other day. She also forgets to add ghee in the dal these days,' he had said, looking mournful.

The doctor who had come to see Yuri also insisted he was confused because he could be in the early stages of senile dementia.

'But, doctor, Yuri was fine last week when we left him at home and went to the spice farm. I heard him singing when he was shaving. How can you get dementia in one day?' Deven had asked.

'It is all in god's hands. He is watching us all and sending his bolts of lightning to torment us. We are helpless. Old age comes to everyone. Senile dementia, gout, tooth decay and baldness come to all of us,' the doctor had said, raising his hands to the sky.

'At his age people have a tendency to fall and injure themselves. It could be some other age-related problem.' He had then taken Rs 500 and left.

But they knew someone had attacked Yuri and the bill Leela had found under the almirah belonged to that person. It was definitely a stranger's since no one in the Happy Home ever got their clothes dry-cleaned.

The address on the bill had led them to this area at the other end of Trionim. This villa with a huge garden and impressive iron gate had the same address Bobby had shown them: 45 Greenside Villa.

This was the villa where the dead woman had once lived.

Everything they had learnt so far led them to this place, to this grand, red-roofed villa in an expensive part of Trionim that none of them were familiar with even though it was not very far from the Happy Home. Why was Inspector Chand not questioning the man who lived here? If they had found a connection surely he too must have figured it out by now. They were not sure where exactly it was going to take them but they had to follow this trail and find out. 'This Inspector Chand is really not interested in solving the case. He told Maria that the woman had come from Mumbai, not Delhi. Apparently he found a Mumbai address in her jacket pocket,' said Cyrilo. Deven shook his head. 'I think that was placed there to mislead the police. We will find out.'

Deven and Cyrilo wanted to jump into the van and rush to the villa as soon as they were shown the dry-cleaning bill but Maria had told them not to. 'We might get chased by the guard. I don't want you two to get hurt,' she had said and quickly rushed out and got into Bobby's car before Deven could say anything.

He shook his head angrily and watched as Bobby's car drove out of the Happy Home gate.

'What does she mean? We have been doing so much work on this case already. We found that slip with the address. Well, Leela found it. That fat inspector has done nothing at all except trying to arrest Yuri. Why does he not question this Russian girl? Maria should have taken us with her. This is not fair,' Deven told Cyrilo in his room as they sat drinking tea. For a few moments they sat silently brooding and then they suddenly looked at each other. They knew at once that both of them had the same idea.

'Come on. Let's follow them,' said Cyrilo. They left quietly and got into their van. Cyrilo took the shortcut through the narrow, muddy lanes between the rice fields and soon they were on the main road. There was not much traffic but they could not see Bobby's car. 'We should catch up with them. This Bobby drives so slowly,' said Cyrilo, changing gears roughly. The little van groaned in protest and stalled, almost bumping into two girls riding past on a scooter. 'Grandpa, drive carefully,' one of them shouted.

'Who is she calling grandpa? Must be you, Deven. You should start dyeing your hair,' said Cyrilo, laughing.

'Shut up. Just concentrate on driving or we'll lose them. Do you remember the address on the bill?' asked Deven.

'It is one of those new villas near the Chapora river. I pass them every morning on my way to the fish market. We can stop on our way back and pick up some prawns,' said Cyrilo.

'Listen, we are trying to catch a murderer but you always turn all our attempts into a jaunt. Forget about the fish and try to remember the number of the villa,' said Deven.

'No harm in picking up some fish since we will be passing by the bridge. The boats come in exactly at this time and the prawns are really fresh. The murderer is not running away but prawns get stale so fast.' Cyrilo overtook a bus from the left, honking loudly. The driver leaned out and waved.

'Oh. He is from our village. Did I tell you how he drove his bus over my grandmother's chickens one day but not a single one died?'

'I don't want to hear about your grandmother's chickens again. I am fed up with them. Please pay attention to the traffic and let me think. I am trying to connect this address to the other clues,' said Deven, tapping his fingers impatiently on the car window.

'Pity you did not bring your blackboard along. Helps you think better. When we catch the murderer, you must show him the blackboard and your jottings. He'll be really impressed.' Deven did not reply and looked out of the window as they left the main road and turned into a lane. The red-tiled roofs of the villas sparkled in the sunshine and uniformed guards stood at every gate. Cyrilo slowed down and began counting under his breath as they passed each villa. The van groaned and rattled as if it was not happy to be in this unfamiliar part of Trionim.

'Even the dogs look rich here,' muttered Cyrilo and stopped the van with a jerk under a large banyan tree. They could see 45 Greenside Villa on the opposite side of the road and Bobby's car was parked in front. But they couldn't see him or Maria anywhere.

Maria lifted her head and looked at the man who had just come out of the house. Alfie, who had joined them on the way here, was right behind her, while Bobby hid behind the garden wall. The man was very short and was wearing tight jeans, a bright red T-shirt and dark glasses with blue frames. He looked like a middle-aged man dressed like a teenager. His hair, dyed with blonde streaks, stood out all over his head as if he had just had an electric shock. 'I will go and talk to him. You stay here,' she told Bobby.

'No. I don't want you to go alone. I'm coming with you,' he said, suddenly sounding so assertive that Maria was surprised. Timid Bobby had turned into a tiger.

'Listen, Bobby. Let me go talk to him. I'll pretend to be a housekeeper looking for a job. It's very easy to fool these people from Delhi.'

'I can pretend to be a gardener looking for a job. I can act as well as you. Remember the play we did in school? Shakespeare's *As You Like It*,' he said and smiled.

'Make up your mind, you two, otherwise this fellow will drive off. There is no time for chit-chat about plays and silly things. The guard will come back soon and chase us away.' Alfie threw his cigarette into the shrubs. 'If you want I can go and talk to him. I know him quite well. I often do cleaning jobs for him when he has a party. They leave the house in a real mess but he gives good tips. How much they fight, those two. That Russian girl once poured a bottle of whisky over his head.' Alfie laughed.

'Alfie, you can go home now. Thanks for your help. We will handle this. We need to find out who he is and what is the connection between this house and the Happy Home. We can't just roll up at his doorstep and ask him these questions. He might get suspicious, so I will pretend to ask for a job and then snoop around,' said Maria. She was feeling a bit nervous but did not want to show it and was very glad Bobby was with her. Alfie turned around and walked away as Maria opened the gate, her heart thumping with fear. Bobby followed her silently.

# CHAPTER TWELVE

RANA THOUGHT HE heard a car and came out to see if Olga was back. He was now really anxious. The sudden visit from the police inspector earlier that day had given him a shock. Why had this man turned up at his house asking questions? He tried to remember what the inspector had said but his mind was a whirl of confused thoughts. He should really stop taking those yellow pills Olga kept giving him but they made him feel so happy and he desperately needed to feel happy. The inspector had shown him a photograph of a dead woman. Her face was all swollen and black. 'Do you know her?' he had asked.

'Why should I? I have never seen her,' he had said, quickly looking away, but there was a frightening thought at the back of his head. Who was the dead woman? Why was the inspector asking him?

'May I ask you, sir, where is Mrs Rani Hooda, your wife?' the inspector asked.

'In Mumbai. She is in Mumbai. I just got a message from her.' The message had come from an unknown number. 'I have lost my phone and messaging you from the driver's phone. I am going for a few days to Dubai. Will call later. Love, Rani.' Rather an odd, curt message but he did not tell the inspector that. He wanted this sweaty policeman to go away before Olga came home. The man was snooping around the room and Rana was afraid he would see the packets of grass lying around. Olga was so careless.

'Do you have a photograph of Mrs Rani Hooda?'

Rana shook his head. Olga had removed all Rani's photographs. Then he remembered the old one on top of the bookshelf. He pointed at it. Rani had just had her new face done and looked so unlike herself that even Rana couldn't recognize her. The inspector looked at her for a while and wrote something in his notebook. Rana looked at him impatiently and said he had to make an urgent phone call and got up. The pain in his head was killing him and he wanted to go back to sleep.

As soon as the inspector left, Rana went upstairs and lay down. His hands were shaking and he was dying to take a pill but restrained himself. He needed to clear his head. He must talk to Olga when she came back. Why had Rani sent him that peculiar message? It did not sound like her at all. She never signed off with 'love' ever. Why had she suddenly taken off for Dubai?

Rana shut his eyes and then heard the doorbell again. He got up with a groan and went downstairs, almost tripping over Olga's shoes. He cursed under his breath as he opened the door, hoping it was not the policeman again. He was not going to look at that photograph. He had shut his eyes when he had thrust the crumpled picture at him; the dead woman's face was so distorted and ugly.

Rana shaded his eyes and opened the door. He saw a girl and a young man standing near the gate. The girl was very pretty with long curly hair but was dressed shabbily in an old skirt and white blouse. Maybe she was collecting money for charity. Olga always told the guard to send such people away but he did not mind helping them. The guard was not around and this girl looked so pretty and innocent standing in the sunlight, her hair shining like a glossy mane, that he wanted to help. He took a deep breath of fresh air and felt his pain ease slightly.

'Yes? Do you want something?'

'Good afternoon. I am Maria Souza and this is my friend Bobby Menezes. We are looking for part-time work. We live nearby in Trionim,' said Maria, her heart beating fast. She had never told a lie like this before. She was quite sure this man would find out that she was fibbing and order them to get out but he stared at her through the dark glasses as if he had not quite understood what she was saying. She was about to repeat herself when he spoke in a croaking, rough voice.

'Okay. Please come in. This sunlight is too strong for my eyes,' he said and moved aside to let them in. Maria saw that his T-shirt was stained with oil, as if he had sat on a plate of greasy curry. The man opened the glass door that led into the house and as soon as the air conditioner's cool air touched her face, Maria felt she had been transported to another country.

The room was huge, with glass windows that went all the way up to the ceiling. The walls were painted white but a glossy, blinding white Maria had never seen before. The bulging leather sofas with massive silver feet were white and the carpets were black and white. There were at least two dozen black and white cushions strewn all over the place. For a moment Maria felt she was surrounded by a herd of baby zebras. Black-and-white paintings of naked bodies hung on the wall and giant silver vases filled with artificial white lilies were placed on the tables. A chandelier with pieces of shining glass leaves winked at her from the ceiling. Beyond the windows, a swimming pool shimmered and a pink plastic raft shaped like a woman's body floated on its surface. Two crows were perched on its head.

The man picked up a chiffon scarf and pair of high-heeled shoes from the sofa and sat down with a groan. Maria and Bobby kept standing near the door. The room was a mess. There were marigold garlands strewn on the floor and a lamp had overturned, spilling oil on the white, marble floor. A strong smell of incense and something rotten floated in the air and Maria began to feel a bit sick.

'What kind of job are you looking for, Miss . . .? I forgot your name, sorry.' The man mopped his face with a red handkerchief that had 'RH' embroidered on it in gold.

She had seen a handkerchief like this before. But Maria could not remember where. Who had shown it to her? Was it at the Happy Home or the Tip Top Cafe? Where?

'I can do housekeeping and cooking. Bobby here is an expert gardener with a degree in botany from Goa University. We often work in big houses like this during the summer to earn some extra money. I have an old mother whom I am looking after. Medicines are so expensive now,' said Maria, on a roll. Once you started telling lies, it got quite easy. She was no longer feeling nervous and she pushed Bobby forward. Why was he standing so quietly? He should help to get some information too.

Bobby cleared his throat and said, 'Your garden really needs a total overhaul. Those shrubs are dying. If you like I will do a soil analysis and give you a report of what kind of plants are suitable for your garden.' The man took off his dark glasses slowly and looked up at them. His eyes were bloodshot and puffy and Maria could now smell stale alcohol on his breath. 'Please sit down, Miss Mary. I am Rana Hooda, by the way. I cannot offer you tea or anything since the servants seem to have vanished. You can see everything is a mess,' he said. 'I would like to employ you both. It is so difficult to find good staff in Goa though we pay so much. They just keep running off. My wife lives in Delhi. Can you cook Goan food?' he asked. 'I love Goan food but Olga hates it. She says it gives her a stomach ache. These Russian girls can drink a bottle of vodka happily but a bit of chilli scares them. Olga is my . . . err . . . she is my personal trainer,' said Rana and suddenly burped loudly.

'Sorry. I am not feeling too well. I don't know what I ate last night. Some Russian food Olga had made. Half-cooked chunks of meat. Olga is the only person I know who can burn meat and still leave it uncooked.' He frowned and twisted the heavy gold chain around his neck with his fingers.

'Olga?' said Maria softly. Could this be the same Olga who had come to the Tip Top Cafe with the bundle of stolen jewellery and tried to frame Yuri? There were so many Russian girls in Goa but still she must ask him.

'Is Olga living here too? I think I met her the other day. Tall girl, very beautiful?' asked Maria, trying to sound casual, holding her breath.

'Beautiful? Yes. Olga is very beautiful but she is a greedy, cruel-hearted bitch. She is an evil Barbie doll. Do you think you could make me some tea and toast? I am feeling a bit ill. If I eat something, I might feel better. By the way, we are hosting a party this evening for some very important people from abroad. Come and help to serve the drinks. I will pay you . . . pay you whatever you ask. Ten thousand . . . twenty thousand rupees. Wear a black dress. Olga will give you an apron. She loves uniformed servants, though she is a bloody peasant herself.' Rana lay down on the sofa. He yawned a few times, snapping his fingers in front of his mouth.

Maria nodded. 'Sure. We are free this evening. I will make some tea for you now. Can you show me where the kitchen is? Okay, don't worry, I will find it,' said Maria as Rana gave her a confused look. She went out of the drawing room and opened the first door she found. It was a gym with a row of machines and a giant television on one wall. There were blown-up photos of Hollywood stars and one of a small dog on a bicycle.

Maria came out and turned into the corridor. She opened another door and almost tripped over a heap of wet towels as she stepped into a large bathroom with a shining marble floor. The ceiling was painted with flying cherubs and a black, round bathtub sat like a giant spider in one corner. The taps were golden. Maria was very tempted to jump into the bathtub and turn the golden taps on. This luxurious bathroom belonged to a movie star. The perfect setting for a bubble bath scene. There were large bottles of various green and red gels, a basket of multicoloured soaps and a tall vase filled with fake lilies. The bathroom mirror was steamed as if someone had just had a bath. Maria could smell a strange, unpleasant aroma of burnt oil and flowers. The next door she opened led into a dining room with a glass table balanced on four silver legs shaped like a tiger's paws. Golden chairs with swans painted on their backs surrounded the glass table and Maria felt she was in a magical zoo. She quickly shut the door and came back into the drawing room.

'Excuse me, Mr Hooda, but I cannot find the kitchen,' she said.

Rana Hooda was sprawled on the white sofa, snoring loudly with his mouth open. His shirt buttons were open and his hairy chest rose and fell with each breath, reminding Maria of a gorilla toy she had once seen that grunted when you pressed its stomach.

'Great. Now we have to wait till he wakes up to ask him about this Olga. I am sure it is the same girl who came to meet me at the cafe,' said Maria as she looked at Rana.

'Now what should we do? Shall I wake him up?' asked Maria as Bobby came and stood next to her.

'No. Let him be. This is perfect. We can have a quick look around while he is asleep.'

'Glad to know you're still here with me. You really impressed him with your garden talk, Bobby.'

'You are much better at talking than I am, Maria, and you know it. Come on. Let us look through the drawers

over there. We might find a letter addressed to this Olga.'
Bobby pointed to a large desk.

"No, I'll go upstairs. If Olga lives here, her bedroom
must be upstairs. I might see a photograph of her. She
looked like the kind of girl who takes pictures of herself all
the time, though she probably has to hide them when the
wife turns up,' said Maria, turning towards the stairs.

Her footsteps made an echoing sound on the marble
floor and Maria tried to walk softly, holding on to the wall.

A giant stuffed leopard standing in the corner gave her
a start and she stopped and touched its head. 'You poor
creature. I hope the person who shot you gets punished,'
she said, patting the leopard's rough, dusty head. There was
a door to her left but it was locked. Maria went to the door
next to it and tried to turn the knob.

It opened at once and a whiff of strong perfume hit her
face as she walked in. There were clothes lying all over the
bedroom floor and the large bed too was covered with silk
scarves, underwear and gowns. The carpet was black and
white but covered with red stains. Maria was not sure if it
was part of the design or someone had spilled red wine on
it. A fine white powder covered the glass on the dressing
table that was loaded with jars of perfume and make-up
bottles.

Maria picked up a silver-framed photograph of a
woman lying on the floor, half hidden under the bed. It
was not Olga. This woman was much older and had beady,
suspicious-looking eyes. Could this be Rana's wife? She
looked familiar but Maria could not remember where she
had seen her. She looked around but there were no other

photographs. An ashtray filled with cigarette butts lay on the floor. Maria walked out of the room, closing the door gently behind her. She stood for a moment wondering where to go next. She suddenly heard someone calling out downstairs.

Maria quickly tried to open the door on the other side of the staircase. She hoped Rana was still sleeping, otherwise he would think it very odd to see her wandering about the house like this. Maria looked out of the window in the corridor and saw Cyrilo gazing up at her. He smiled and waved and she lifted her hand and waved back at him in surprise. Then she saw Deven getting out of the van. 'They must have followed us. I knew they would.' She opened the door and went into the next bedroom.

It was much bigger than the last one and the ceiling was covered with silk drapes like a stage. A large, heavily carved four-poster bed sat in the middle of the room and there were at least twenty soft toys huddled on the pillows. As Maria stared at the pink and blue velvet rabbits, woolly cats, puppies and monkeys she heard a soft whimpering sound and quickly turned around.

A large rat was watching her from under the bed. Maria opened her mouth to scream and then she saw it was not a rat but a very small dog. She went closer and the dog began wagging its stump of a tail and looked up at her with sad eyes.

'You poor thing. Someone has chained you to the bed.' Maria stroked the dog's head. She saw it was a female and wore a collar with 'Armani' written on it in diamante studs. The dog began to whimper, and Maria untied her chain and pulled her out. She ran to the bathroom and made a big puddle on the black marble floor.

Then Maria looked up and saw the photographs.

Olga, the same Olga she had met at the Tip Top Cafe, was staring at her from the bathroom wall, naked as a newborn baby except for a fur stole wrapped around her neck. There was another photograph of the ugly older woman but someone had put it behind the cistern. Olga had probably switched the photographs around as soon as the wife left. 'My personal trainer', he had called her. What a complicated life this Rana Hooda led. No wonder he looked so miserable and unhappy.

The dog began running around in circles near Maria's feet, barking loudly. Maria filled water in a mug and placed it on the floor. She took a half-eaten bun from her pocket and gave it to the dog, who sniffed at it but did not eat it. 'Fussy thing you are. I have to leave you now, sorry.' She quickly shut the door. She did not want the dog's high-pitched barks to wake Rana.

Maria opened the bedroom door quietly and went out. She noticed there was one more photograph of Olga beyond the corridor but in this she was wearing a beautiful, formal gown and heavy diamond jewellery.

The girl obviously liked her diamonds.

'This man is still asleep. What should we do? I cannot find anything in the study. Shall we look in the other rooms?' asked Bobby when she came back into the drawing room.

'No. I have found what we were looking for. Olga lives here. Olga is the connection to the Happy Home. She is connected with the woman's death,' said Maria. She heard a faint bark again and wished she could take the little dog home with her.

'Look, Cyrilo and Deven are in the garden,' said Bobby.

'Yes, I saw them from upstairs. I was going to ask them to come in. They would love to see this house. It's like being in an old Hollywood movie. What on earth are they doing? Why are they crawling?' Maria went to the window.

'Probably searching for clues like true detectives. You know, cigarette butts, torn bits of cloth, lost shoes.' Bobby smiled.

'I will call them in,' said Maria, walking to the door.

As soon as she touched the door handle she heard Rana mutter in his sleep and she quickly turned around. He was still fast asleep, his cheeks puffing up with each loud snore. His face was glowing with sweat though the room was freezing with all the air conditioners on full blast.

'I think he is on drugs. This kind of heavy sleep is not natural. It is certainly drug-induced,' said Bobby, staring at him.

'There was a sprinkling of some white powder in the bedroom upstairs. Do you think it's cocaine? I didn't want to touch it. I think we should let him sleep. Now that he knows us, we can always come back later in case we need to find out anything more,' said Maria. 'And he has employed me. I have to help with the party in the evening. You are coming with me, Bobby.' She opened the door. The dog was still barking upstairs but Rana Hooda slept on, dead to the world.

Cyrilo circled the villa and came back to the van. He was happy to have spotted Maria inside the house. Hopefully that meant she had found out something important. Luckily there were no guards around and he had had a good look at the garden. He tapped on the window of the van now and said to Deven, 'The coast is clear but first I need to do a small job.'

'Why is your bladder so weak? You must learn to control yourself. There are some yoga exercises I can teach you,' said Deven, coming out of the van as Cyrilo got up too.

'It can wait. I am not going to start doing yoga here to control my weak bladder,' muttered Cyrilo and disappeared behind a shrub.

Deven looked around. It was so quiet here. They could not hear the sound of traffic at all though the main road was not very far. The new villas already had green gardens with fully grown trees. Deven wondered if they had all been transplanted from the forest to create an instant garden for these rich people. When you had money you did not have to wait for anything.

Cyrilo came back, humming, and then saw Maria waving to them from the door of the villa.

'Come in. Be very quiet. The guard is still not back,' she whispered.

'I have no control over anything. My bladder is weak, my blood pressure is high, my hearing is bad and my eyesight is weak. My blood sugar is high and my libido is low. But I am alive and kicking. I am sixty-nine years young,' sang Cyrilo, walking into the villa.

Deven followed, took one quick look around and said, 'There has been a puja in this room. I can smell sandalwood agarbatti. Why has this man passed out like this?' he asked, pointing to Rana slumped on the sofa.

'You smell agarbatti everywhere. This man looks happily drunk to me,' whispered Cyrilo, opening the door nearest to him. 'I am going to check out the rooms. Wow. Deven. Look. What a bathroom! I might take a quick shower here while you glare at that blissfully drunk man on the sofa. Let the sleeping drunks lie, I always say.'

'Everyone looks drunk to you,' muttered Deven. 'I can see something very strange is going on in this house. Why is there so much stuff on the floor? It seems someone has done a puja but then someone has also smoked marijuana in this room.' Deven touched the wet surface of the glass table. It was oily and a brass lamp lay on the floor. He quietly opened a drawer next to the table but then heard footsteps behind him and quickly shut it.

Cyrilo came out of the bathroom a few minutes later, his hair wet and plastered to his head. He was reeking of strong perfume.

'I had a quick wash with some imported soap but it really smells foul. Look at that old chandelier. They must have bought it from one of those old villas in Goa. This table is antique too. My grandmother had one just like this,' Cyrilo said, looking around.

'I could never live in a house like this. It is like a hotel. Not very clean either. Look at all the mess on the carpets.' Deven went towards the door that led into the garden.

'Well, I don't think you have to worry about that. How can we ever live in such a house? It's only for millionaires like this fat fellow. Anyway, I love the Happy Home the best. Who needs costly chandeliers? But I wouldn't mind having a giant TV like that. Watching football on that screen would be so great,' said Cyrilo, following him into the garden.

Maria wanted to show them the dining room but they heard Rana muttering loudly as he turned restlessly on the sofa. 'Time to depart,' said Bobby and quickly pushed all of them out. He shut the door quietly behind them and walked out. He opened the car door and waited for Maria to get in. She shook her head and laughed. 'Don't spoil me like this, Bobby. I am not used to it.'

Bobby opened his mouth to say that he wanted nothing more in life than to spoil her, give her all the comforts she ever wanted, but he said nothing. As they drove off, he began practising what he would say to her later, as he had done so many times at home. He had sat day after day by the water lily pool and thought about laying his heart bare to Maria. He had told her how he had fallen in love with her from the first day he saw her at school with her long curly hair tied up with a blue ribbon. He had long imaginary conversations with her as he walked around the spice garden and he was sure all the trees, shrubs and flowering plants knew every word he had spoken to Maria. Everyone knew so well what was in his heart, except Maria.

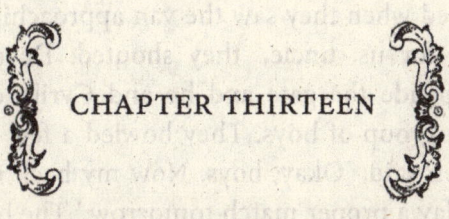

## CHAPTER THIRTEEN

'WHAT A GRAND villa. It's like something out of a Hollywood movie. This Rana Hooda must be loaded,' said Cyrilo as they walked to their van parked farther down the road. The guard had now come back and was staring at them suspiciously. 'We could have robbed the whole house if we wanted to. This guard fellow is useless.' Deven gave the guard such a stern look that he promptly jumped up to salute him. 'All made with black money,' he added as he turned the van around. The street was empty except for a big red car under a tree. A stray dog slept in its shade and a few urchins were trying to look at their faces in the side mirrors. Cyrilo waved to them and they ran away. As they drove back, Cyrilo kept talking about the villa they had just seen but Deven said nothing. 'What are you thinking about?' Cyrilo finally noticed and asked.

'I will tell you when we get home. Don't be so impressed with this kind of showy wealth. A simple life is a noble life, remember,' said Deven, not taking his eyes off the road.

'I am okay with a simple life as long as I have five good friends and a giant TV,' said Cyrilo.

Soon they were near the lane that led to the Happy Home. A few small boys were playing cricket near the gate and shouted when they saw the van approaching. 'Come and bowl for us, uncle,' they shouted. Deven parked the car outside the gate and he and Cyrilo obediently joined the group of boys. They bowled a few times and then Deven said, 'Okay, boys. Now my back is hurting. We will play a proper match tomorrow.' The boys began complaining loudly but then soon went back to their game and forgot all about them. Their frequent excited cries of 'Out' reached the veranda and Cyrilo wanted to go back and join them again but his back was giving twinges of protest too.

'I wish I was young and could play cricket all day long,' he said with a sigh. He reluctantly turned to Deven and asked, 'Maria said she saw photographs of the Russian girl Olga in the bedroom. How can that Olga live there? Doesn't the man's wife mind? My wife would have killed me if I brought a Russian doll home,' he added.

'My wife was a saint,' said Deven.

'So was mine. She prayed all the time but she would still have taken a knife to my throat if I brought another woman home,' said Cyrilo. 'Not that I ever wanted to. One wife is more than enough. It must be tough to keep them separate from each other.'

'Wait till I show you what I found,' said Deven.

'What? What did you find? Diamonds?' asked Cyrilo.

'Just look in my jacket pocket,' said Deven.

Cyrilo slipped his hand in and pulled out a syringe. 'Hey. Where did you get that? Have you got diabetes now?'

'Don't be stupid. My blood sugar is perfect. I don't drink or eat sweets. I found this under the sofa. It must have fallen out of Rana Hooda's trouser pocket. This is the kind of syringe drug addicts use,' said Deven.

'Do you think he takes drugs? He's so rich,' asked Cyrilo, surprised.

'You think rich people don't take drugs?' asked Deven. 'You need to get your head examined. Either that man asleep on the sofa or someone in the house takes drugs. Serious drugs.'

'Imagine having a TV that size and a fabulous bathroom and still wanting to take drugs. Some people are mad.'

'While you people were busy admiring bathrooms, TVs, chandeliers and antique tables, I had a quick look around. There were a packet of letters in Russian and a Russian passport. I think it was that girl's passport but I couldn't get a good look because Bobby pushed us out,' said Deven.

'That Rana Hooda must be married to both of them; no wonder he takes drugs. Which man can remain sane with two wives squabbling over him?' said Cyrilo. 'Do you think we should show this syringe to Maria and Bobby?'

'No, I want to do some thinking. When we have a meeting this evening I'll show it to everyone.' Deven started going upstairs.

Cyrilo nodded his head and smiled. He knew that Deven wanted to show off, and why not? After all, he had found the syringe and not Maria or Bobby. Deven had sharp eyes and a very sharp brain and deserved all the praise he was longing for.

Cyrilo turned to go to his room. Then he saw Rosie sitting alone in the veranda and went up to her. He sat down on the wooden bench and began telling her in great detail all that had happened that morning, adding his own bits and pieces to amuse her. They both laughed when he told her how keen Deven was to hold an evening session with his beloved blackboard.

'He is probably longing to go back to his schooldays. That was the happiest time of our lives. I still think about my schooldays. I remember the name of every child in my class. Their faces often come to me in my dreams,' said Rosie. She did not add that the faces of her dead husbands too floated around her as she lay awake at night.

'You know, Cyrilo, at our age, memories are like old friends. They cling to you, comfort you. They feel sad if you neglect them. Memories flow upon memories, a tall hill rises of our past life as we grow old,' said Rosie. She was feeling happy now that Cyrilo had told her what he had done all day. Suddenly she felt a part of the group again and knew in her heart that tomorrow too would bring fresh memories for her to store and look at during the long, lonely nights. She patted Cyrilo's hand and they sat together for a long time, chatting and watching the dragonflies chase each other all over the garden. It was good to feel a human presence next to you; to listen to another voice besides the one in your head. Even if you sat silently, it was so good to have a person by your side. She would never feel lonely in the Happy Home with Maria, Leela, Yuri, Cyrilo, Deven and even that sulky Prema around. She smiled at Cyrilo, feeling glad she had worn her best scarf today and dotted a tiny drop of her precious French perfume on her fragile wrists.

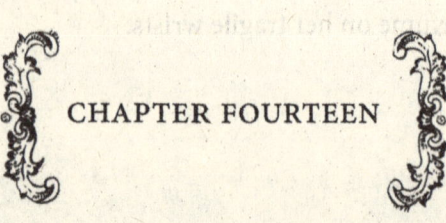

# CHAPTER FOURTEEN

'THE TWO WIVES quarrelled, and that is why we were able to catch him, sir,' said Robert, smiling proudly as he jabbed his stick into the man's stomach.

Inspector Chand looked at his fingernails. He had stopped biting them long ago but the scars remained. The IG's visit had passed off well and now he could relax once more.

There had been a case of robbery on the Vagator road that morning but they had caught the man before he could escape. He stood before them now, his hands tied behind his back.

'How long have you been doing this?' asked Inspector Chand. He was wondering if he should go to the Happy Home and tell them there was no further update on the case and they should stop their sleuthing. He was quite fed up with their questions.

Inspector Chand gazed out of the window. Maria might ask him to stay for tea. He was quite sure that the IG was going to recommend him for a promotion and then he could ask Maria to marry him. Inspector Chand suddenly saw his mother's face in his mind's eye, her eyes blazing with anger. He quickly got his mind back to the present.

'I started stealing only last month, sir. I was a shopkeeper before that but my wife said I could make more money this way. My second wife said that. My first wife was happy with the shop. We sold underwear and socks,' said the man, rubbing his nose on his sleeve.

'Is your second wife a thief too?' asked Inspector Chand, quite interested now.

'Yes, sir. She started with simple pickpocketing tricks and then got trained by a master robber to dupe tourists. He was arrested in Mumbai last month so she told me to take over.'

'Take over his area?' asked Robert.

'No. His area is huge. She meant all the beaches in north Goa, sir. I cannot manage so much so I only took a part of Vagator beach. Easy stretch and I could finish work by 7 p.m. I don't like working late.'

'How much did you make every day?' asked Inspector Chand.

'On weekdays during the season we made almost a thousand a day and sometimes more. People drop wallets, watches, mobile phones and shoes on the beach. We did not have to steal them at all. I told the constable here that I never stole. Things just dropped into my hands from heaven. God's gift to me,' said the man and began to sob.

'Should we bring his wife in, sir?' asked Robert. 'The second one, not the first. The first one is a god-fearing woman, I am told. The second wife is the main culprit. She cheats innocent women by asking them to show her their gold jewellery, pretending she wants to buy it. She takes them to a quiet place and then vanishes with the loot.'

'I should never have married her, sir. My first wife is such a good woman, a better cook too. This one throws pots and pans at me if I say there is too much salt in the fish curry,' said the man, sniffing. He tried to wipe his nose on his shirt but could not turn his head.

'Untie his hands, Robert. Let him wipe his nose. You can go but if I catch you stealing again, I will send you off to Panjim jail at once. Understand?' said Inspector Chand.

'Yes, sir. God bless you, sir, and you too, Constable. You are a great man.' The man bowed to them as he rubbed his hands together.

'I am going to the Happy Home to tell them that the case is closed and they should stop looking for a murderer. I should have a talk with that Russian too and ask him how he got the jewellery, but what is the point now? That fellow is half-mad. Anyway, we have closed the case. We will take the jeep and go along the river path and stop at the fish market. If they have fresh crab, I might get one for Miss Maria. She will make nice, spicy Goan crab curry for us,' said Inspector Chand.

\* \* \*

The twinkling lights danced like fireflies all over the garden and Olga, dressed in a long silver dress, sashayed about on the lawn like a mermaid. She was quite unsteady and drunk already, though the party had just begun. A few guests, not very important people according to her, had arrived early and were standing near the bar, clutching their glasses and talking self-consciously to each other. A tall, good-looking man was standing alone, talking on his phone. Olga walked towards him. 'Hello. Have I not met you before?' she asked, trying to keep her voice low in case Rana was around. She had slipped him some more intoxicants to keep him under control and he was still very confused about what had been going on.

'Yes, you have. I am Francis. We met at the casino last month,' said Francis, smiling and crinkling his eyes. He knew women could not resist his smile and he often practised it at home in front of the mirror to keep it in good condition.

'You have such healthy white teeth,' said Olga, leaning towards him. Francis smelt the wine on her breath. He wondered what to say to her. He was not sure if she or Rana Hooda's wife was the hostess tonight. He decided to play it safe and said, 'It is quite cool this evening though the monsoon has just ended.'

'Oh no. Not another monsoon freak. Why must you Indian men only talk of the monsoon?' she cried, slapping her head with her hands. Francis stepped back. She looked very drunk and he did not want to cause a scene. Rana Hooda was watching them, he noticed, from the corner of the garden. Francis turned to go away but Olga put her arm out and caught his sleeve. 'Hey. Where are you going? Have a drink with me,' said Olga in a whiny voice. The image of the beautiful mermaid disappeared. Francis, feeling trapped, tried to free his arm and then saw Rana walking towards them, a glowering, dark look on his face. The music suddenly became very loud and Olga put her hands on her ears and began to sing loudly as she swayed to the music. A few other Russians appeared from the shadows and began to dance with her, laughing and slapping each other like playful children. They were all very drunk.

Just then, the lights went out inside the house and the twinkling fairy lights faded into darkness. The music stopped and the garden now only had the light of the moon. Only Olga's golden hair glowed like a flame, surrounded by fireflies.

* * *

Minutes earlier, Maria, uncomfortable in her tight black dress and frilly white apron, moved towards the bar with a loaded tray of empty glasses. Her legs were already aching. Guests were still streaming in. She had never known that so many rich and famous people lived in Goa. She had already served drinks to three minor Bollywood movie stars, four models, two designers and a famous man whom she often saw on television, though she was not sure what his name was. Bobby, dressed in a black suit, was hiding behind the bar, pretending he was washing glasses. Maria filled up her tray with several glasses of wine and turned carefully. She was not used to carrying such heavy trays.

As soon as she turned, she saw Francis. She did not want to go up to him in case he began to question her disguise. She was surprised to see him here. He looked so smart in his designer jacket and gelled hair. He seemed to know everyone. Maria wondered if he had brought Tina the bitch with him. *I will make sure to spill a glass of wine over her*, thought Maria, turning her face away. *Not that I care any more who he is dating.*

'Maria. Maria. Hi,' cried a shrill voice. Maria turned. Tina was right behind her, waving her hands. 'What are you doing here? Why are you dressed like this? Did the invite say fancy dress? Come here, Francis. Look, Maria is here.' Tina had a kilo of make-up on her face. The diamonds in her ears flashed like searchlights and Maria blinked. She saw Francis walking up to them and her heart began to beat very fast. What would she say to him? Why was she here? She could not tell him that she was playing detective and trying to spy on Rana Hooda's Russian girlfriend. The tray in Maria's hand shook and the glasses clinked in protest as she tried to move but her heels sank deeper into the grass and she stood frozen.

Then the lights went out and she dropped the tray. Maria watched with horror as the glasses shattered with a loud crash on the stone table. She tried to move her arm to pick them up. Just then, Rana Hooda began to shout. Maria looked up. He was holding his face and running towards the house. His nose was bleeding and his white shirt was already stained red. People stopped talking and stared at him but nobody moved. He stumbled over the garden steps and a woman tried to help him but he pushed her away, groaning loudly. Olga was nowhere to be seen. Maria looked around helplessly, trying to pull her shoe out of the lawn, a pile of broken glass all around her feet and on the table.

Bobby called out her name and she quickly left her shoes and ran towards the bar. He was crouching behind the table. He pointed to the window of the bedroom upstairs. Maria looked up. It was the same bedroom she had been standing in this morning.

The moon suddenly came out from behind the clouds and they saw Olga standing in the room, a lit cigarette in her hand. She seemed to be looking right at them, her blue eyes narrow and sharp, as if she knew what they were up to.

'We should have never come here. It was my stupid idea. Sorry, Bobby. I dragged you into this,' said Maria as tears welled up in her eyes. They took advantage of the commotion and ran to the car.

'Hey, don't get so upset. We were trying to find out who this Olga really is. Why did she try to frame Yuri? We were just curious. No need to get so agitated,' said Bobby, driving away quickly. They were soon back at the Happy Home. He parked the car outside the gate. They could see the lights on in the kitchen. The residents of the Happy Home were still awake, probably waiting for them, but he needed to talk to her. He knew this was the right time. He must seize his chance, otherwise all would be lost. The stars in the sky were in his favour and he had to speak to her now.

'Are you upset because Francis was there with his fiancée?' he asked quietly.

'Fiancée . . . Tina is his fiancée?' cried Maria and then burst into tears.

'I thought you knew. Everyone in Trionim knows. The wedding is next month. Sorry. I did not think you would get so upset,' he said.

'I am not upset. I do not care. I was just surprised, that's all. I left my shoes behind.' Maria wiped her nose on the handkerchief Bobby had given her. After she blew her nose a few times and wiped her face, she waited for her anger to abate. How dare he get engaged to Tina and not even tell her about it. Maria suddenly found she really did not care. She could not believe that she no longer felt any pain jabbing at her heart. She was free of him. Francis with his smart designer suits and sweet talk did not matter to her any more. He was like a bit of fluff that the wind had blown away . . . forever. He was a liar and a smooth-talking philanderer and she hoped Tina would give him a rough time. Her rich father would set his goons on him if he tried to cheat on her. Maria suddenly thought of Rana Hooda.

'Bobby, that Rana Hooda's face was covered in blood,' she said.

'Yes, I saw that. He had a severe nosebleed. I'm sure he's a cocaine addict,' said Bobby, looking at her nervously. He reached for his handkerchief and when their hands touched he looked away. 'Here, I picked up your shoes.' He bent down in the dark to put them on her feet. His hands touched her ankles and lingered gently for a few fleeting seconds.

Maria gave his handkerchief back to him, laughed and said, 'You are the only man I know who still uses a fine cotton handkerchief with your initials on it.' Bobby turned to her, his eyes twinkling softly with a strange look, and she felt her heart jump.

'I am old-fashioned, Maria. I am boring and I am dull but I love you very much. I have loved you since we were in school. I remember when I saw you the first time swinging in the school garden, your hair tied with a blue ribbon, and I decided then I wanted to marry you some day. I know I have nothing much to offer but I love you more than anyone else in this world. Will you marry me?' said Bobby in a rush and held his breath. The trees swayed in the darkness and the cicadas began to call. Far away, an owl hooted. Bobby wondered if it was a lucky omen. A strong scent of frangipani floated into the car. He could hear his own heart thumping so loudly that he was sure Maria could hear it too.

Why didn't she say something? Did it take so long to say no? She would say no. He was sure of that. She would never say yes because she was still in love with that creep Francis. Rich, smart and clever Francis who had stolen his bike in school; Francis with his perfect white teeth and the sly smile that all girls loved.

The moon looked down on them as Bobby waited. His entire life seemed to be on hold. Then he took his courage in his hands and turned his face to look at Maria. Her eyes were sparkling. Tears ran down her cheeks.

'Yes, Bobby. Yes, I will marry you,' she whispered.

* * *

The house was in darkness when Maria finally came into the living room and took her shoes off. She heard Bobby's car drive away and wished she had asked him to stay. They could have celebrated with a glass of wine. But it was very late and she knew he had to wake up very early to attend to his plants at the spice farm. She could see Rosie was still awake because a faint light was shining under the door. Maria wanted to rush to her and tell her what had happened. She had to share her news with someone and Rosie was the only person she could trust. She did not want to tell the rest yet because then the entire village of Trionim would come to know. She wanted this murder mystery solved and then she would tell everyone. It was terrible to have the shadow of death hanging over the house. It was like a dark cloud weighing them down, trying to choke them with poisonous fumes.

Maria walked into the dining room, not bothering to put the light on, drank a glass of water and then knocked on Rosie's door.

The room was empty. The bed was covered with sheets and pillows as if Rosie had just woken up. 'Rosie,' called Maria, keeping her voice low so that Prema in the room next door would not hear her.

'I am here. By the window,' whispered Rosie and then Maria saw her.

She was sitting at the window and looking out. Her face was full of terror. She pointed her finger and Maria looked out into the garden. The trees swayed in the gentle breeze and the moon was hanging like a huge lamp above them.

A man was sitting slumped on the edge of the garden wall, right next to the well. He was dressed in a white shirt and black pants. Even in the dim moonlight they could see the red stains on his shirt. His head was bowed as if he was asleep.

'My god. Who is he? What is he doing there?' said Maria, forgetting to keep her voice down.

'How awful. Is he dead?' asked Rosie, turning her face away.

The lights came on in the veranda just then and they heard footsteps and Deven's voice shouting, 'Cyrilo. Cyrilo. Come with me. There is someone in the garden. Bring the torch.'

'Please, god. Let it not be another dead body,' said Rosie.

'He looks pretty dead to me. He could be a ghost,' said Prema, coming out of her room. 'The Happy Home should now be called the Dead People's Home,' she added and yawned. 'Soon the entire village will be lying dead in our backyard. We'd better reserve our own plots from now otherwise we will not have place.'

'Stop it, Prema. Don't wish evil on our home,' said Rosie as Maria turned to go out of the room.

Prema followed her but Rosie stayed near the window. She began to pray softly under her breath. 'Our father thou art in heaven . . .'

The wind whistled through the branches as Deven walked into the garden. The light from the torch cast a beam of bright light and a few birds fluttered in the trees above them, angry to be disturbed. Cyrilo hesitated and remained standing near the door. He was wary of going too close to the man. 'What if he is dead?' he said to Deven. 'We should call the police.'

'Don't be stupid. I'm just going to check if he is all right,' said Deven and went ahead.

As Cyrilo, Maria and Prema watched, Deven bent down and touched the man on his arm. Nothing happened. Deven gave him a gentle push and the man suddenly moved his head. Maria gave a start and took a few steps back into the house. Prema laughed and Cyrilo shrugged his shoulders nervously.

'The fellow looks alive to me,' he said, and walked out to join Deven.

'Must be drunk,' said Prema loudly.

The man lifted his head and stared at them. Maria gave a gasp. 'Oh my god. He is Rana.'

'Rana Hooda! What are you doing here at this time of night?' asked Deven, shaking him roughly now.

'You gave us a fright. We thought. You were . . .' muttered Cyrilo.

'We thought you were yet another dead body. We found one right here last week,' said Prema loudly.

Rana lifted his arms to the sky and began to wail. 'I killed her. I killed my wife. I know, Olga told me you found her body in this well. I am a murderer. I just wanted to see where she had died and now I will go to the police. I will tell them I am a murderer. I killed my wife. I thought she was in Dubai, shopping. She had sent me a message. Everything is so confusing. I cannot think straight any more. My mind is going. I have killed Rani,' sobbed Rana.

'You did not kill her. We found her body here but it was not in the well. You are mistaken, Mr Rana,' said Cyrilo.

'I killed her. Olga said I killed my wife. I did not know I had killed her in a fit of madness. I am a murderer,' cried

Rana, looking up at the tree. The crows, disturbed by his voice, moved restlessly on the branches.

'Yes, we heard you the first time. But why did you hang her up on the tree?' asked Deven.

'Tree? Which tree? I killed my wife. I am a murderer.' Rana banged his head on the stone wall.

'If he says that again I will kill him and announce to the world that I am a murderer. What is he? A bloody parrot?' said Prema.

'Listen, Mr Rana Hooda. Calm down. Your wife's dead body was not found in the well. We found her hanging from this tree,' said Deven, pointing to the mango tree.

Everyone stood silently as Rana lifted his head and looked at the tree. His face was wet with tears and blood dripped from his nose, staining his shirt.

'How could she hang herself? She was dead. I killed . . .' he mumbled and then shut his eyes.

'Yes. Yes. Yes. You killed her. You are a murderer. We know it. You have told us a hundred times.' Prema had come out of the house now. Maria followed her.

'Mr Hooda, I think you are not feeling well. You nose is bleeding very badly. Please come into the house and rest. I think you have had a shock,' said Maria.

Rana looked at her blankly, as if he did not know where her voice was coming from. He could hardly focus his eyes and kept jerking his head about.

'I killed my wife. I am a murderer,' he slurred, and then Prema rushed up and yanked him up by his arm. He looked at her, his eyes shocked and bewildered as he tried to pull his hand away. He began to whimper.

'Listen to me, you idiot. You will stop this rubbish talk and come into the house with us at once. Otherwise we will drag you inside by your feet. You have told us a hundred times you have killed your wife. Say it again and I will give you a slap. Come with us, right now,' she shouted as Rana cowered, trying to hide his face.

'Don't stand there. Follow us,' said Prema, wagging her finger.

Rana bowed his head and quietly followed them into the house. They all went into the drawing room. As soon as Cyrilo switched the lights on, a pigeon flew out. 'Oh my god. A bat. I hate bats,' shouted Rana Hooda, covering his face.

'Relax, man. It's only a pigeon. We hardly ever use this room so the pigeon has claimed it,' said Cyrilo, gently pushing Rana into the room. Maria quickly ran upstairs and brought a blanket from her bedroom while Deven helped Rana take his shoes off. He noticed they were covered in mud. He stopped and stared at the pointed leather shoes. They were the same expensive, imported leather shoes the dead woman had been wearing. He had seen the constable pick them up from the garden that day when they had brought the body down from the tree.

Deven stood silently as Prema gave Rana a wet towel to wipe his face and when he just sat still, sobbing and whimpering, she wiped his nose roughly for him as if he was a child. Then she threw the towel down and walked away muttering, 'Stupid fool. Thinks he killed his wife. He can't even wipe his own nose.'

'Let him be. Poor fellow. He's in a bad state. I think he is having hallucinations. Now, Mr Hooda, you just lie down and go to sleep. We will sort it out in the morning. Okay, Mr Hooda?' said Cyrilo. When Rana obediently lay down, Cyrilo pulled the blanket over him and patted his head.

'Go to sleep now,' he said. 'We will talk in the morning.'

'Don't leave me. She will come and get me. She won't forgive me. She is waiting for me in the well,' Rana began to whimper again, his face hidden under the blanket.

'We will sit here. You go to sleep now. Nobody is coming to get you,' said Cyrilo. And as Deven and he watched, Rana shut his eyes. His hands trembled as he clutched the blanket and then he began to snore, his bloodstained face distorted and crumpled with fear.

# CHAPTER FIFTEEN

ROSIE WAS THE first person to wake up. She lay in bed for a few moments, listening to the birds calling in the garden, and then suddenly remembered last night's incident. She opened her eyes at once. It took her a while to get ready since the water was still cold, her clothes had not been laid out by Leela and her wheelchair got stuck between the bed and the dressing table.

For once Rosie did not bother to put her make-up on, and just washed her face with cold water. She looked at her face in the mirror and decided she looked quite good for her age even without make-up, and, wrapping a thin shawl around her shoulders, she wheeled herself out into the veranda. Deven was already up and looking very worried. 'He has disappeared,' he said as soon as he saw her. Rosie knew at once who he was talking about and moved her wheelchair towards the drawing room. The blanket lay crumpled on the sofa and the pigeon was pecking on something glistening on the floor. It was a gold watch.

'I think that man is in a state of shock. He should not be left alone. He might harm himself,' said Rosie.

'What can we do now? I was planning to ask him a few questions and then call the inspector but he has vanished. Look, he has left his Rolex gold watch behind,' said Deven.

'He must really be in a state of shock,' said Cyrilo, coming into the room.

'I think you should both go to the police station and tell the inspector about him,' said Rosie.

'Good idea. I will get ready quickly and then we can go. On the way we can stop and buy some . . .' said Cyrilo.

'Shut up. I know what you were going to say. We are not stopping by the fish market. We are going straight to the police station and I am going to drive,' said Deven and walked away.

Cyrilo stared at him and then made a face like a sad clown. 'Grumpy old Deven. Grumble. Grumble. I was just planning to go via the Siolim church. I have some books and toys for the children.'

'Better not annoy him or else he will complain about you to Maria. You know how he likes to get us into trouble. I am going to check on Yuri to see if he needs anything. Leela can push my wheelchair up the ramp. Poor Yuri. He still can't talk properly. Do you think he really had a stroke?' said Rosie.

'Can't tell. Whatever happens to us at this age, people blame it on old-age problems. If I fall into a well tomorrow that stupid doctor will say it was due to old age. I'd better get ready quickly or else Mr Deven Grumpy will start yelling again.'

Rosie moved her wheelchair slowly to the kitchen and began helping Leela with breakfast. She carefully peeled boiled eggs, buttered toast and spooned jam into small bowls. 'You are the only one who helps Miss Maria and me,' said Leela, smiling at her. 'The others just sit around doing nothing but chatting and demanding tea.'

'I want to help more but you both don't let me. I cannot walk but my hands work very well, you know. Listen, Leela, I want you to take me up to Yuri's room. We will make some scrambled eggs for him and feed it to him with a spoon. He must be tired of soup,' said Rosie.

Maria joined them and they worked quickly to get breakfast ready before the others arrived. The oven was giving out a delicious aroma of cinnamon buns but Rosie was not hungry today. She kept worrying about Yuri. Would he ever recover?

'You know, that man might be telling the truth,' said Leela.

'What do you mean?' asked Maria, still feeling sleepy and tired. She had slept very badly last night, dreaming about Francis and Tina. The image of Rana Hooda's face with blood dripping from his nose kept popping up. Then Bobby had made an appearance and taken her away in a boat made of coconut palm leaves. She had finally fallen asleep planning her future life with Bobby. She must stop thinking about Francis. He was out of her life, over and done with.

'He could have killed her and hung her dead body in our garden to make it look like suicide,' said Leela. 'She looked like an evil, bad-tempered woman. I would not have liked to live with a woman like that.'

'Do not speak badly of the dead, Leela,' said Rosie.

'You should hear the women in the parlour. They do nothing but talk about all the dead people they know. They also wish some of their relatives were dead. As I polish their nails and scrub their feet, I have to listen to all this. But it is great fun,' said Leela, putting a large vessel of milk to boil on the gas stove.

'Do you like working at the beauty parlour? I'm glad Joni is paying you now,' said Maria, taking the buns out of the oven.

'I love working there. One day I may open my own parlour. Who knows,' said Leela, laughing.

'You will, my child. By god's grace, you will. I will help you,' said Rosie.

'You can open a parlour next to the Tip Top Cafe. There is plenty of room there,' said Maria.

Leela looked at them and smiled, her eyes sparkling with happiness.

'Yes, ladies can have coffee and cake and go for a pedicure, or the other way around. Okay, now I have to peel potatoes for lunch. Beauty parlour dreams can wait,' said Leela.

\* \* \*

The police station was crowded with a group of tourists when Deven and Cyrilo arrived. There was no place to sit so they went back their van, which they had parked in the side lane.

'I wonder why there are so many people here today,' said Cyrilo.

'Must have lost their luggage or wallets. Tourists are always losing things. I hate tourists. Why don't they stay at home like us?' said Deven.

'Tourists are good for Goa, they bring money, but they should not spoil our village by throwing all their junk around. By the way, do *you* think Rana Hooda was telling the truth? So many husbands kill their wives. You read about it in the papers every day.'

'Quite a few wives murder their husbands too,' said Deven.

'Yes, especially the quiet types. They suffer silently for years and then suddenly one day erupt like a volcano and choke their husbands to death.'

'It's easy for a wife to kill her husband. She can add a lethal dose of poison in his tea, push him downstairs or electrocute him while he is shaving.'

'A husband can push her downstairs too or throw her off the roof. He can add poison to her tea . . . but very few women allow their husbands to make tea for them. Too fussy. I would just throw her off the train. Easy and neat,' said Cyrilo.

'You sound like an expert. How many wives have you killed?' asked Deven, giving him a cold look.

'Not a single one. My beloved wife died peacefully in her sleep. God bless her kind soul. I was just chatting, killing time. I think that Rana Hooda was just rambling on. He seemed to be not quite sane. Do you think he had taken some drugs? These rich people are always doing party drugs, I am told.'

'Yes, he did seem a bit deranged. His eyes had a peculiar gleam, like a person who's hallucinating. Why did he come to the well? Do you think that girlfriend is trying to get him to confess to a murder he never committed? What does she gain from it, I wonder?' said Deven, tracing his fingers on the window.

'Missing your blackboard and chalk? It is so boring just sitting here. Shall we go home? Maria can call the inspector and he will come running at once. I need to go to the bathroom again,' said Cyrilo.

'Not again. We have just come from the house. Why didn't you go then? Look. The tourists are leaving. Come, let's go in before some other people turn up.' Deven opened the door of the van and got out. Cyrilo looked out as the crowd of tourists walked past the van and saw that none of them were wearing shoes. They were limping and hobbling as the gravel jabbed their bare feet, muttering angrily in a foreign language.

Constable Robert looked up and smiled at them as they walked into the police station. 'Welcome to the Trionim police station. How can we help you today?' he grinned and lisped in his girlish voice, his huge hands folded in a clumsy greeting.

'What is the matter with you? Are you training to become an air hostess?' asked Deven, rudely rushing past him.

'We have been ordered to say this when someone comes into the station but most people never stop to listen to me,' mumbled Robert, looking sheepishly down at his feet.

Inspector Chand was standing at his table gazing at a map of Goa on the wall. He was tracing an area with his baton and did not turn around when Deven greeted him.

'If you have been robbed of your rubber slippers, sandals or shoes from the temple, please report to Constable Robert. Do not bother me. I am busy.'

'We have come from the Happy Home to report what Rana Hooda has said to us. It is very important,' said Deven curtly, and Inspector Chand quickly turned around.

'Oh. It is you again. Mr Sherlock Homes of Trionim and his sidekick. What do you people want now? Have you found another dead body in the Happy Home? You should rename your house the Unhappy Home,' he growled. 'I feel sorry for Miss Maria, having to put up with you crazy lot day after day.'

Deven stood silently for a few moments and then cleared his throat.

*He cannot talk unless he has his beloved blackboard in front of him*, thought Cyrilo.

'Miss Maria has sent us here with a message for you,' he said, and Inspector Chand immediately turned around.

'Why didn't you say so earlier? Come. Sit down.' He grinned.

'She said to tell you she is getting married soon,' said Cyrilo with a smile.

'Married to whom?' shouted Inspector Chand so loudly that Robert rushed into the room.

'You called, sir?' he asked, saluting smartly.

Deven glared at Cyrilo and turned to Inspector Chand. 'We want to tell you about Rana Hooda. We found him in the Happy Home garden in the middle of the night and brought him in. He was very upset and kept rambling in a confused manner. He said he had killed his wife and was coming to confess to you. He had stopped on the way at the Happy Home to see where she had died,' said Deven.

'What are you talking about? Are you mad? At your age you should be singing bhajans, not trying to solve a murder which was never a murder. For your information, Rana Hooda's wife just came to report that he has been missing for two days. He went to Tiracol in his private boat and has not come back yet. She says he has been kidnapped by some drug dealer called Ziriko with whom he had illegal dealings,' said Inspector Chand. 'I was looking at the map of Goa. Tiracol is almost in Maharashtra. This is a matter for the Maharashtra police. Not my area at all.' He pointed to the map with a broad smile.

'Tiracol is in Goa. The last fort in Goa,' said Cyrilo.

'It is touching the border of Goa. They must have taken Rana Hooda across. Kidnappers prefer Maharashtra to Goa. The beaches are less crowded,' said Inspector Chand.

'They are kidnappers, holding a person for ransom, not tourists looking for a scenic spot to sunbathe. Anyway, we told you we saw Rana at the Happy Home. He talked to us,' said Deven.

'Please get new spectacles all of you. You can charge it to Goa Police if you want,' said Inspector Chand. 'I have closed the case and it is none of your business now. Please don't waste my time. Are you sure Miss Maria sent you here? I don't believe you. Please leave. We have to go and look for this temple shoe thief now. He has gone off with 121 slippers.'

'Why steal an odd number of slippers?' asked Cyrilo as Deven frowned at him.

'One man's foot was bandaged so he wore only one slipper to the temple,' said Inspector Chand. 'We were wondering too but Robert here figured it out. He is very smart.'

As soon as his name was mentioned Robert smiled and saluted again and said in an excited voice, 'The man who stole the slippers has come, sir. Asking us to lock him up. He wanted to teach his wife a lesson since she keeps buying new sandals every week so he gave her all the slippers he had stolen from the temple.'

'Poor fellow. Let him go with a caution. I feel sorry for a man with such a spendthrift wife,' said Inspector Chand.

As Deven and Cyrilo walked out they bumped into a small, thin man. He was wearing a straw sun hat and dark glasses. His feet were bare but next to him was a pile of shoes and slippers.

'The slipper thief,' said Cyrilo. 'Marry in haste and repent at leisure,' he whispered to Deven and the man heard him. He took off his dark glasses and nodded his head. 'She is my third wife. So I can repent till I am your age, sir, if I am still alive,' he said.

* * *

Yuri looked at his hands. They were still trembling. He put the brush down. What was happening to him? Had his brain really gone as the doctor said? He could remember everything clearly but still couldn't speak. Words came out in an incoherent jumble when he opened his mouth. A wave of fear swept over him. Would he never be able to speak again? What would he do now? He could not live like this.

Yuri tried to pick up the brush again and this time he noticed his hands were trembling less. He dipped the brush in ink and very slowly drew a faint line. Gradually, as he looked at the paper, his eyes following the shaky line he had drawn, he began to feel calmer. He raised his head and looked out of the window. The garden was bathed in gentle, golden sunlight and all the shrubs seemed to have been washed clean with rain. A few yellow butterflies flitted about and one flew in to sit on the window frame. It lazily opened its wings and Yuri saw it was deep orange like the early morning sun.

He knew he would be all right. As long as he could draw, as long as he could see all the beautiful images around him, he would be fine. Who cared if he could not speak clearly? His few friends could still understand him. Olga had not even bothered to call him. Did she know about his accident? Someone must have told her. Maria had said she met some Russians at the Tip Top Cafe and they were asking about him. Olga must know.

Suddenly Yuri knew what she was trying to do. Why had he not seen it before? He had been so blinded by his infatuation for this beautiful girl that he had closed his mind to what she really was. What an old fool he had been. Yuri shut his eyes and Olga's beautiful face floated up in the dim light. She seemed to be laughing at him, her painted rosebud mouth leering and cruel. Yes. She was behind all this. She was trying to trap him for that woman's murder. She wanted him out of the way so that Rana Hooda could marry her. He was rich and had palatial houses in Delhi and London. He had expensive cars and owned a racehorse too. He had everything Olga wanted.

'Soon I will be a very rich woman and I will live in London and throw garden parties. You can come too and be my butler,' she had said to him one day. He had thought she was being silly and daydreaming like all the young Russians who desperately wanted to become rich overnight. They were children of turbulent times in their country and felt no loyalty like his generation did for the motherland. Getting rich very fast was their motto.

*I must tell the others about Olga right now. She must not get away with this. Olga must have sent that fellow to beat me up,* Yuri thought as he looked at the window. He saw that the paint had been scratched near the windowpane. It must have happened when that man jumped into his room. Yuri shut his eyes and tried to think. It was difficult. At first everything was blurred and then gradually the images in his head cleared and he saw the man's face. He was thin with a long, scrawny neck like a turkey. His eyes were so deep-set in his head they looked like black hollows. The nail on his little finger was like a misshapen claw and painted bright red. He had held his scarred hands over Yuri's face and tried to smother him with a pillow. 'Why don't you die? You dirty old goat. Leave Olga alone. She is mine. Say goodbye to her now because I am going to send you to your grave,' he had whispered, saliva dripping from his mouth. Then someone had shouted from downstairs and the man had run away, leaving Yuri bruised and gasping for breath. He had not managed to kill him but those claws had damaged his windpipe. They had taken away his ability to speak. It was as good as being dead.

Yuri heard a noise and saw Rosie pushing her wheelchair into his room. He shut his eyes. He felt so tired but he knew he had to tell Rosie what had happened. She was patient and kind and she could help him write it all down. Yuri tried to raise his head and look at Rosie but found he did not have the strength. He lay back helplessly as tears ran down his face.

*He is sleeping. I'd better not disturb him,* thought Rosie, stopping her wheelchair near the door. She pushed the handle on her chair and began turning around and then heard a whimper. She looked back and saw Yuri staring at her with desperate eyes.

Rosie moved forward. She stopped near the bed and put her hand out to touch Yuri's arm. 'Is something bothering you, Yuri? I will wait here. You can tell me slowly. Can you speak a little now?'

Yuri grunted a reply which she barely understood.

'That is good. Much better than before. Try once more. Make a long sound now. Think you are a cow mooing,' said Rosie with a smile.

Yuri smiled back at her and opened his mouth. His voice filled the room with a long, trumpet-like sound. Then he barked a few short words, and even though they made no sense to Rosie, she clapped her hands. Yuri began to call out over and over again, his eyes sparkling with joy. He mumbled incoherently for a while and then fell silent and shut his eyes.

'You rest now. We will practise talking some more again tomorrow.' But Yuri was already fast asleep with a quiet smile on his face. Before he had been injured, Yuri would very often sit with her in the veranda at night since they both could never catch that elusive creature called sleep. They would watch the moon travel across the star-studded sky. Yuri would talk to her about his childhood and then sing Russian songs. 'You remind me of my dear mama,' he would say, kissing her hand. Rosie was not happy to be compared to his mother, who she felt must be a hundred years old, but she let it pass. *Poor Yuri. I hope he gets well soon. It takes so long for our bodies to heal at this age. Everything is slow. Our minds work slowly, our blood flows slowly but not our heartbeats*, thought Rosie.

\* \* \*

The newspaper was wet with the rain that had fallen at night. Leela went out to fetch the milk and the day's newspaper. She wiped her hands on her dress and glanced at the headlines as she put them on the table. Then she began to scream. She ran to the dining room and threw the paper on the dining table. Everyone stared at her.

Deven picked up the newspaper and began to read. 'Rana Hooda, Delhi builder, found dead in the swimming pool of his villa,' shouted the bold black letters. A photograph of the villa was splashed on the front page along with a small inset of Rana.

'I cannot believe this. We just saw him last night. He was sitting right here,' said Maria. 'How terrible. I must call Bobby and tell him at once.'

'He must have seen the newspaper too though I doubt he gets one at the remote spice farm. They are not saying how Rana died. At least he didn't die on our doorstep,' said Prema, reaching for another piece of bread. She spread a generous spoonful of jam on it.

*The terrible news has not spoilt her appetite,* Rosie thought as she imagined the dead man's face. 'Do you think it was an accident?' she asked, pushing her coffee cup away.

'I think he was on drugs. Remember I found that syringe in that house, right under the sofa where he was sleeping. Did I not show it to you?' Deven asked.

'No, you did not. Anyway, you should have given it to the policeman,' said Prema.

'I was planning to. Come, let us not sit around wasting time. We'll go meet Inspector Chand again and see if he has any more news. I want to know exactly what happened. I think he must have overdosed and drowned,' said Deven, pushing his chair back.

Maria was still on her phone. 'I cannot get through to Bobby,' she said.

'Why don't you call Francis? You said he was at the party too that night. He might know something,' said Prema.

'No, I don't want to call him . . . ever,' muttered Maria and walked out into the garden, still looking at her phone.

'That means Francis is out and Bobby is in. Good riddance to bad rubbish,' said Prema.

'I will tell you a secret,' said Leela, coming in with a mug of coffee for Maria. 'She is engaged to Bobby but wants to keep it a secret for some time.'

'How do you know?' asked Cyrilo.

'I heard them talking. I was putting the garbage out and I heard them talking and . . .' Leela giggled. Then she remembered they were discussing a man's fatal accident and kept quiet.

'We must not pry into Maria's personal life. She will tell us when she wants to, Leela. I cannot believe we have another dead body. What is going on in Trionim? Why are all these Delhi people rolling up here to die?' asked Rosie.

'Forget them. Do you think what Leela is saying about Maria and Bobby is true? She's always eavesdropping. Real sneak, that girl,' said Prema.

'She is not. She is a very smart girl and we would all be lost without her. She cooks for us, washes our clothes and gives us our medicines,' said Rosie and turned away from Prema.

She was trying to recall the details of Rana's face. He had been sitting on that sofa just the previous night and now he was dead. How fate struck people, taking them unawares. What a horrible way to die. Could he have really killed his wife or was he imagining it? He seemed an unstable and odd fellow. Rosie tried to put these thoughts out of her mind. She wanted to only think about the good news. She was so pleased about Maria and Bobby. She wished all these terrible things would clear up soon and they could celebrate with chocolate cake and home-made wine. But death was hanging over the Happy Home. First that woman from Delhi, and now her husband. These clouds of tragic events were casting a gloomy shadow over their home. All this evil darkness must be cleared away. The sun must come out again in their garden to chase away the shadows and then Maria and Bobby would be blessed.

'A rich man like him must have had many enemies. There is always someone waiting to put a bullet through important people. You read it in the newspaper every day,' said Deven.

'Poor fellow. He looked so distraught and confused last night. That Olga had convinced him that he had killed his wife by pushing her into the well. I can't believe a woman can be so cruel. Do you think he committed suicide or he was pushed into the pool?' asked Cyrilo.

'The newspaper report does not say much. He was certainly taking drugs. Everyone in that house was an addict. Maria even found traces of cocaine on the tables. He could have overdosed,' said Deven.

'That Olga woman could have pushed him in,' said Cyrilo.

'He could have jumped in himself. Killed his wife and then committed suicide. Matter finished. Why do these Delhi people have to come all the way to Goa to pop off? I wish they would do all these horrible things in their own homes and not spoil the pure air of Goa. Now let us get on with our breakfast. My mother used to say we must not talk about death during breakfast.' Prema tapped her fingers on the table impatiently.

'So when is it a good time to talk about death, Prema?' asked Rosie.

'At our age any time is bad. Death is waiting to pick us up any minute. Have you all made your wills?' asked Prema.

'I have nothing to leave and nobody to leave it to. I am a happy man,' said Cyrilo.

'You know, we should find out if Rana Hooda had made a will. He was such a rich man. His wife is already dead so who is going to inherit his houses and cars?'

'Yuri told me Rana has a yacht too. How does he know? Yuri can talk a bit now but it is difficult to make out what he is saying. He tried to write but his hands are still shaking badly. But he can hold a brush and paint a few strokes. He keeps asking me to tell you that Olga is behind all this,' said Rosie.

'I will go and see him right away. Will you come with me, Rosie? I can push your wheelchair up the ramp,' said Deven.

'All that money and he drowned in his swimming pool. Poor fellow. We should have locked the door and made sure he stayed with us last night. We could have saved his life. I am feeling very bad about this,' said Cyrilo.

'His time had come so he went to his maker. What is there to feel sorry for? God has taken him,' said Prema.

'What if his time had not come? What if that woman pushed him into the pool? We have to go to that villa again. We have to find out what that Olga woman is up to now,' said Cyrilo.

'Wait till Deven comes back. Yuri might tell him something important now that he can communicate a little bit,' said Prema.

'No. I'm not going to wait for him. He's too bossy and does not let me do anything on my own. I am going right now but don't tell him where I have gone,' said Cyrilo, quickly going towards the door.

'I will tell him. How dare you ask me to lie to Deven, our chief detective?' said Prema. 'In fact, I will go up to Yuri's room and tell him right now.'

'Go on, Miss Tattletale,' shouted Cyrilo, slamming the door shut. The lights on the wall shook and a picture fell down. Leela heard the van spluttering noisily as it struggled to start and looked out of the kitchen window. She saw Cyrilo, still dressed in his trackpants driving off. *He's in a great hurry. Did not even ask for his second cup of coffee today,* thought Leela as she washed the breakfast dishes. Maria was upstairs in her room and the others too had all disappeared. It was unusual for them to rush off like this right after breakfast. They always sat around talking, reading the newspaper over and over again, arguing about small items they had read. Each one would think he or she knew better than the others. If Cyrilo said the monsoon had arrived, Prema would say it was late by ten days. If Deven said foreign tourists were bringing a lot of money to Goa, Rosie would say they were making the prices go up for locals. *It must be very relaxing to be so old. Nothing to worry about since life is almost over. No worries about the future,* thought Leela, putting the teacups away on the shelf.

Leela heard a scratching sound on the kitchen door. She ignored it at first, thinking it must be cats but then the sound became louder. Leela opened the door and looked out. There was no one. The cats were sleeping peacefully in the shade of the guava tree. 'How strange,' muttered Leela.

She was about to shut the door when she saw someone. The little boy Tony was standing behind a pile of chopped wood. He was so still that for a moment Leela thought he looked like a wooden statue.

'Hello! What do you want?' asked Leela, smiling and waving her hands. The boy looked at her shyly and then came forward. Leela saw that he had a phone in his hands.

'Is it your phone? You want to show it to me?' she asked, pointing at the phone and then at herself.

Tony nodded and handed her the phone. Leela was shocked to see that it was a very expensive phone, like the iPhones she saw advertised in the newspapers. Where had he got it from? Leela wondered if Tony had stolen it and suddenly felt afraid for the boy. She gave the phone back to him and shook her head.

Tony smiled at her as if he could read her mind. He gestured to himself and then spelt out 'Alfie' on his palm with his fingers.

'Alfie gave you this phone?' asked Leela.

Tony nodded with a broad grin. He pointed to the ground and mimed picking up something.

'He found it on the ground and gave it to you.'

Tony nodded.

'But that is not right. He should have handed it to the police. This phone does not belong to him or to you. Do you understand me, Tony?'

The boy gave her a puzzled look and put the phone back in his pocket.

'You give this phone to me. I will see if I can find out who it belongs to. Okay?' Leela put her hand out.

Tony stood still, looking at her uncertainly, and then brought the phone out of his pocket. He touched the smooth surface and then reluctantly gave it to Leela.

'Thank you. You are a good boy. I will buy you a phone one day when I have enough money,' she said.

She pressed a round button on the phone. The screen lit up and Tony clapped his hands.

A face popped up on the screen. It was the lady she had seen in the beauty parlour, the lady who had been murdered right outside the Happy Home. The cruel eyes seemed to be screaming at her angrily. Leela switched the phone off. She ran upstairs and left Tony staring at her. She knew it was the dead woman's phone and she must tell Maria at once.

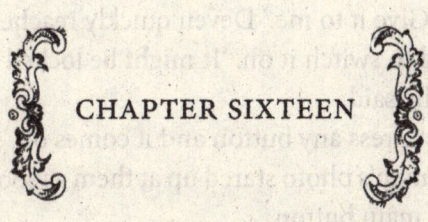

# CHAPTER SIXTEEN

DEVEN PAINSTAKINGLY WROTE down what Yuri was saying. He was still slurring but by stringing together the words they could understand, Rosie and he could put together sentences. Something about Olga . . . the Russian girl wanted to marry Rana Hooda . . . so what? Deven stared at Yuri. His face was still very swollen and his eyes could not focus properly. Poor chap. He could have been murdered too. Had his brain been affected by the blow to his head?

'Yuri, you rest now. We will go to the villa and talk to Olga. Find out what she's up to,' said Deven.

Yuri shook his head and muttered something. His face was contorted with fear and his eyes began to water.

'What is it?' asked Rosie, gently touching his arm.

Yuri cried out, slapping his hand on the bed.

'Police. I think he is trying to say police,' said Rosie.

'Don't worry. We will tell the police. Now you sleep for a while,' said Deven and covered Yuri's feet with the blanket. They heard him whimpering and crying as they left the room.

241

Leela was racing upstairs just as Deven was pushing Rosie's wheelchair down the ramp. 'Deven, sir, please see this. I can't find Maria. Alfie has found the dead woman's phone. Tony brought it to show me.'

'What! Give it to me.' Deven quickly reached for it.

He tried to switch it on. 'It might be locked and need a password,' he said.

'No, just press any button and it comes on,' said Leela.

The woman's photo stared up at them as soon as Deven pressed the main button.

'That is her. The same woman. I can recognize her, though her face was all swollen when we saw her that day,' said Rosie.

Deven pressed the message icon and began to read.

'You bastard. You are a liar and a thief. I will tell the police about your shady deals in Russia. I know everything so don't try any tricks.'

He read on.

'I will never divorce you. I will never let you marry that cheap Russian tart. Over my dead body.'

Deven stopped and looked up.

'He must have killed her because she would not agree to divorce him,' he said.

'No, wait. These are messages that were forwarded. Look at his sent messages,' said Rosie.

'Darling Olga. I cannot live without you. You see the mad woman I am married to. See how I suffer for your sake,' read Deven.

'What an idiotic man to forward his wife's abusive messages to his girlfriend. What was he trying to do?' asked Rosie.

'See, here is her reply. "You are a stupid, weak man. I will fix your wife. Don't worry, all will be well, my snowflake."' He scrolled down further.

Deven stared at the phone.

'What does she mean? Fix her. How? We must go to the police at once. Come on. Call Cyrilo,' he said.

'He is not here. I forgot to tell you he has gone to the villa to meet Olga,' said Prema.

'Why did you let him go? It is not safe. That Olga is dangerous. We must rush there right away,' shouted Deven.

'How will you go? Cyrilo has taken the van,' said Leela.

They all stared at the empty space where the van was usually parked. 'You can go on the scooter. Miss Maria can take you, Deven sir. I will go and call her. Maybe she is in her room. Wait.' Leela ran upstairs.

* * *

Cyrilo parked the van under the shade of the old banyan tree. Sunlight was dancing on the iron gates, making the gold paint shine, and the guard was fast asleep. *Poor man. Must have had a late night*, thought Cyrilo as he went in quietly. There was no one about. The door to the villa looked firmly locked. Cyrilo hesitated for a few moments and then walked through the garden, stepping carefully over the paving stones. He was heading towards the door at the back. He had seen it the last time they had come to this villa. That door was shut too. He stood on his toes and peered in through the kitchen window. Then he saw that the window was half open. He reached in to open it wider but his hands would not reach the latch. He looked around and spotted a large stone under the tree. He picked it up, groaning under his breath, and dragged it closer. He placed it right under the window, stepped on the stone and pulled himself up. He managed to slide his hand in and open the window. 'Still quite agile, old man,' he muttered to himself as he carefully entered the house. The muscles in his lower back gave a brief, complaining twinge but he ignored it.

Cyrilo slowly lowered himself on to the floor and wiped his hands on the seat of his pants. He was breathing quite heavily and he leaned against the wall to rest. He waited to hear if someone was in the house but he couldn't hear a thing. He was feeling a bit dizzy but he willed himself on; he was going to solve this case without any help from Mr Smarty-pants Deven. He would prove to everyone that Cyrilo was not just a happy-go-lucky man, only good at playing merry tunes on the piano. He would show them that he had a sharp mind and a cunning brain, capable of solving all kinds of mysteries. He would confront this Olga woman and make her confess everything. They would all be so amazed. All of Trionim would applaud him and maybe the Goa police would give him a medal. Cyrilo shut his eyes and saw Inspector Chand's face staring at him, his jaw dropping with surprise as the IG pinned a huge shiny gold medal on Cyrilo's jacket. *I must order a new suit at once. A dark-blue one and a new light-blue shirt to match. Maybe some new shoes too.*

'What should I say to the Russian girl?' he whispered to himself. 'I must be very, very careful of what I say or else she'll suspect something fishy and not fall into my trap. I have to get her to spill the beans. I must remember to switch the phone on to record when she starts talking.' He felt a nervous rumble in his stomach and his hands began to sweat. Would he be able to do that? Which button did he have to press on the phone to switch on the recording? Leela had shown it to him the other day but he had not practised it on his own ever. What if he pressed the music button by mistake? What if Olga caught him recording her?

Cyrilo's mouth suddenly felt very dry and he could hear his heart beating very fast. Why had he come alone? What if the police were watching the house? They would think he was trying to steal. Now it was too late. He might as well see if the Russian girl was here and confront her. *You want to be a hero so you'd better go out and be a hero, Cyrilo. This is your only chance, man.*

The shimmering chandelier winked at him a hundred times as he looked up and Cyrilo touched the phone in his pocket nervously. Though he could not see anyone in the room, there was a strong scent of perfume and marijuana in the air. Cyrilo wiped his hands again and tried to breathe slowly. He hoped his blood pressure was not going through the roof.

He suddenly spied golden curls cascading all over a cushion and almost tripped. Olga lay on the sofa with her thin, languid arm stretched out, holding an unlit cigarette.

'What do you want, Cyrilo? Do you have a match?' she asked in a girlish, nasal voice.

'Good afternoon, Miss Olga.' Cyrilo was surprised she knew his name.

'You are Yuri's best friend. Aren't you, Cyrilo? He always says you are the kindest, cleverest man in Trionim.' She did not lift her head as Cyrilo went closer. He found a matchbox on the table and leaned forward to light her cigarette. He saw that her eyes were red as if she had been crying.

'You know my husband is dead? Poor man. We were hardly married for a week. I brought him bad luck it seems,' she whispered and began to laugh. 'He brought me lots of good luck, though. I say a big thank you to you, Rana.' She pointed to the ceiling, as if her late husband was hovering above, watching her. 'This is all mine now. I am Mrs Rana Hooda. I own everything now. Can you imagine?'

'You are really lucky. I wish I had a rich wife too,' said Cyrilo. He wondered if that was the right thing to say.

'That is the trick. You are a clever man. Yuri was right. You see, Rana had a rich wife but she died and now he has a rich wife again. Simple as that.' She giggled and waved her hands about.

'I must congratulate you,' he said and smiled, anxiously checking the phone in his pocket. He pressed what he hoped was the record button.

'Why are you grinning at me like an idiot? You think it was easy for me to get here? You think all this just dropped in my lap?' said Olga, suddenly getting up from the sofa. She was dressed in a thin, crumpled nightdress stained with red wine. She took one step forward unsteadily and sat down on a chair.

Cyrilo saw at once that she was quite drunk. He hoped she had not seen him pressing buttons on his phone.

'I worked hard for this. I planned for months, almost two years. I knew I could get away with it but then that moron Ziriko almost blew it. He got jealous and tried to ruin everything. Men are so stupid,' she said, pouting like a child.

'He attacked Yuri, didn't he? He came to the Happy Home and tried to strangle him,' said Cyrilo. He was making a wild guess but he had to keep Olga talking. He prayed that the phone was recording her voice but he did not dare check it.

'Yuri. Poor, silly Yuri. He fell in love with me. I like him but he's so poor and so old. Maybe now I will keep him with me. He will be useful to have around the house.'

'Won't Ziriko mind that?'

'Ziriko is my pet dog . . . he does what I order him to.'

'Did you order him to get rid of Rana's wife?' asked Cyrilo, his heart racing now. Olga turned to look at him. Her blue eyes were like two pieces of broken glass. She threw her cigarette on the floor and came towards him.

'Why are you such a nosy man? You people at the Happy Home have made things really difficult for me. I hate old people. Always snooping around. You just get out now before I set my dog Ziriko on you. I will call the police and get them to lock you all up. I am Mrs Rana Hooda and they will listen to me,' she screamed, slapping her hand on the sofa. A diamond ring flew off her finger and she quickly ran to retrieve it from underneath the sofa, muttering abuses in Russian.

Cyrilo suddenly wanted to use the bathroom desperately and ran to the first door he saw. He heard a soft whine and as his eyes adjusted to the dark he could make out a white shape. The whining became louder and the shape rose in a weird, distorted way. It started moving towards him. Cyrilo froze in terror and opened his mouth to scream. He did not see the fist coming at him but he did feel the blinding pain as his head hit the floor. A red curled claw was going for his throat and Cyrilo tried to push it away with all his strength but he felt his hand slipping over cold flesh. It felt like a giant fish was attacking him. A wet hand clamped on his mouth. He began to choke and slowly sank into the quiet darkness.

* * *

Deven sat precariously behind Maria on the scooter, trying to hold on to the rack behind him. His arms had a painful cramp but he hung on, craning his neck forward to keep his balance. He did not want to put his arms around Maria's waist. 'Hold on to me, Deven. I don't want you to fall off,' shouted Maria as she went headlong into the traffic. The scooter jumped over a few potholes and turned sharply, and Deven had no choice but to put his arms gingerly around Maria's waist. *She is like my daughter. She won't mind*, he thought. Aloud, he said, 'Why has that stupid Cyrilo gone on his own to Rana Hooda's villa? What is he trying to do?' Deven felt a pang of fear jolt him and he almost slid off the scooter. What if something happened to Cyrilo? As the dark thoughts rushed into his head Deven could hardly breathe. *What if that woman kills him? No. No. That can't happen. Cyrilo is the only friend I have in this world. He is the kindest, most honest man but he is too trusting. He does not know how wicked and cruel this world is. That evil woman will destroy him like she destroyed two men. Yuri has still not recovered and Rana Hooda is dead. Cyrilo has gone willingly into a snake's pit. Why? Why did he do such a foolish thing? Why did he not wait for me?*

As Maria took a sharp left turn, Deven shut his eyes and began to pray. The last time he had prayed was more than sixty years ago when he was a child and had gone to the temple with his mother. He could not remember if god had heard his prayers then. 'I am praying to you after sixty years and I will not ask for another sixty years of life. Please keep my friend Cyrilo safe,' he muttered. 'What?' shouted Maria, slowing down. They had almost reached the lane outside the villa. Maria stopped the scooter in a shady spot under a tree. They stepped off and walked towards the gate. Deven's knees felt stiff but he forced himself to walk fast. The guard was talking on his phone and when he saw them he lifted his hand to wave them away.

'I am working here. Madam Olga has asked me to come today to clean,' said Maria.

'But she did not tell me anything,' said the guard, spitting a stream of betel juice on the ground.

Deven stepped forward and said to the guard in a curt voice, 'I know you are from Balia. You should not talk on the phone while on duty. Miss Olga will not like it,' he added in the chaste dialect of the region. The guard broke into a nervous smile and bowed. He thumped his chest proudly and began talking very fast as Deven opened the gate and Maria slipped in. After Deven spoke a few more words to the guard he ran forward to open the main door.

The drawing room was empty except for a tiny dog running around in circles. It did not bark when they walked in and instead came running up to Maria and tried to lick her hand. 'Shhhh. My friend,' she whispered. Maria heard someone coming down the stairs and quickly hid behind a carved wooden screen. Deven crouched near the window, pulling the curtains around himself.

'The old creep will be out for some time. Get rid of him. Do it fast. Don't go loitering on the beach with your dopehead friends. We still have work to do. I have to collect my London ticket today,' said Olga.

'You have already booked your ticket? You said we would have to go to Mumbai and fly from there. Safer that way, you said,' a man's voice replied. Deven could not see him but he guessed it must be Ziriko.

'What do you mean we?' said Olga, raising her voice.

'You and me,' said Ziriko.

'You are staying here. Someone has to look after this house.' Olga had reached the drawing room. Her heels clicked noisily on the floor and Maria held her breath. She was so close that Maria could smell strong perfume and marijuana on her. She hoped the dog would not come to her again.

'Olga. You promised me. You said when all this was over we would go to London and live there together,' said Ziriko.

'Me live with a junkie like you? Are you mad? They are very strict in the UK. They will throw you in jail at once.

You are not going anywhere. You must stay here and look after this house. Keep an eye on the construction work too. There is a lot of money to be made there. I need you to manage it if you can stay off your magic juice. Go get me some cold tea,' she said, lighting a cigarette. 'Go on. Don't stand there like a moron. Get rid of that old man too while he is still unconscious,' she shouted, blowing smoke out through her mouth and coughing.

The smoke began to irritate Deven's throat and he stifled a cough. He wondered exactly where Maria was hiding. He could only make out blurred shapes through the curtain. He saw Ziriko pick up a heavy vase. 'You lying bitch. I did all your dirty work and now you think you own me. You will listen to me now. I am not staying here. I am coming to London with you,' he shouted, his voice shaking with rage.

'Put that vase down, you idiot. It cost a fortune. You did my work and you got paid for it. You made a mess by hanging that woman on the tree dressed up in Rana's clothes. "It will look like suicide," you said. You are a crazy fool. You should have dumped her in the sea like I told you to. Now get lost or I'll call the police and tell them who you are and what you did. Get out of my sight, you dirty, stinking swine,' said Olga, throwing her shoe at Ziriko. Maria and Deven heard a strange whining noise. Ziriko lifted the glass vase high in the air and smashed it on the floor, narrowly missing Olga's foot. 'I can fix you too. I can talk to the police. Tell them things about you. I can break your pretty neck in one second,' he shouted.

Olga ignored him. She picked up a shard of the broken vase and waved it in front of Ziriko's face. 'You come near me and I will cut your throat. Don't think I am afraid of you. I don't need you any more. Get out.' She screamed so loudly that Deven could feel his ears hurting.

While Olga's face was turned Maria quickly crawled out from her hiding place and, staying low on the floor, slid under a table near the window. The tablecloth with its long tassels hid her from view and she could see Deven's feet peeping out under the curtain right next to her. 'We should get out of here while they are busy fighting. It's our only chance,' she whispered.

Ziriko began to upturn all the tables and chairs. 'You bitch. I will call the police right now and tell them what you did. You killed Rana. You gave him an overdose and pushed him into the pool. I saw you. I will call the police right now.' He took his phone out of his shirt pocket and suddenly dropped it and began to tremble. As he stood glaring at Olga, his eyes began to blink and he shook his head from side to side. His arms were twitching frantically. He groaned and slid to the floor.

Deven moved the curtains aside and Maria put her head out from under the table. She crawled swiftly to Deven behind the curtain. 'He is having a fit. Let's make a dash for the front door while Olga is still distracted,' she whispered.

Olga leapt up on the sofa, the sharp piece of broken glass in her hand, and yelled at Ziriko. 'Go on, tell them. I don't care. Who will believe you? Call the police from your phone. By the way, I sent Rana text messages from his wife from your phone. They will pounce on you at once. They will throw you in jail and forget about you for the next fifty years. That is how it works here. I just have to give the right amount to the right person. So stop talking shit and go get rid of that old man. Then I will get you your fix. You are beginning to fall apart, you dopehead. Get out of my sight,' shouted Olga, picking up the broken vase and throwing it at the wall. It missed Ziriko by an inch and shattered into pieces above his head but he ignored it. He was shaking badly now, his body rocking. As Deven and Maria watched, Ziriko's tall figure crumpled and he collapsed on the floor. Olga gave an angry shout and got up from the sofa.

'I can smell something strange in this room; a woman's perfume. Have you been bringing women here, you creep?' Olga kicked Ziriko. He gave a loud moan, curled up and hid his head in his hands.

'Oh, you are useless. I will have to deal with that old fellow,' said Olga and began walking towards the dining room.

Suddenly, she stopped. She turned her face to the window and stood very still. Maria knew she had seen them.

* * *

Cyrilo lifted his head and put his hands out to touch the clouds. Then he looked down. His body was lying on the floor, surrounded by tiny clumps of grass. Then he was floating in the sea, the waves tickling his toes. A girl with golden hair was calling out to him and when he went near her he saw she was spitting blood. Then he was in a room again. A dark room lit only by lamps. People were singing and dancing all around him and he too wanted to join but found he couldn't move a muscle. Cyrilo began to laugh and then he could not stop. He heard his loud laughter echoing all over the sky, sinking in the sea and then coming up to engulf him in discordant notes. He tried to shut his eyes but the light was still blinding him. He did not want to hear his laughter any more. It sounded ugly and harsh. His heart was aching with a strange sadness now, and he wanted to go to sleep and never wake up. He could not shut his eyes.

Cyrilo touched the cold marble under his hands and looked around. He remembered that someone had struck him and he felt the lump on his head. It wasn't hurting at all and he actually felt very alert. 'Nothing like a blow on your head to clear your brains.' He slowly pulled himself up and entered the hall, taking care to be as stealthy as possible. He could hear a lot of screaming from the living room. He had to take the chance. He climbed out of the window and gingerly lowered himself into the garden, then walked as quickly as possible towards the van. The vehicle grunted and rattled as he drove out on to the road. His eyes could not focus too clearly but he was sure the old van knew the road and would get him to the Happy Home safely.

* * *

'Look who's here.' Olga pulled the curtains apart. She began to laugh.

Deven and Maria stood awkwardly. Maria felt her hands tremble as a wave of fear swept over her.

'I did not know we had guests. I am sorry but we cannot offer you any tea or cakes now. My servants have gone and this idiot here is going into convulsions since he has not had his dope,' said Olga. She put her hands out and roughly pulled Maria out.

'We came to look for Cyrilo and we . . .' muttered Deven.

'And you hid in my house to spy on me. You old creeps from the Happy Home are getting on my nerves. But I'm so happy you have come. Now I can get rid of all three of you at the same time. It's a pity Yuri and Rosie are not here to join you.' She gave Maria a push. Deven wanted to reach out and save her but he could not. He felt tears roll down his cheeks. He knew he did not have the strength to deal with this woman and he felt overwhelmed.

Maria went mad with rage when she heard Olga talking about the sweet old folks that way. She forgot all her fears and, rushing forward with an angry shout, hurled herself at Olga with all her strength. Olga tripped and fell on the floor and Maria turned and ran towards the door, dragging Deven with her. They were about to open the door but then saw that Ziriko had crawled forward on his knees to block their way. His face was drenched in sweat and he was twitching madly. Maria saw that he had a broken piece of glass in his trembling hands.

'Good boy. Don't let them out. Guard them and I will get you your shot,' shouted Olga and ran upstairs.

Maria and Deven stood close to each other. Ziriko
was watching them like a guard dog, following their every
move. He looked a mess but his eyes were alert, with the
expression of a dangerous wild animal about to attack its
prey. Maria felt dizzy with fear. There was no way they were
going to get out of this house. She heard Deven breathing
heavily next to her and knew he was just as frightened.

Maria heard Olga's high heels clicking on the stairs and
turned her head. Deven whispered something to her but
she couldn't understand. 'Just don't say anything. Okay?'
he said a bit louder. She nodded. What was there to say
now? They were all doing to die. This crazy drug addict
was going to stab them any minute. Poor Cyrilo must be
lying unconscious somewhere in the house. Maria wished
she had called Bobby before coming here. Now she would
never see him again. She would never be his bride. She had
got all of them into this mess.

Maria felt the tears roll down her cheek and Deven
looked at her and pressed her hand gently. 'We will get
away. Just stay calm.'

Olga came and stood before them. She twisted a strand
of golden hair around her finger and smiled.

'You poor things. Now I'm going to be very sweet and
I'm going to allow you two to choose how you want to die.
I can get my mad dog Ziriko to neatly slice your throats but
he is drooling for his fix so he might make a mess. Or I can
shoot you with my pretty little revolver. Look,' she said,
taking out a small gun from a velvet bag.

Ziriko got up from the floor unsteadily, gave a loud
groan and began waving the broken glass in the air.

'Ziriko, wait. Don't be in such a hurry. I got the shots for you. I want to ask these two clever people some questions first just for fun,' said Olga.

'You know. I cannot help admiring you, Miss Olga. You are really a very clever woman. You had us fooled. You fooled the inspector too,' said Deven.

'I know. Men think I am just a pretty doll. They don't know I have a sharp mind too. How did you guess that Rana had not killed his wife?' Olga asked.

'We were suspicious at first since he was the only person to benefit from her death. They had no children. Then he came to the Happy Home that night and we realized he had no idea how his wife had died. He thought she had drowned in the well. Either the police had told him nothing or he did not understand what was going on. He really thought his wife had gone missing from Mumbai and the woman found in the Happy Home was some other person. After all, even the inspector did not know who she was till just two days ago, though Yuri kept trying to tell him,' said Deven in a firm voice, suddenly sounding like his old self.

'Rana was a fool. Like our darling Ziriko, he too liked his cocaine. He kept having hallucinations. When did he come to the Happy Home?' asked Olga, narrowing her eyes.

'The night before he died. He came and talked to us. Poor man. He was so unhappy. He told us you had doped him and arranged this marriage. He told us how you were forcing him to make a will in your favour. He told us how much he hated you,' said Deven softly.

'Listen, you old fool. I never forced him. He was chasing me for months. He made the will to please me, the idiot.

Now he is dead and everything is mine. You two . . . oh, I forgot, there is another old creep in the house . . . you three can all stay here and starve to death. I will not kill you, just shoot you in the leg so you cannot escape, and then I will lock the house and leave. This is what happens when you start poking your nose into other people's business, you stupid woman,' she said and lifted the gun, pointing it at Maria's legs.

Maria shut her eyes. She felt sweat running down her spine. Her legs had gone numb, as if the bullet had already pierced her flesh.

'Wait,' said Deven.

Olga turned to him. 'What? You want to be shot first? How gallant. Maybe I will shoot you right in your tender heart and send you to heaven right away. Your time has come, in any case. By the way, you should call me Mrs Olga Hooda. I am the rich Mrs Hooda now. All this is mine now.'

'You are not really married to him. You do realize that, don't you?' said Maria.

'What do you mean, you stupid bitch?' said Olga.

'This kind of wedding with marigold garlands and some chanting is not really a proper marriage,' said Deven.

'It is. I have seen many Indian people get married like this. The priest told me it was all proper.' Olga looked furious.

'You need 101 witnesses and a proper ceremony. You also need to register your marriage at a government office. Now, alas, it is too late. Your so-called husband is dead. You killed him too soon, Miss Olga,' said Deven.

'If you are planning to go to the UK to grab his house, forget about it. They will never accept this sham marriage there,' said Maria, remembering what Yuri had told her about Olga's schemes.

Ziriko started crawling towards Olga.

She gave him a sharp kick. 'Don't come near me. I must wash my hands. I must wash my hands right now. You are all liars. I am married. I am Mrs Olga Hooda.'

'I want to tell you something else,' said Deven.

'I have heard enough of your rubbish. I am leaving now and you can bleed to death. I have wasted too much time,' said Olga, pointing the gun at Deven.

'Then you will never know the number of Rana's Swiss bank account. How sad. All that money lost,' said Deven, very softly.

'What . . . what are you saying? Rana did not have an account in any Swiss bank. He would have told me,' she said, looking around as if she expected to see Rana standing behind her. Her eyes flicked uncertainly over Deven and Maria. Ziriko was still guarding the door.

'He showed us the account number on his watch. He told us we should give it to his wife's sister,' said Deven.

'What! How dare he. Where is the watch? Show me. If you are trying to play a trick on me you will get a bullet in your brain. Understand?' shouted Olga hysterically, waving the gun in Deven's face.

'The watch is at the Happy Home. It is a gold Rolex. The number is engraved on the back in Hindi so that no one else can get it. You saw it too, didn't you, Maria?' said Deven.

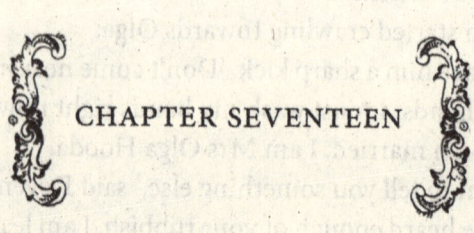

## CHAPTER SEVENTEEN

FOR A FEW moments no one spoke. Maria quickly nodded a few times. She did not dare speak in case she said something wrong and ruined Deven's game.

Olga stared at them, her large blue eyes brimming with suspicion, anger and greed. Finally, greed won and she lowered the gun. Maria said a silent prayer. She tried to move her legs but they seemed to have gone to sleep. She bent forward to rub her ankle with her foot.

'Don't move or I will shoot. Listen, you two. We will go to the Happy Home and you will get that watch for me. You will not try to escape. I will keep this girl as guarantee in case you try to do something silly on the way. I must wash my hands first,' she said, grabbing Maria's hand and pushing her towards the door.

Ziriko began to shout and wave his hands frantically. Olga took out a small plastic packet of white powder from her pocket and threw it on the floor. Ziriko pounced on it and began to tear it with his teeth, saliva dripping from his mouth.

'We cannot leave Cyrilo behind,' whispered Maria.

'I saw him in the garden a little while ago. I heard the van too,' replied Deven in a low voice as Olga turned to open the door. She seemed to have forgotten about Cyrilo and was now rubbing her hands with soap over and over again.

Deven drove the BMW very slowly. Olga had pushed Maria into the back seat, with the gun held close to her neck. Deven had never driven such a powerful car before and Olga kept shouting at him to go faster.

'Drive faster. I don't care if you ruin the car. I am going to dump it at the airport when I leave. I am so rich now. That fool Rana was so scared to divorce his wife. So scared to lose her money. Now he is with her too. All I did was give him a little extra-strong magic pill. I don't care if I'm not married to him. I am still rich. I have all the diamonds. I have all the cash he hid behind the bathroom mirrors in the Goa villa.' It was as if she was talking to herself now.

'Yes. Now you will have the money in the Swiss bank too. You should thank us,' said Maria under her breath.

'Shut up. Don't you dare move,' shouted Olga. 'I am quite happy to put a tiny bullet into your neck. You interfering bitch.'

The red BMW passed green fields, busy roads and crowded markets. Maria saw people shopping and drinking tea in roadside cafes. Many drove past them on scooters and in cars. None of them could guess that her life was in the hands of this crazy woman. She knew any minute Olga might change her mind and shoot her. It was only her greed for Rana's Swiss bank account number that was keeping

Maria alive. Deven had saved her life with this clever trick but for how long?

\* \* \*

The sky was a peculiar shade of crimson red with grey streaks and the wind was whistling through the trees. Rosie was sitting by the window combing her hair and watching birds pick up grains from the lawn. They were fighting bitterly and occasionally huddling close together to share the spoils. The mango tree was in the shadows. Rosie heard a blaring horn and then saw a red car drive in through the gates, almost crashing into the pillars. It came right up to the door in a flurry of dust. She was surprised to see Deven in the driver's seat of the expensive-looking car. A Russian girl was sitting in the back with Maria. They were sitting very close together for some reason. Maria looked very upset and did not raise her head. It was an odd scene. Deven parked under the tree near the steps and then waved to her and smiled, showing all his teeth. Rosie knew at once that something was terribly wrong. Deven never smiled in this way like a clown. She wondered if he was trying to send her a message. He lifted his hand and twisted his fingers into the shape of a gun for a few seconds. Then he put his hand down quickly and got out of the car.

Rosie's heart began to race. She sat frozen for a few seconds, unsure of what to do, and then turned her wheelchair around as fast as she could and went into the veranda. She could smell another fragrance along with the faint scent of roses from the garden, something sharp, hot and biting. She saw a flash of red on the veranda table, as if a carpet of crimson had been laid out. Leela had powdered all their home-grown chillies on the mortar and pestle and put the powder out to dry in the sun.

Rosie suddenly had an idea. *Will it work?* she thought, her hands trembling nervously as she moved her wheelchair towards the table. She held her breath and reached for it. The table was not quite within her reach, so she lifted her stick and pushed it. The table was very heavy and hardly moved an inch but Rosie kept pushing with all her fragile strength till it was closer. She leaned forward, forcing herself to bend down as much as she could and picked up a handful of red powder.

The strong aroma of chillies flew up to sting her eyes painfully and she quickly shut them. The skin on her fingers began to burn as if she had dipped them in boiling water. Rosie took four handfuls and spread them on her scarf. Then she moved her wheelchair back. She went near the door and waited. She was not sure what she was waiting for but she knew that something terrible was happening outside and she must somehow protect the Happy Home. She began to pray silently. Suddenly, a loud ringing echoed all over the house, startling her and making her hands fly to her face. The chilli powder bit into her skin like acid.

Why was Deven ringing the doorbell? He knew it was always open.

Then the door opened and Deven rushed in. Rosie could tell from his face that he was really frightened. 'Deven, what . . .' she began but he lifted his hand and told her to remain silent.

He bent his head very close to her and whispered, 'Tell Leela to call the police. Maria is in danger. That woman has a gun. Go quickly. I have been stalling her by telling her I could not find the key to the front door,' he said and walked quickly towards his room.

Rosie gave a loud gasp but swung into action immediately. She knew there was no time to waste. She called out to Leela, who was washing clothes outside the kitchen. 'Leela, run and get that phone of yours. Call the police inspector. Tell him it's urgent. Maria is in danger.'

'What happened to Miss Maria?' asked Leela, her soapy hands suspended in mid-air, her eyes filled with horror.

'Just run. Quick,' said Rosie, turning her wheelchair around. Deven was still standing on the stairs.

'Maria is being held hostage by that Russian girl. She has a gun. I am trying to fool her. Don't know if I will succeed, Rosie,' said Deven.

'You will. You are very clever and brave. You will manage somehow,' she said, though she was still not sure what was going on.

'I am going to fetch that watch Rana left behind. I will try to bluff my way out of this. Might not work but I have to try. It is our only chance.'

Rosie opened the door slightly and saw that Maria was sitting in the car, huddled close to Olga. Rosie pretended to smile and wave to her but Maria did not show any sign of having seen her. Her face was a frozen mask of sheer terror. Deven opened the door and came out of the house, not looking at Rosie. He walked towards the red car very slowly, his back bent. He looked as if he had aged ten years in the last few minutes. He held out his hand with the gold watch. Olga reached out through the car window and snatched it from him but the watch dropped to the ground. Olga banged on the car door and yelled profanities at Deven as he bent to pick up the watch. Rosie suddenly caught a flash of metal and saw the gun in Olga's hand. Her heart began to knock against her ribs and she felt a flood of terror wash over her.

Rosie had never managed to move her wheelchair down the three steps that led to the driveway by herself. Someone always carried her down. She had never gone out on her own beyond the front door. Her arms did not have the strength to move the wheelchair down the steps. But now she put her two frail hands firmly on the wheels and gripped them as tightly as she could. She took a deep breath, ignoring the loud thumping of her heart, and hurled herself forward with all her feeble strength. For a moment, she caught a fleeting glimpse of the green leaves as she landed near the car with a loud crash. Before she hit the ground she threw a handful of chilli powder in the air. It made a rainbow of red, orange and crimson as it flew in an arc over the car. Her head hit the ground.

Someone screamed and there was a crash as the wheelchair collapsed. The horn of the BMW began to blare and the gun went off at the same time with a deafening blast. Smoke filled the air and the crows began to screech hysterically as if they had been shot, though the bullet was wedged in the roof of the car. Deven, pulling his cap down to protect his eyes, dragged Maria out of the car as she blindly waved her hands, trying to wipe the chilli powder

from her eyes. Olga sat trapped in the back seat of the car.
She began hitting her head on the window, screaming in
Russian. Her golden hair looked as if it was on fire and
streaks of chilli powder ran down her pale face, turning her
into a strange red creature, a creature that belonged to the
devil's own clan.

* * *

Later, they would all laugh at Rosie's Olympic high jump,
as they now called it, but for days she was in agony. She
had broken both her ankles and had a deep gash on her
forehead. Despite the lack of sensation in her legs, the
phantom pains tore her entire body into shreds.

Rosie did not mind the pain. She was happy she had
saved Maria. She still did not know how she had got the
strength to hurl her wheelchair down the steps. God
gave you strength when you really needed it. It was she
who had caught the murderer though till this day Deven
claimed he had done it. She let him believe it. Men
needed to believe in something grand to feel good about
themselves. She knew in her heart what she had done
for Maria and Maria knew it too, and that was enough
for her.

Olga, totally blinded by the chilli powder, had tried to
run away. 'You cannot prove anything, you old creeps,' she
had shouted, blood dripping from her earlobe where the
bullet from her own gun had grazed her. She had almost
fallen into the well as she tried to escape but Deven had
caught her. He had quickly snatched the gun away from

her. She struggled furiously, biting and kicking him, but he had managed to tie her with a rope to the mango tree.

A crowd had quickly gathered after hearing the commotion. The news spread fast in Trionim about a mad woman being captured. 'One more murder,' some people shouted in glee before stopping at the gate. 'No dead body. Look. This one is alive, kicking and screaming.' They jostled each other for a place close to Olga and soon settled down to gape at her. Each time she screamed an abuse they replied with one of their own. Everyone was thrilled. Trionim had never seen anything like this. The branches of the mango tree trembled as Olga screamed, spit running down her chin. She kept twisting and turning, trying to free herself, but Deven had tied her firmly.

Cyrilo walked up to her and whispered something in her ears and suddenly Olga fell silent and started sobbing instead. 'What did you tell her?' asked Deven, surprised. He had been trying to make her shut up for a long time. The police had still not arrived, though Leela had called them half an hour ago.

'I told her that I have recorded her lovely voice singing on my phone, saying very ugly things to me about killing her so-called husband Rana Hooda and his wife,' said Cyrilo, patting his shirt pocket. Deven could see a small mobile phone there.

'She sings very well. The police will love her songs,' said Cyrilo to the crowd. Olga began to wail.

The crowd gave a sudden roar as they heard the police siren outside the gate. Now they would see some action. Inspector Chand got out of the jeep, straightened his jacket and walked in through the gate. He looked around, waving his stick in the air like a warrior going into battle. He was shocked to see Olga, the beautiful Olga, in this terrible state. Her golden hair was blood red and stood up around her head all tangled up. Her face was swollen and red, her puffy, misshapen lips twitching away like a fish about to die. She reminded him of a woman from a horror film he had seen recently. The woman had turned into a monster just like this. Inspector Chand gave a loud gasp and then heard Constable Robert echo his breathless hiccup right behind him. Inspector Chand looked around and wondered what to do.

Deven stepped forward and whispered something in the inspector's ears as he handed him Olga's gun. Inspector Chand, holding on to his stick for support, stared at Olga for a few moments. Then, very slowly and reluctantly, he reached for the handcuffs in his pocket and moved forward to clasp them on Olga's hands. He thought of saying a few soothing words but she spat at him.

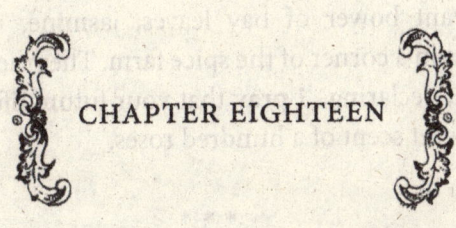

# CHAPTER EIGHTEEN

BOBBY WAS SORRY he had missed all the excitement. 'You were in such danger and I was not there to save you,' he said over and over again.

'You can save me some other time. We have the rest of our lives to save each other,' said Maria. Bobby nodded but secretly hoped he would never have to do such a fearful thing. He was not sure he was as courageous as Rosie. They said she had flung herself on that woman holding a gun. What a brave thing to do. What if Olga had shot her? Or Maria?

Then he would have died too. He could not live in a world without Maria. He could not bear to even think of it. Bobby shut his eyes. His life was now lit up with a joyous, golden light and dark thoughts had no place in it. This terrible business at the Happy Home was finally over and now they could start their new life together. No more excitement of the evil kind. They would plant a new garden of flowering trees and fragrant shrubs. They would walk in the spice garden every dawn and newly opened buds would greet them. He would grow all kinds of fruits for Maria and she could make jams and jellies. He hoped she liked making jams and jellies. Now he could finally start the life he had waited for for so long.

Maria and Bobby were married in a quiet ceremony in a fragrant bower of bay leaves, jasmine, roses and lemongrass in a corner of the spice farm. The priest blessed them both, declaring, 'I pray that your future life be filled with the sweet scent of a hundred roses.'

\* \* \*

Deven, Cyrilo, Prema, Rosie, Yuri and Leela sat in the veranda at the Happy Home the morning after the wedding. The table was laid out with tea, leftover wedding cake and freshly baked cinnamon buns. A fierce argument was going on, all of them speaking simultaneously. Each one thought they were responsible for solving the murder. Half-eaten pieces of cake lay forgotten on the table, bees buzzed and sparrows picked up crumbs as their angry voices rose in the air. Only Yuri sat silently brooding, picking paint off his fingernails.

Finally, Leela jumped on the bench and banged a wooden stick loudly on the table.

'Listen to me, please. We all had a part to play. Shut your eyes and think back to the beginning. Who found the body?'

Everyone looked at her, taken aback.

'Tell me. Come on. Think. Who?' she asked again, sounding uncannily like Deven.

'That boy who cannot speak. Tony,' said Cyrilo.

'Who found out the name and address of the dead woman?' asked Leela, tapping her stick on the rose bush, sending a shower of rose petals on their heads.

'Well, you did,' said Prema, frowning.

'Yes, I did, and Bobby helped too. Remember he met that woman at the spice farm,' said Leela.

'I found the dry-cleaning bill under the cupboard in Yuri's room,' she added, patting herself on the back and grinning at them.

'Listen, you cheeky girl. We all helped too. Yuri told us the dead woman's name. Deven and Maria discovered the connection between her and Olga. They were brave enough to go to that villa to confront her,' said Cyrilo.

'You went there too, all alone, and you recorded her confession on your phone, Cyrilo,' said Yuri, who had made a full recovery. 'That was very clever of you, my friend.'

'Well . . .' mumbled Cyrilo, suddenly looking sheepish.

'What do you mean? You said you taped her voice as she spoke to you about paying Ziriko to kill Rani Hooda. Once she knew you had recorded all that on your phone, she just broke down and confessed,' said Deven.

'I was bluffing. I had actually pressed the wrong button and erased her voice from my phone. Anyway, Olga the witch never guessed that, did she?' Cyrilo grinned.

'She thought she was clever but obviously not that clever,' said Leela.

'She almost managed to fool Inspector Chand. He was quite ready to let her go but fortunately Constable Robert kept her locked up till she confessed in writing,' said Deven.

'Inspector Chand is heartbroken about Maria's marriage. I heard he has been transferred to Ponda. I hope he finds a suitable girl there. And it's so good that Constable Robert has been promoted. He informed the Panjim police and they managed to arrest Ziriko at the airport. He was trying to catch a flight out of Goa,' said Cyrilo.

'His dreams of living in London with Olga are shattered forever. He will now spend a long time in jail,' said Yuri. 'I'm ashamed to say I was once crazy about that woman.'

'We all make mistakes. Thankfully that woman could not harm you, Yuri. You escaped,' said Cyrilo.

'Greed brought them to this sorry end. God made Olga a beautiful woman but he poured a cauldron of wickedness into her. Life is a long, difficult journey, as all of us know. Wicked deeds drag us even deeper into a well of despair,' said Rosie. She turned to Leela. 'Leela, my girl, you are young and innocent. I want you to remember that kindness, compassion and a generous heart: these are gifts that make it easier to travel along this long life. How does it matter how much wealth we have if we are too mean to share it? My body will slowly become useless, my mind might go but my love and affection for all of you will never fade as long as there is light and air on this earth. I will hover in the sky and send my good wishes down to you all.'

'We will all join you and send happy thoughts to all those we love,' said Cyrilo.

'You can all go and hover like helicopters. I am not ready to fly to heaven yet. I'll be here for at least ten more years,' said Prema. 'You go fly in the sky while I sit here and eat delicious cakes.'

'You must have my wedding cake too. I want all of you to stick around for a long time. You can also have free beauty treatments and haircuts when I open my beauty parlour,' added Leela.

The five aged residents of the Happy Home looked up at Leela. A ray of sunshine filtered through the trees and, looking at them, she smiled. They all began thinking of the days ahead and wondering what flavour Leela's wedding cake would be.